BLOOD & GOLD

ALSO BY T. G. AYER

Young Adult Paranormal

THE VALKYRIE SERIES

Dead Radiance
Dead Radiance Audio
Dead Embers
Dead Embers Audio
Dead Chaos
Dead Chaos Audio
Dead Wrath
Dead Silence
Joshua - Dead Radiance
Joshua II - Dead Embers
Joshua III - Dead Chaos
Joshua IV - Dead Wrath
Joshua V - Dead Silence

THE HAND OF KALI SERIES

Fire & Shadow
Blood & Gold
Time & Fate
Fury & Virtue
Spirit & Soul

THE DARKWORLD ORIGINS

Pyros (Logan)

Ailuros (Kailin)

~

THE DARK SIGHT SERIES

Dark Sight

Cursed Sight

Vissarion

Shadow Sight

Dark Prophecy

Cursed Prophecy

Shadow Prophecy

~

THE APSARA CHRONICLES

Immortal Bound

Gods Ascendent

Dominion Falling

Vengeance Born

Last Legion

~

A SEASON OF ASH AND BONE

Heartfyre

~

INFINITE
INK
BOOKS

Blood & Gold

USA TODAY BESTSELLING AUTHOR

T.G. AYER

Hindu Mythology is a living religion.
Like, Christianity, Islam, Judaism & Buddhism, Hinduism has millions of followers around the world. Fiction featuring Hindu gods is not merely a matter of choosing a god, and placing them in a fictional situation, mainly because you risk offending that deities devout worshippers. Unlike the Greek, Roman, Egyptian & Norse Pantheon, Hindu & Buddhist gods must be treated with the utmost respect in any fiction. I hope I have maintained this ethic within my series.
I have tried to maintain as much respect as possible while still using fiction to both entertain and educate the reader. The Kali series is filled with details of the various deities currently worshipped across the world.
Some rituals and powers are fiction, of course.

There is much in the Kali series that is part of my own journey in life. I hope my travels in India have lent some level of authenticity to the Indian scenes.

Some of the gods featuring in this series, like Chayya and Bhumi, are ones who are not currently as popular. They are still worshipped, but belong to the older generation of gods, which would explain why not every Hindu reader would be familiar with them.

Demons, Zombies, Undead & other creatures and spirits are as per mythology texts and are available online to research. Much of how to eliminate these creatures is anecdotal & fictional. Sorry guys, if you come across a Vitala, you're on your own.

CHAPTER 1

*D*arkness and shadows bled into the fiery twilight sky, while a fat line of blood red sat ominously on the distant horizon.

Maya sighed.

She was beginning to regret tagging along on this round of her parents' client visits. What had come over her to offer to accompany them? Worse, she couldn't believe they actually agreed to bring her along. But then again, this was exactly the type of thing they would want – for Maya to get more involved in whatever it was that the Kali followers got up to. She'd been curious. Now, something told her she would probably be paying for that curiosity soon enough.

The call had come through not half an hour ago and they were already on the move. The information her dad received had seemed a bit mysterious and strange. A name and address given, a brief history told and Dev and his wife were expected to go rushing off to attend to the matter. He'd briefly explained what he could to Maya so she was guessing he wouldn't know the finer details of the situation was until he got there. Maya glared out the window at the closely built homes. Not a supremely affluent area, but not poor either.

They drew up in front of a small two story house. Although brightly lit, the building was blanketed by an almost tangible somberness. No sounds emanated from the house, no music, no voices. Just silence.

Someone had died.

Maya's stomach twisted. She'd known it was a funeral they were attending, and she'd still agreed to come. What had come over her? She hated funerals. All the sadness, and the awkward conversations that usually meant nothing to either party. People milling around smiling blank smiles and offering blank commiserations. The few funerals Maya had attended in her time had been excruciating for her. And here she was willingly attending another one.

They parked a few doors down after driving up and down the block looking for a spot. Cars filled the street and had even flowed onto the side road. The number of vehicles were at odds with the silence emanating from the house. Something else that creeped Maya out.

She followed her parents up the drive, fiddling with the long chiffon scarf around her neck. She smoothed down the dress of the salwar kameez she wore, another reminder of things she hadn't liked doing. In the past she hadn't been a keen wearer of all things Indian. Give her a jeans and teeshirt and she was a happy girl.

But her stint in Patala had given her a little more appreciation for the attire after having been forced to fight in the garments. Today what she wore was boring compared to the jewel-encrusted skirts and blouses she'd worn in the Underworld not so long ago.

Dev knocked on the door, two raps so soft Maya wondered if anyone would even hear it. But only seconds later a woman opened the door. Her make-up-free face was lined, almost haggard, the red dot on her forehead smeared slightly, as if she'd just rubbed her brow without realizing it. Her hair was held away from her face in a serious bun, not a single strand escaping the knot at the base of her head. She wore no jewelry, and her sari was the statutory white, unadorned by either color or sparkle.

Maya's father introduced himself and it seemed that was all she needed to let them in. Maya watched her but the old woman's tear-swollen gaze returned to the floor as she stepped aside, allowing them to enter. She shut the door softly and waited while they removed their shoes and placed them next to the dozens of pairs already occupying the floor of the entrance hall.

Once they were ready the woman turned, pulled the length of her sari tighter around her and led them deeper into the silent house. Maya followed her parents as sedately and quietly as she could. She kept her eyes downcast, forcing herself not to look around. But despite her demure behavior she managed to get a good sense of the place.

The air hung thick with smoke, and from somewhere inside the house rose the cloying smell of frankincense. Maya's throat closed. There wasn't anything wrong with frankincense. In fact, Maya had always liked the smell – associated it mostly with babies. People burned a lot of frankincense when babies were born. It was just that this place held such a sense of foreboding that Maya's bones hurt. The whole building seemed to bear down on her, but even though she wanted to turn and run she continued to play the dutiful daughter and followed her parents in silence.

They were on the job and she was curious what the job actually was. For the first time she would see her parents in action, doing whatever they did as Kali followers. They'd responded to the call from the family – people in need of their help. So her parents must have a reputation of helping those who needed their kind of help. She hadn't thought of that.

The pall of mourning clung to the house, clung to the people the deceased had left behind. The family had lost their daughter-in-law three months ago. She had died in childbirth but strange things were happening and the family was concerned that the girl had returned and was haunting them.

In the car on the way there, Maya's mom had explained how a pregnant woman, unhappy or ill treated by her family, could often return after death and wreak vengeance if she dies in childbirth. This kind of spirit was called a Churel. Maya shuddered at the thought. She'd always thought these types of stories belonged in horror movies and not in real life. And today Maya was here to see the vengeful spirit in action. She blinked, surprised to discover that her parents were the equivalent of supernatural hunters. The purpose of the Kali followers had just risen in her estimation.

The sounds of soft crying and hushed sobs filtered through the house and Maya cringed. She hated funerals and death and anything to do with crying and consoling the grieving. She breathed deep. She'd killed demons, surely she can handle normal humans.

She tried to calm herself as they were ushered into a large furniture-less room, thick with smoke. A picture window on the right wall sat wide open to help the dense air filter out. Not that it helped. Maya's eyes stung as she glanced around at the sea of people seated before her.

The old woman took a small path that ran through the crowd and Maya and her parents followed. It seemed all the members of the family had gathered within this one room concentrating their fear and worry and grief into an almost living thing. The path led to the center of the room where the body of a man was laid out on on a pallet, wrapped in white fabric.

The man's face was deeply lined and wrinkled, the skin papery thin and mottled with age-spots, and sagging at the throat .The hands crossed at his chest were gnarled and twisted with age and arthritis. He was ancient. And he was so painfully thin, as if someone or something had sucked the flesh right out of him.

A hush fell over the room as the Raos reached the body. The sniffling and crying came to a stop as the gathered family watched them. The air seemed filled with expectation. And Maya didn't like it. Dev and Leela knelt beside the shriveled corpse. Maya wasn't entirely sure what to do with herself. Should she kneel too? In the end she just stood behind them and watched.

Her dad turned to speak to the old woman – who Maya now assumed was probably an important female in the house. A mother or grandmother maybe. Maya studied her a little closer, knowing the family suspected they were being haunted by their dead daughter-in-law. If that was the case, had this old woman been party to the mistreatment of the girl?

Dev was still speaking to the old woman and Maya heard the soft, hushed words as he asked her, "Is it okay to check?" His tone was somber but it wasn't a question. The old woman's eyes widened and she glanced over at another older man seated on the other side of the corpse. He gave a small almost haughty nod, his pale brown eyes regarding them coldly, and the woman turned to Maya's father and nodded too.

Maya's heart gave a little twist as if some precognition told her that what her dad was about to do would surely upset a few people. He bent closer to the corpse and moved some yellow and orange flowers away from the old man's neck. His movements were slow and respectful as he unbuttoned the man's shirt and pulled the collar forward. A low gasp ran around the room, the gathered mourners unhappy with Dev's desecration. But despite their unhappiness nobody moved to stop him.

Dev leaned forward, and Maya's could tell even from his profile that he didn't like what he saw. He nodded to himself then motioned for Leela and Maya to come forward, to see what he saw. Maya tipped her head forward and blinked at the sight.

A single puncture wound sat near the jugular. It looked raw

and red and even in death it seemed ready to bleed. Maya swallowed as bile rose in her throat. She wanted to breathe but all she would inhale would be smoke and the dead man's odor, so instead she held her breath.

Maya shook herself. She really shouldn't feel disgusted by the sight. She'd seen worse. The sight of dying demons were definitely worse. Even the smell of the Rakshasa, living or dying, was worse than the odor of the sad room filled with sad people. A few moments later, and after Dev had returned the dead man's garments to their former status, Maya's parents rose and nodded at the old woman. Dev bent to her and again spoke in her ear. Then he turned and motioned for Maya and her mom to leave.

They maneuvered through the crowd and Maya felt the stares on the back of her neck, felt every eye on the curved of her spine as she passed. She shuddered but kept the movement delicate. In the front hall they found their shoes and left the house unimpeded. Once outside, Maya gulped the fresh night air, relieved to have smoke-free lungs again.

Then she turned to her father, not liking the sober expression on his face. "Now what?"

"Now, we go to the grave," he said. He spoke so matter-of-factly that Maya thought at first she'd misheard him. But his face said otherwise.

"Are you serious?" she asked, her brow creasing with a frown. She pulled her chiffon shawl closer around her, not that the action would have relieved the sudden chill that had run up her spine.

Dev nodded. His lip curled as he glanced at her, clearly amused by her trepidation. "Yes, there are a few things we can do to bind the Churel. We need to stop her before she moves on to the next man in the household."

Maya frowned as they climbed into the car, her thoughts still with the shriveled corpse of a dead man. "How old was he?" she asked as she shut her door and drew her seatbelt around her.

"Eighteen," said her mom from up front, the streetlight giving her a pale, ghostly countenance. "He was the youngest son. The Churel habitually begins with the youngest and then moves upward. They must not have treated her very well at all. The worse the treatment, the more vengeful the Churel is. The angrier she is, the harder it is to stop her." Leela's voice was grave and her eyes a little far away as her thoughts seemed to remain on the abused girl.

Maya cleared her throat, the taste of frankincense still in the back of her nose. "And these rites, will they really work?"

"They've always worked in the past." Dev nodded, his eyes flashing with confidence as he gunned the engine. "There's nothing to say that they won't work now."

"Come," said Maya's mom. " We need to get moving. The faster we do this the better."

Maya looked out of her window as their car pulled away from the curb. She stared at the brightly lit house. Despite the lights, the house exuded a darkness that Maya still felt in her bones. What had they done to the girl while she'd lived there? How badly had they treated her for them to deserve this kind of punishment? Had the young man also ill treated her?

Or was he an innocent bystander caught within the net of vengeance?

CHAPTER 2

As they entered the graveyard Maya had to force herself to hide a smile. In all her wildest dreams she never would've thought she'd be sneaking into a graveyard in the dead of night with both her parents. And on a serious job at that.

They had visited the house at nightfall and that had seemed so creepy. Yet now, just entering the graveyard under cover of the growing darkness, sent shivers up Maya's spine.

They parked in the little graveled lot at the entrance of the cemetery. Maya got out with her mom, her feet crunching the stones underfoot. The sound echoed so loudly around them that Maya flinched. Her mom watched her with a raised eyebrow, and Maya rolled her eyes. They waited as Dev removed a small suitcase from the trunk of the car. He shut the lid, then retrieved something from his trouser pocket. He held a little piece of paper in his hand and though Maya wanted to ask what was on it, she gritted her teeth and followed in silence as he headed off into the darkness of the graveyard. No one stopped them, and Maya guessed that Evergreen Hills Cemetery, with it's unusually high wrought-iron fences and bright security company logos, was not exactly overrun with grave robbers and kids playing midnight pranks. She could just imagine the Rao's getting tossed out for trespassing.

They walked further into the cemetery, with just a small torch and the tiny electric lamplights lighting a thin path way through the trees. Maya shivered. The thought that they were surrounded by hundreds and hundreds of dead bodies creeped her out. Not that Maya should be creeped out the first place. Killing demons was a hard enough job but demons were far worse than dead people.

Still, she guessed she'd also run and hide at the first sign of the zombie invasion.

At last they reached the dead woman's grave, a plain site marked with a unadorned, simple headstone. Grass had begun to creep across the ground in front of the headstone. Grass that shriveled up and died as the blades reached the area directly above the grave.

Maya stared at the grave, a hollow feeling in her chest. "Is there any way to prevent this from happening?" she asked.

"Well honey, the family must have known there was a possibility that the girl would turn into a Churel. Everyone has heard the warnings, which is why most people usually treat expectant mothers with care and gentleness. But perhaps this particular family didn't want to admit the possibility because an admission would mean they would have to admit, at least to themselves, that they were abusing the girl. That in itself is not an easy thing to do." Leela's face was dark with anger as she looked at the bare grave. "There are a number of things they could have done after she died to make sure she didn't become a Churel. But I have a feeling that in this particular family nobody would've admitted any wrongdoing in the first place."

"Yeah, the best prevention would've been that they should have treated her well in the first," said Maya, her voice bitter and hard.

Dev laid the suitcase down at one corner of the grave. Crouching, he clicked the locks and flipped it open, and Maya raised an eyebrow at its contents. They seemed to have come quite prepared. He withdrew four nine-inch nails and lay them beside him. Then he took a plastic container and laid it on the grave. Next he moved a brass tray to the center of the raised mound of soil and placed a small clay lamp on it, along with what looked like frankincense and camphor.

Maya glanced at her mother who stood beside her, her pale pink sari fluttering in s sudden breeze. She was just as silent as her husband. It seemed the whole idea of the pregnant woman being abused really troubled Leela. But, before Maya could ask her mother any further questions, Dev motioned for her to join him. That left Maya standing alone at the foot of the grave. As creepy as ever. She glanced around her, staring through the trees up the path and behind her down a small gully. Nothing moved, nothing stirred.

Maya watched as her dad handed her mom the nails, which Leela proceeded to place at each of the four corners of the grave. Dev open the large plastic container and removed what looked like a number of small red-flowered plants complete with root and soil. He handed them to Leela who placed two of the plants alongside the nails at each corner. Then Dev followed, quickly leaning over and dropping a small leaf, some camphor and frank-incense at each corner as well. Before closing the bag he removed a small-handled shovel.

He rose and dusted the soil from his knees, then came to stand at the foot of the grave. He removed a piece of paper from his pocket. Maya peered closer to see what was written on the paper. Sanskrit. A language she could not read. She waited, and soon her dad began to chant, repeating the words from the paper in the same singsong way that the priests of the temple used. Strange hearing her dad speak that way.

After chanting the incantations Dev turned to his wife and

nodded. She rounded the grave placing little clay lamps at each corner filling them with frankincense and camphor. Then Dev went back to the first corner. Withdrawing a small hammer from his pocket, he began to dig a small hole into which Leela placed two of the small red plants. Once buried Dev grasped a nail and hammered it into the soft soil at the corner of the grave site while Leela lit the camphor and frankincense.

They continued to plant the flowers and hammer in the nails at all the other corners. Soon the scent of frankincense wafted around the grave-site, hanging like a thick white blanket. Not a breeze stirred now, yet Maya felt as if someone was trailing cold fingers up her spine. She shook the feeling off and tried to pay attention to what her parents were doing.

At last Dev returned to the bottom of the grave and completed his incantations. Then he nodded his head and stepped a few feet back from the site. Done, they hurriedly put the shovel and container away and headed back to the car.

Maya frowned as they reached their parked vehicle. She stared back at the dark tree line that hemmed in the graveyard. Already she had no idea where the gravesite was."We left the grave pretty quickly," she said, a question in her statement.

"It's best to leave as soon as we are done. The last thing we need is for the Churel to follow us. It's likely that might happen so we have to take precautions," said Dev and he stepped into the car, seemingly unperturbed at the possibility of being followed by an undead demonic force.

"You mean that thing could actually follow us home?" asked Maya, her voice cracking as she spoke. She jumped in and buckled up, waiting for him to answer her.

"It's possible," replied her mother as she shut her door. "The Churel naturally seeks a male member of her family to wreak vengeance on. That's not to say that another male wouldn't suit her purposes, especially when he is in her way."

"You mean Dad could be in danger?" asked Maya, her heart thudding as she glared at her father's eyes reflected in the rear-view mirror.

"Yes, it is possible." Leela spoke, looking out of her window, and the fingers of cold crept along Maya's spine again.

"Then why did we get involved? Especially when it could endanger Dad?" Maya asked vehemently. She couldn't believed that they would willingly face such dangers to their own lives just to help people who mistreated their family. In this case as far as Maya could tell these people probably deserved what they were getting. She gritted her teeth.

"Honey, you have to understand that we have to do our duty first, even if it puts us in danger. The family needed us and we did what we had to do," Dev said, meeting his daughter's eyes in the mirror.

Maya's neck remained stiff as she folded her arms. "I don't see how they needed you that much considering what they did to her when she was alive. She would never become a Churel in the first place if it weren't for them."

"I understand what you mean and I agree with you, but that young boy could have been totally innocent. The Churel will seek her vengeance on the family as a whole. When she returns from the grave she is no longer capable of seeing a difference in any of the men in the family, whether they have ever hurt her or not. That is one of the biggest problems with the creature. We may understand her point of view. No one likes the idea of a pregnant woman being abused. But once she turns into the demon she loses all sense of humanity and fairness. She becomes a demonic killing machine."

Maya nodded, although she wasn't entirely convinced. "I can understand that. Okay, let's be careful then. Is there anything that we need to do?"

Her parents shook their heads as Dev backed out of the

parking lot. He said, "We've done what we can. We just have one more thing to do before we go back to the house."

Maya remained silent as they drove back towards the area in which the family lived. Just before they crossed the suburb line, Dev pulled up at the side of the road, not two feet away from a giant-sized sign proclaiming Richfield Gardens as the perfect place to live. Dev got out of the car and withdrew another nail and the small hammer from his pocket. He walked to the edge of the sidewalk where he crouched and began to pound the spike into the soil beside the sign.

When he returned to the car Maya asked, "What was that about?"

"I just placed a nail in the suburb line. It should keep the Churel out. We can only do what we know how to and just hope it works." He slid into the car, seemingly unperturbed by the whole episode.

Yeah, Maya thought, let's just hope it works. The last thing she wanted was for that demonic creature to come after her dad. The entire drive from the graveyard Maya had the distinct feeling that if she glanced out the back window she would see ghostly, skeletal fingers reaching out for their car, as if the graveyard wanted them back.

Dev started the engine and drove off, returning to the house which was still brightly lit and still deathly quiet. He got off the car and said, "You two wait here. You don't need to come with me." Then he left, hurrying up the entrance stairs to knock on the door. It was opened within seconds by the old woman. This time though she seemed a bit more pleasant, a smile turning the corner of her lip as she spoke to Dev.

A shiver ran up Maya's spine as she watched the woman. Something about her seemed off. She watched them talk and in the end the old woman nodded and opened the door wider. Dev retrieved another nail from his pocket and bent to hammer it into one end of the threshold. Once done he got to his feet and dusted off his pants, nodding at the woman. She spoke a few more words and Maya assumed she was thanking him. Then he left to return to the car.

CHAPTER 3

*D*ev got back into the car and shut the door, an odd expression on his face. For a long moment he just sat in the front seat, his hands on the wheel

"What's wrong?" asked Maya her eyes not leaving his face.

Dev turned to look at her. "I'm not sure. Just something didn't feel right."

Maya nodded. "You felt it too?" He gave her a sharp glance, then started the car.

"Let's not get too complacent. Let's just all be aware and careful. You just never know what could happen." Leela spoke and instead of calming her down her mom's words just put Maya more on edge.

They drove through the tree-lined streets, through the darkness of the night, and Maya wondered what other horrors the shadows held. These days nothing should surprise her. She'd been through so much in the last few weeks, so much that it all seemed so unbelievable at times. But the strange thing was it was getting less and less unbelievable as time went. Funny how that happens.

Another shiver ran up Maya's spine and she looked around.

She turned in her seat and stared out the rear window at the long stretches of dark road behind them. Nothing. Just darkness and shadows and night.

Finally, there were home. Dev turned into their driveway and cut the engine. Maya knew she should be relieved but she still felt strange. As if she expected something to happen but she wasn't exactly sure what was going to happen. All she knew was that it was inevitable. Her gut churned and she swallowed hard as she got out of the car and shut the door. She scanned the shadows around them. Still nothing.

Leela unlocked the front door and went into the house while Dev rounded the car. He opened the trunk to remove the suitcase of ghost-hunting paraphernalia. Maya followed him. Something in her was reluctant to leave him alone.

And then she stiffened.

Something made her sniff. She turned to smell the air that wafted around her. An odd scent floated on the night breeze. A gust of wind blew through the trees, sending all the leaves around them aflutter, as if even the wind knew something was going to happen.

Something bad.

Maya jumped as her father shut the trunk with the bang. He looked at her, winked then turned to walk off when Maya got the scent again. This time it was stronger, thicker, more cloying. More demon-like. Maya scanned the darkness frantically looking for a demon.

Nothing.

That's not true.

Maya narrowed her eyes, staring hard at the spot next to the oak tree beside the driveway. The air shimmered as if Maya had something caught in her eye. She blinked and breathed. The demon smell was strong; raw flesh and incense and something else. The smell of the dead. The smell of freshly turned soil.

Maya turned to her dad as he walked off. She glanced back at the shimmering in time to see it slowly begin to take the form of a woman. Her hair spread open behind her, blowing on an invisible breeze, her dark eyes Kohl-lined and as black as death. The woman would've been pretty once, with her high cheekbones and almond shaped eyes. But now she stood there in the shadows of the trees with the cloying odor of rotting meat around her. Maya could see nothing of beauty, just everything of death.

The woman glided towards the house and that one movement set Maya in motion.She began to run towards her father. Dev had seen and heard nothing, his back still to Maya.

And to the Churel.

He was walking slowly back to the house. Maya's knees felt like rubber, as if of fear had decided to bind her legs. She grunted. She wasn't going to let that happen. She ran, pushing herself forward on feet she could barely feel. And as she ran the ghostly shadow-woman ran too.

The Churel was fast. Faster than Maya ever imagined she would be. The wind lifted the woman's hair as she flew towards Dev.

"Dad," Maya screamed as she ran. "Run," she yelled hoping he would get away but he didn't listen. Instead he turned around, a frown on his face, mouth half open as if he wanted asked Maya what was wrong. Now he could see for himself what was wrong.

The Churel was almost on him, hands outstretched, clawed fingers reaching for his face.

Maya knew she wouldn't reach them in time. Frustrated, she stretched out her hand called on her fire. A ball of flame appeared in her upturned palm. She tipped her hand and aimed at the Churel, flinging the fiery ball at the demon.

The fireball missed the ghostly woman, flying past her head, singeing her hair as it disappeared into the night. It was enough to get the Churel's attention, though. The demon-woman turned to glare at Maya. Her eyes glowed red and she bared yellow spiked teeth when she sneered at Maya. She snarled, then tipped her head in Dev's direction. Her oily hair hung over her face, as she glared at him, her fiery eyes gleaming. And then, in the blink of an eye, the Churel sped towards Dev grasping at him with her viciously long claws.

Dev grunted and held onto his stomach. Maya stomach hurt too, dread filling her slowly. The Churel had gotten to him. And Maya was just standing there like an idiot, watching as her father was attacked by a monster. She had to do something.

In one smooth move, spurred by her fury and her fear, Maya drew another ball of fire and aimed it at the Churel. She didn't wait. This time she immediately drew another ball of fire and sent a stream of them, aiming straight at the Churel's face. It was too close to her father but there was nothing she could do about it now.

"Dad, duck!" she yelled. She had to get the Churel away from him and the only way she knew how was to kill the creature with her fire. A little voice inside her head asked her 'what if it doesn't work?'. But she couldn't listen. She had to trust her firepower.

The first ball of flame hit the Churel, slamming into its neck. The smell of burning meat rose through the air as the fire dissipated in a small puff leaving a blackened scar behind on the demon's leathery skin. The second ball of flame hit her in the chest, burning the fabric of the sari in which she'd been buried.

Fear rippled through Maya. For a moment she thought that the blasts of fire was not working and all she could smell was that demonic odor of the woman. In a fit of fear she sent three balls of fire at the Churel one after the other. She put all her strength and her might into them, hoping they would at least give her father time to flee. And this time, when the fire hit the Churel it set her clothing ablaze.

But it seemed Maya's flames didn't deter the creature. The demon turned to Dev and grabbed a hold of him, grasping the fabric of his shirt with her sharply-tipped fingers. She pulled him closer. The demon possessed an inordinate amount of strength and though Dev struggled in her grip he couldn't get away no matter how hard he tried. The Churel tipped her head to one side, staring at him with her glowing eyes. She gripped his chin, pushing it upwards and baring his neck to her. She raised her free hand, holding it close to him and Maya watched as a vicious looking nail extended from the demons fore-finger. The Churel grinned, her sharp-toothed leer sending chills through Maya. Then the demon looked at Maya.

Maya screamed and ran forward a few steps. "Stop you don't have to do this."

But the Churel just looked at Maya as if she was the one that was crazy. It turned its attention back to Dev and pressed its nail against his jugular. A thin red line appeared as the sharp edge cut into soft flesh. Blood rose to the surface of the incision and the Churel lowered her head to it. Her tongue extended, ready to lap up Dev's lifeblood.

The sight of the extended tongue of the ghostly woman awakened Maya's fury. She extended her hands and dug deep down for the fire. She pulled it from every cell of her body and from deep within her mind, channeling it to her fingers, directing it straight at the Churel.

This time Maya's fire streamed forth so strong and so hot that even Maya herself was surprised. Again, the fire was too close to her dad but she had to take the risk. Even if her fire singed him, he might still make it out alive.

The fire spewed from Maya's hands, straight into the Churel's chest. The demon screamed and for one short moment Maya was afraid. What if all the neighbors heard? What if they came running? Then Maya snickered. They will just have to be ready for the fright of their life.

Maya's fire continued to stream from her fingers, burning deep into the demon's torso. The stink of charred flesh filled the air and wafted around Maya. Her mother, hearing the scream, came running out of the house. And stopped in her tracks, her mouth hanging open in horror. She took a step forward and stared at her husband. But she hesitated. Dev was too close to the fire and he was too close to the demon.

Only Maya could save her father now.

Maya continued sending her fire into the demons chest. The fire power of Kali poured into the body of the dead woman and Maya began to see a certain glow around the ghostly woman's limbs and neck. The demon screamed again, a spine chilling sound that brought goosebumps to Maya's skin and scraped the inside of her ears raw. Maya winced but did not let up the fire.

The demon threw back her head and Maya could see a fiery glow in her throat. She turned and looked at Maya. The red glow in her eyes had faded. Now only Maya's fire glowed in her eye sockets, as the flame coursed through her body. The demon's fingers relaxed, releasing Maya's dad. The Churel let go and stared at her hands in horror. The skin on her arms and fingers began to peel off, flaking away and floating around her until it touched the ground and turned into dust. Her skin fell away in patches, revealing what lay beneath. Bones and dried tendons. Reminding Maya that the woman who stood before her was dead. A living corpse. A true zombie.

A zombie that was now burning up in front of Maya's eyes. The Churel's entire body glowed softly. The yellow gleam was strangely beautiful. Maya shook the thought from her head. Her father fell to the ground blood gushing from his neck. He pressed the heel of his hand against the wound. She channeled more fire straight into the demon. She had to get this done and fast. Leela ran to him, uncaring that the Churel was so near, uncaring that the ghostly woman was burning up not two feet away from her.

Maya took a step towards the Churel focusing her fire on the Churel's chest. The ghost stepped back, as if she wanted to leave, as if she wanted to escape but Maya was not about to let her. This was going to end and it was going to end now. No matter what had been done to the woman while she was alive she had no right to hurt innocent people. And now that she had chosen Maya's dad as a target she had just made her first mistake. And her last. Maya had no sympathy for her any longer.

Flame flickered through the Churel's hair, and the creature that now stood in front of Maya had lost most of its skin and most of its form. It was now one column of flame with the demon somewhere within it. The Churel screamed but the sound of the scream faded into the fire.

And then with a sudden crash of flame the demon fell into a pile golden glowing dust. Maya raised her eyebrows at the unfittingly beautiful end to the horrible creature. A breeze drove through the street, a stray gust of air sending the remains of the Churel into a whirlwind of embers and ash.

And the Churel was gone.

Maya rush to her father's side and he looked up at her with a wry smile. "That's one way to fix a Churel problem," he said.

Maya wanted to laugh. Trust her father to come up some smart-ass comment when all she wanted to do was hug him. She'd come closer to losing him than she'd ever done before. A shiver of fear ran through her as she raised her eyes to meet her mom's gaze. The worried look on her mom's face mirrored her own feelings.

They had almost lost him.

CHAPTER 4

After the excitement of the evening Maya was glad to just be alone in her room. She sat on the bed cuddled up with *Expelling or Disposing of Household Possessions & Demons: A list of cases* trying to concentrate on the words and failing miserably. Not that the book was boring. She'd had it waved in front of her at dinner, a gift from her father for killing the Churel. It's probably wise for Maya to read up anyway but as much as the content was fascinating, her mind still buzzed with thoughts of the Churel and more especially how close her father had come to death.

The Churcl case had been a routine one ; something her parents had done dozens of times before. But what if Maya hadn't been with them this time? She hated to think of what would've happened. The only reason her father was alive today was because *Maya* had killed the Churel. Her parents were powerless against such creatures; and always will be. They relied on ritual to ward off the demons or ghosts, on incantations to kill them. In reality, there was nothing they could to physically defend themselves since weapons and ammunition didn't work so well on this branch of demonic creatures.

The more Maya thought about it the more she began to dislike the idea of her parents and their hunting. It didn't matter that they had experience. As far as she was concerned this one hunt proved that they were not powerful enough to hunt alone.

Maya shifted in her seat, the book lying forgotten on her lap. What also worried her was it had taken far too long for her fire to build up in strength. And it wasn't as if she wasn't practicing. Even though Nik was not here she still did her training every day but she was beginning to wonder when he was going to return. They had to work on advancing her training. They had to. The Churel had been so strong that Maya had doubted her ability to kill it. And that was not good at all.

Her stomach twinged. What if Nik had decided he no longer wanted to train her? What if he decided to stay in Patala? What if Yama had found something else, something better for him to do with his time? Maya wasn't sure what she'd do should that be the case.

Then she shook her head and laughed at herself. She was beginning to get far too paranoid for her own good. He'd promise he'd return and he would. No matter what. Even if his assignment had changed he would come back first tell her. Nik would never just abandon her.

Maya's thoughts flickered on everything that Nik meant to her. He'd been with her since the first moment she'd used her fire and burned Byron, the demon, in seconds. He been the easiest thing to believe when she'd been surrounded by gods and hell-hounds.

Nik had always been her one constant.

When they'd returned from Patala a few weeks ago Nik had promised Maya would always have him in her life. She couldn't keep him all to herself though. Being the son of the God of the Underworld couldn't be easy. The last thing she wanted was put pressure on him and demand that he spend more time with her.

He had other commitments. Ones probably more important than Maya.

But Nik was taking his responsibility for Maya and her training seriously. All she had to do now was to let him do his job. He'd be back soon. She knew he would. For now she would just practice and wait. Oh, and kill any demon that threatens anyone she cares about.

That was all.

CHAPTER 5

The next morning Maya's walk to school seemed surreal. Sparrows soared and dived in the clear blue sky, and the sun was beginning to warm up the day but she couldn't help wondering why she was going to school in the first place?

Wasn't there something better for her to do than to be sitting in class all day learning stuff that will never help her in the future? It's not as if she was going to grow up to be a doctor or lawyer. She snorted at the thought. What a waste that would be of the powers she wielded.

Demon hunting was something that was *in* her blood. And it was the power of Kali that she was destined to wield. She'd finally come to terms with the reality of being the instrument of the goddess Kali. She'd ceased rebelling against it weeks ago.

But even as Maya silently cursed the necessity of attending school, she accepted that, on one level it could be a wise move. They'd all had to continue as if nothing had changed. Nik had said Yama and his informants were not sure how close the mastermind controlling the Rakshasa was to Maya. The last time she'd had to battle the demons they'd come way too close too quickly. She had to be on high alert at all times.

Maya was so deep in thought she almost walked right into Joss.

So much for being on high alert.

"Hey, watch where you're going," said Joss, her blond hair hung open, grazing her shoulders and framing her beautiful face. She raised an expertly tweezed eyebrow while giving Maya a happy grin. "What's the matter with you?"

"Just thinking," said Maya, reluctant to elaborate.

"You look like you were doing some pretty serious thinking." Joss fell into step beside Maya and nudged her with her elbow. "So what gives?"

Maya laughed and knew she'd have no choice but to give in soon. "It's not as serious as it looked. I was just wondering as to the advantages of wasting time attending school instead of being out there fighting demons."

Joss cast her eye around them, taking in the bustling pathway and the school across the street up ahead. "I don't see any demons standing around right this minute, so why not go to school in the meantime?"

Maya shook her head, her mind on her father. "There are plenty of demons out there to fight. You just gotta know where to find them." Then she shrugged, a little deflated. "Besides, you just never know when one will jump out and surprise you."

"So you're telling me you know where to find all these demons," asked Joss, her expression clearly indicating she thought Maya was joking.

But Maya met Joss's gaze head on. It was probably time her friend knew what had happened to Maya's father the night before. In a low voice, Maya related the story, as they weaved through the school crowd. Maya watched Joss's expression closely. Her friend looked horrified and Maya understood that very emotion all too well. She was still horrified herself that her father had come so close to death that she had almost not been able to save him. Her heart clenched every time she thought about it.

"Wow," said Joss the lines of her face dark with concern, she'd gone so pale Maya could see the blue smudges below her eyes through the makeup. Joss was having trouble sleeping again. She didn't want to bring it up but she suspected being revived from the dead would do odd things to a person. Maya paid attention to Joss again, glad she hadn't missed any of Joss's comments. "Sorry, that's all I have. Just wow."

There was a short silence in which both the girls crossed the street side-by-side and hurried up the steps into the school. Then Joss asked softly, , "Is he okay?" her face still worried. She'd grown close enough to Maya's parents that such a close call would worry her as much as it did Maya.

"He's okay now. The bleeding stopped. She just missed his jugular, thankfully. She did manage to give him a triple slides to the abs though. He's got three thin cuts across his tummy. Says it adds character." Maya snorted.

"Good grief, Maya. He could have died if those injuries had been an worse." Joss shook her head, her eyes flashing. "Wasn't he was just doing one of those run-of-the-mill checks? Something they've done all the time?"

Maya nodded vehemently. "Exactly." Then after a short pause she said, "I have an idea. " Joss looked at her, waiting. "I think we should join them, you and me go with them whenever they go out to any of the day hunts or whatever it is that they call it."

"So, what exactly is it that they do?" asked Joss.

"Well, people have these problems with ghosts and spirits and stuff. They get in touch with my parents who go to investigate to see how they can help. So when my parents get there they assess the situation and do what they need to do. Usually it's pretty cut and dried - they do the rituals, chant the chants and it's all done and over and everyone's happy."

Joss smiled. "Sort of Sam and Dean but without the blood and guts and possessions." Maya grinned and nodded. "But last night it wasn't cut and dried?" Joss asked.

"Nope. And put a question mark on the possession statement. I think some of the stuff they deal with can end up possessing the person trying to fix the problem."

"Okay, then. A touch more Sam and Dean than I initially assumed." Joss's face was serious as she nodded her head. "Sounds like they put themselves in danger each time they work a case."

"That's why I think we need to go with them. The way I see it the more eyes and hands the safer they will be. I just never realized until now that their work was this serious, or this dangerous."

Joss nodded as the two girls weaved their way through the crowded hall. The volume around them had slowly increased as the school began to fill up. "I totally agree. Plus it would be pretty cool to see all these ghosts and stuff in action."

"I don't think you'll think that it's pretty cool when you come that close to death," said Maya, her tone a little on edge

Joss flushed. "Sorry, I really didn't mean it like that."

Maya shrugged. "That's okay. I'm a little bit too sensitive today, I think," she said as she reached her locker. She dug around inside it for her books and waved at Joss as they both headed off to separate homerooms.

CHAPTER 6

The day crept along, pretty normal and as boring as it could possibly be. Maya had expected to see Ria at school, but even though she'd kept an eye out she never saw her quiet friend. Ria's fiance Viren had assured Maya nothing would change. Even Ria had said everything would be normal and that she would still come to school, that she would finish school before she got married. But Viren hadn't owed Maya a thing. Her stomach tightened.

She'd known.

At the time she hadn't believed them and it seemed her gut instinct had been right. Ria was nowhere to be found.

Maya settled into her seat in English, trying to put thoughts of Ria and Viren out of her head for a while. She glanced up, expecting to see Mrs. Bane, but it looked like they had a substitute, or a new teacher. Disappointment filled Maya; she'd liked Mrs. Bane. The woman, dressed in a slim fitted navy suit, her hair curled into a dark bun at the back of her neck, tilted her neck as she wrote her name on the board. The chalk scraped as she curved her letters and Maya cringed as the sound seemed to cut right into her brain.

Ms. Harris.

It shouldn't matter to Maya. English was easy enough no matter whom the teacher was. She bent her head over her book, waiting, like the rest of the class until Ms. Harris was ready to address them. As with any new teacher she introduced herself and confirmed they would no longer have our old teacher for the class. Apparently poor Mrs. Bane had a few health issues to resolve.

Then the teacher requested introductions from each student via roll call. More than a few rolled their eyes as each student raised their hand and answered banal questions like how long had they been at XX High and what they liked about English. When Maya's turn arrived she lifted her hand and waited.

Ms. Harris had been walking the aisles, reading the names of her sheet, and the closer she came to Maya the more Maya began to feel uncomfortable. The hairs at the back of her neck stood on end and her skin prickled with goosebumps.

"Maya Rao." She spoke the name loudly. "What is your chosen career path for tertiary studies?"

Maya was stumped. She struggled to find the words, then said, "Graphic design." She let out a soft sigh. It had been on the tip of her tongue to say demon-hunter. Then she stiffened as the teacher came to a stop beside her, so close Maya's shoulder almost brushed the curve of Ms. Harris's hip.

How had Maya missed it?

The scent of meat and incense wafted to her and Maya held her breath. It was that or choke on the odor. It couldn't be. Not again. Not right here in school, out in the open for everyone to see. But the longer the teacher stood beside her the more certain Maya became.

Ms. Harris was a Rakshasa.

Maya kept her body stiff as the demon walked past her. She couldn't understand it. Her senses were meant to be on high alert after the attack of the Churel. She should have detected the smell of meat and spices the moment she'd entered the classroom. Now her stomach turned, the odor making her want to vomit. But she couldn't react. Instead she pretended to read as the demon made a circuit of the room,

When the Rakshasa reached Maya again, she slowed almost imperceptibly. And that was when Maya knew. They knew she was here and they had sent someone. *They should actually know better*, she thought. *The last time they sent someone she'd killed them.*

Maya still felt bad that both Byron and Amber's human forms were killed in the process and even though Nik had convinced her that the demons had taken over the bodies of the humans for so long that there was no human left, she still didn't feel comfortable with the idea of killing people, no matter what form that took.

For now she watched the demon's back as it strolled to the front of the class and turned to face the students. Maya tamped down the twinge of fear that began to rise within her. Showing fear was a bad, bad idea. They'd smell it like a shark smelled blood. There was only one thing that she had to do and try to do well. She had to pretend she had no idea that Ms. Harris was a demon. She had to let them think she hadn't recognized the Rakshasa for what she was. This could be some sort of reconnaissance, and it was probably best to let them think they had the upper hand.

As the lesson continued, Maya began to wonder who the mastermind was behind the Rakshasa search for her. Kas hadn't seemed like he was the one. Not that Maya had gotten the chance to ask him before he'd disappeared into thin air, but her gut was telling her that he wasn't the demon lord sending the Rakshasa's to her.

Someone powerful and very angry wanted Maya, and she suspected they were after the powers given to her by Kali. But what was the point really? All she had was firepower and the ability to detect demons. What difference did it make and what would they use that power for? Although it confused her, she knew they were after her and now they were too close to getting what they wanted.

Hopefully all her training would pay off if they decided to snatch her. A bubbled of laughter welled within her. She'd known coming to school was a bad idea. She just hadn't figured on how bad.

The bell rang and the students rose and filed out of the class. The Ms. Harris demon was good. After her initial question, she never once made eye contact with Maya. She'd behaved normal, did nothing out of the ordinary, not a single thing to let anyone know that beneath the pretty human form was an evil demon.

Maya headed to the cafeteria, choosing a seat near the outside door. It didn't take long for Joss to arrive. At last she saw Joss and waved her over before she could slide into the seat beside her, Maya rose and tucked her hand inside Joss's elbow.

She didn't look around, just smiled at Joss and said, "It's stuffy in here. Let's go outside."

"Okay," said Joss slowly as she eyed Maya and allowed herself to be dragged outside into the the sunlight. Maya pulled her toward the tree that had become their spot, where they used to sit with Ria every lunchtime.

They settled on the grass and Maya pulled out their lunches from her bag. Leela had packed a cold chicken salad for both the girls. Something she'd begun to do more often since Joss began spending more time with Maya's family. As she handed Joss her lunch, Maya said, "There's something I have to tell you." She kept her voice low just to be safe. Now with the Rakshasa around she couldn't be certain if there were more where Ms. Harris had come from.

Joss frowned as she poked a plastic fork into a piece of lettuce. "What's wrong?"

Maya glanced around to check if the coast was clear before she spoke. "The new English teacher..."

"Ms. Harris? She's a bit of the stick in the mud, " said Joss making a face.

"Yeah, she also happens to be a demon," said Maya her tone dry, her heart thumping.

"What?" asked Joss, eyes goggling.

"Eat. Don't let them see you're shocked," urged Maya. "And yeah, she's a Rakshasa. She had the whole raw meat and spices perfume thing going on."

"Crap," said Joss. "They found you." She looked across the field then returned her attention to her food. Maya could tell she was having a hard time scanning their surroundings for potential threats.

"It's not like they didn't know exactly where I was to begin with," Maya said, a wry twist to her lips.

"True. But now they sent someone else for you. Did she act weird? Did she talk to you?"

"Standard questions that she asked everyone," answered Maya. "She was perfectly normal, didn't even bat an extra eyelid in my direction."

"Crap," said Joss, her face dark with worry. "We need to speak to someone. When is Nik getting his ass back to town?"

"Your guess is as good as mine," said Maya, trying to keep her emotions out of her words. "Honestly, I expected him to be back already. I wish I knew what's taking him so long."

"Well, he'd better get back here pronto, before the demons manage to get their claws into you again."

Maya nodded, she couldn't agree more.

CHAPTER 7

The martial arts studio was empty.

Maya and Joss had waited until the afternoon classes ended before heading inside the largest room. Ever since they returned from Patala the two girls practiced as much as possible. Joss was still better at fighting but now Maya's ego could handle it. She was no longer jealous.

Joss threw her bag beside the wall and then swore as three super thick books came tumbling out. She rushed over to it, shoving the books back inside, but not before Maya had gotten a good eyeful of the titles. *Hindu Legends & Mythology, Hindu Gods & Goddesses,* and *The Myths and Gods of India.*

Maya smiled. "Interesting reading material, Joss," she teased.

"Well, I'm taking it seriously you know. It's not easy coming into this with zero knowledge. I didn't know my Asuras from my Avatars until now," said Joss so defensively that Maya burst out laughing.

Maya's mom strode into the room from the inner office. "What's so funny?"

"Nothing," both girls replied simultaneously and Leela grinned.

"Fine then, don't share." She handed Joss a set of gleaming Madu's.

Maya grinned at the look on Joss's face. "You're kidding me right?" she asked as she stared wide-eyed at Maya's mom.

"Not not kidding at all. That's for you. Your very own set." Leela smiled as Joss turned the weapons over and over inspecting it and grinning widely.

"Wow," said Joss, her voice still holding a touch of disbelief as if she couldn't believe that someone had actually given her something that she wanted so much. She of the parents who whored her with every known meta rial object in the hopes that she wouldn't realize they were pretty much absent all the time. "These things are pretty awesome. I wanted my own set ever since I saw yours Maya."

"And now you have one," Maya said, grinning at her friend. "Now how about practicing with them instead of ogling them and feeling them up."

Joss giggled and the two girls moved to the center of the mat. Maya sank into the start position, softening her knees and bouncing on them. She held her Madu's in front of her, turning and twisting them this way and that. She loved the fluidity of the antelope horns. Opposite her, Joss mimicked her movements and soon enough they settled into a fluid dance, moving back and forth away from each other, then towards each other again.

Leela watched for a while, then stepped forward. "Okay, now that you're both comfortable with the weapon's physics there are a few sequences that we could practice to get you more comfortable in using them in a fight. Maya, when you've fought with the Madu's in the past, have you ever had the opportunity to jump and fight with them?"

Maya frowned wondering what her mom meant. "I'm not sure," she said. "I don't think so. Whenever I've had to use then I did so while on both my feet."

Leela nodded. "So, I think it's time you both train to fight with Madu's while doing things like jumping or running or spinning."

"Oh. I see what you mean," said Maya. "Using the Madu, and even while your hand is occupied with them still doing martial arts stuff with the rest of you body."

"Yes, exactly. Now watch me for a moment." Leela sank into her stance and began to perform a series of movements that were so unique and different that both girls were transfixed. She moved with such fluid grace it looked like she was dancing. Maya recalled the first time she'd ever seen her mother practice with the Madu's. Her mother's movements was so beautiful, so small, so intricate that it was a form of dance.

Maya scowled. She had never been much of a dancer. She'd failed to inherited her mom's dancing genes. Probably one of the reasons martial arts came a little harder to her than to the rest of her family but Maya did the best she could in spite of her two left feet.

And she was pretty good, if she said so herself.

Joss and Maya followed Leela's instructions and fell into a routine of practice for the rest of the session. They were both drenched as they sank to the mat in exhaustion.

"Boy, this is harder than it looks" said Joss, the expression in her voice saying she had enjoyed the session as much as Maya. "To be honest I don't want it to end."

"Maybe it should," said Leela. "You girls have done enough. You don't want to overtire yourself. If you're too tired you may lose your concentration and end up accidentally skewering each other with the Madu's. Change and head back to the house. There's roast chicken on for dinner tonight and you both deserve a nice hot meal after all this hard work."

The girls headed off to the showers and Maya grinned to herself. She loved that Joss was spending much more time with her. It was like having a sister. She'd almost lost Joss, and her stomach still hurt when she remember looking down at Joss's pale and lifeless face.

She had lost Joss.

And if Yama had not granted her boon and given Joss her life back, Maya would be alone today.

CHAPTER 8

When the girls returned home after practice at the center, the first thing they did was gulp down their dinner of roast chicken and garlic potatoes. Both tired from their training session they spent the meal mostly in comfortable silence. Then Joss headed home and Maya ran upstairs to check on her dad.

As she entered the room he glanced up from reading the paper. A light blanket lay over his legs and his laptop sat beside him. He didn't look too happy to be confined to his bed. But then when faced with the fury of his wife he didn't have much of a chance.

"Hi," said Maya as she took a seat at the foot on the bed.

Dev smiled. "Hi, yourself. How was school?"

"School was . . . interesting." Maya wasn't sure how best to put it.

"That sounds foreboding," said her father, scrunching up one brow.

"I guess foreboding would be the right word to use when it comes to demons," said Maya.

He frowned and laid his paper on his lap. "What do you mean, Maya?"

"Ms. Harris, my new English teacher is of the Rakshasa persuasion."

Dev's eyebrows shot up almost into his hairline as he stared at her. She was amused to see that he clearly had no idea what to say to that revelation. He sat up straight, folded his paper and set it beside him. Maya watched him unsure what his next move will be. He wasn't taking this news very well and she hoped he wasn't going to overreact and leap off the bed to go on a Rakshasa hunt.

Her dad studied her face, his eyes dark with worry. "Maya, maybe you shouldn't go to school."

"Are you crazy, Dad?" asked Maya. "The moment I stay at home they will know something is up." Maya couldn't believe it. Just this morning she was convincing herself that going to school was the worst idea ever. Now she was actually advocating going to school. But it made total sense. The last thing she wanted to do is to alert the demons that she was on to them.

Her father sat back against the pillows and sighed. "You're probably right, Maya. I really wish we knew what to do. Who is it that's sending these demons to find you?"

Maya shrugged. "Maybe Nik knows something," she said hopefully. "As soon as he gets back I'll ask him." Maya spoke with a confidence she simply didn't have. She had no idea when Nik was returning. But she didn't want her dad to know that she was clueless herself. "And besides, I can take care of myself. If Ms. Harris decides to go all Rakshasa on me I'll give as good as I get."

"I'm guessing you will," said her dad chuckling.

Maya smiled, tugged his big toe through the blanket, and left him to his own devices. Back in her room she flung her bag on her bed and pulled her books out to begin her homework. Soon she found herself staring at the papers in disgust. Homework. Why did she need to do homework? Maya clicked her tongue. It was a never-ending argument. She had to go to school so she had to do her homework. End of story. No point in complaining about it, no point in fussing.

With a little bit of persistence Maya was soon making steady headway when she heard a sound at the door. She looked up expecting to see her mother, a smile already on her face.

CHAPTER 9

*N*ik stood at the door leaning against the door jamb, a cheeky grin on his face. As soon as Maya saw him all she wanted to do was fling herself into his arms. But she remained on the bed and held herself stiff. She was still pretty annoyed with him that he had disappeared for so long without even a phone call to say how long he will be. Sure they had no phones in Patala but surely he could have found a way to let her know how long he'd be. Just because he was now here didn't mean she'd have to go jumping up and down and smothering him with kisses.

Not that she didn't want to smother him with kisses.

So in the end she just smiled at him and sat on her bed. Nik grinned as he walked in to the room. And Maya heard the click-clack of nails on the wood floor. She peered around his legs.

Sabala.

Maya grinned at the hell-hound who looked at her with all four of his big black eyes. He came around Nik to sit at the foot of her bed. Once comfortable he looked up her and tilted his head as if to say 'I'm here, now you don't have to worry about anything.'

But Maya's attention remained on Nik.

"Hey," he said as he sat on the bed beside her.

"Hey," Maya responded. She smiled and her smile was genuine despite the little bubble of anger. "There is something you need to know, though."

"Well, let's just get down to business then," said Nik with a wry smile. She detected a hint of annoyance in his tone and narrowed her eyes at him, but he hid it well and offered her a grin. Maya quickly told him about Ms. Harris, the Rakshasa demon. "She's your English teacher?"

Maya nodded. "And she hasn't given any indication that she's there for me. Didn't even pay me any extra attention."

"Interesting." Nik seemed to be far away as he absorbed the demonic development.

"Is that all you can say?" asked Maya, finally allowing her annoyance to filter through.

"What do you expect me to say?" he asked, the expression on his face one of confusion.

Maya glared at him. "What took you so long anyway?" she asked, keeping her gaze on his face.

Nik's brown lifted with slightest bit and his smile disappeared. "I'm sorry. There were a few things I need to get for you. Sorry it took so long."

"You were getting stuff for me?" asked Maya,her annoyance had suddenly evaporated, repleted with a good dose of curiosity.

"Yes," said Nik as he patted his rucksack. "I'll show them all to you at our next training session."

"And when will that be?" asked Maya pointedly.

"As soon as you can make time," he responded. She hadn't expected that and for a moment she was thrown.

"Now, would be good," said Maya. She raised an eyebrow at him. "You've been gone long enough." She got to her feet, abandoning her books, and headed out the door. Nik and Sabala followed closely. As she passed her father's room she popped her head inside. "Dad, Nik is here and we are off to do some training downstairs."

Her dad gave Nik a welcoming smile and then waved them off. Nik and Maya headed to the garage. Dev had converted the triple garage into a small fire-training area. A more convenient place for Maya to practice controlling her fire power. Maya and Nik usually trained in an abandoned parking garage on the outskirts of town. But it was not always convenient for them to rush off to the garage for training. Sometimes they were just doing focused training which didn't really need to be done in a concrete building. Dev had sprayed the walls of the garage with flame retardant paint in the hopes that Maya will not burn the place down.

Maya hoped it would help to prevent her from torching the place

She led Nik into the garage. He followed closely behind her, although she did notice that he remained oddly silent. How she managed so long without him? She didn't like the idea that she was beginning to feel like she depended on him too much. There had been a time when she hadn't depended on anybody and she'd been pretty happy with that.

The click-clack on the floor confirmed that Sabala was also coming along. Maya scowled, wondering what she would do with the hell-hound when she had to go to school the next day. He'd either have to stay at home or be invisible.

She flipped the light switch and waved a hand at the empty garage.

"Set up wherever you like," she said glancing at Nik. He nodded and walked over to the metal table on the far wall where he proceeded to empty his rucksack of an array of little glass bottles. Maya frowned at the line of tiny bottles. They looked suspiciously as if they contained blood.

Maya didn't like the idea at all.

"What are those," she asked, certain she didn't want to hear his answer.

She wasn't surprised when he responded, "Blood."

"Is that where you were all this time? Looking for blood?" Maya asked with a silent scoff.

Nik nodded. "This is it an important part of your training. It's essential that you know how to a identify the different types of blood."

Maya just nodded, unsure what she should say to that. The idea of working with blood in any shape or form was just gross. With Nik in charge of her training, the last thing she wanted to do was to challenge him.

Once his bottles were all sorted Nik turned to Maya and leaned against the table behind him. He smiled at her and the next moment he was Nik all over again. The same Nik that had helped her after she'd torched Byron, the same Nik who'd guided her through the tasks that Yama had set for her. The same Nik who'd promised that she would always have him.

"So where did you disappear to all this time? Was it really that hard to find blood samples?" She had tried but she'd been unable to keep the accusation out of her voice.

Nik smiled apologetically and shook his head. "I'm really sorry. I know I was gone for a long time without contacting you."

Maya shrugged, "Three weeks isn't exactly the longest time in the world, but I guess you could say that I did wonder where you were and what had happened to you."

"I'm really sorry, Maya. I guess I should've realized that you'd be wondering. I didn't realize how long I'd been gone. I was a little preoccupied." When Maya didn't respond his smile slowly disappeared. "I had to pay my mother a visit."

All Maya managed was a soft "Oh." She was beginning to feel a little guilty pushing Nik for an answer.

"It's been a while since I visited her," said Nik. "I didn't want her to worry."

Maya smiled. "I understand. Maybe someday you could take me to meet her." After the words were out Maya realized how forward that sounded. It's not as if Nik had asked her to marry him. They were just together for now. How does one date demigod anyway? Maya gritted her teeth and chided herself for her big mouth.

But Nik merely nodded and didn't seem in the least annoyed with her suggestion. He smiled and said, "You may be in for a little surprised when you do finally meet my mother."

Maya frowned and was about to ask why when Nik continued, "I'm older than you think. And so is my mother."

She frowned again, "How old are you?" Suddenly, she was waiting for his answerer even though she'd never even wondered at Nik's age. Why had she never thought about it? He was a demigod son of Yama the God of the underworld. Why had she taken it for granted that he was really close to her own age. Now she was more curious than ever.

Nik sighed and rubbed his hand through his hair. "I'm not sure how you're going to take this. I mights as well just come right out and say it." He paused and Maya nodded. "I was born in 1952. My mother is now 81 years old and she has a small place in Florida."

The silence was palpable as Maya absorbed the ramifications of Nik's answer. 1952 she thought. That would make Nik 62 years old. Then she said "Wow, I'm dating an old dude."

"Is that all you have to say," said Nik. Confusion twisted his brow.

"What did you expect me to say?" Maya asked, a soft smile at her lips.

"Well, I didn't expect you to take it so well," he said grinning. Clearly he'd been tense about her reaction. He'd been worried about what she was going to say to his age revelation. Apparently there were two of them who were a little unsure of themselves in this relationship.

"How else do you expect me to take it," asked Maya. "You are the son of the God of the underworld. You're a god in your own right and I really didn't expect you to be human. It's hard for me to get my head around it, I have to be honest. But it's not anything that I can't handle for now." Then she thought of something. "Do you age at all?"

Nik nodded. "I do age but at a very, very slow rate. Most of the gods are immortal but the demigods are not. Unless they partake of the Amrita."

Maya's heart twisted. It was easy to think of him as being a demigod, easy to think of him as being son of the God of the underworld, but it wasn't exactly easy to think of him as not aging. Before her stood a man who was 52 years old. Or more specifically, he'd been around for 52 years. Maya was 16. She was human and she would age and soon she would be just like his mother while he looked the way he looks now. Maya wasn't sure that she could handle that. But maybe that would be something she could think about another time. For now she would just enjoy the moment. Enjoy being part of his life. Enjoy being with Nik. She'd deal with the bigger issues when the time came.

Then she remembered something. "Kas." She frowned.

"What about Kas?" asked Nik.

"Varuni was kept in captivity for decades. How old does that make Kas?"

"I'm not entirely sure of the dates, but we suspect that Kas had generated his rebirth just before the turn of the 20th century. So I'm guessing he would've been born around 1880 to 1890."

Maya nodded remembering what Kas looked like but also remembering that he was a demon and capable of shape shifting. "So he is kind of like you."

Nik nodded. "In essence, yes. Kas is the son of an immortal and even though he used a different method of being born into the world again he still is, for all intents and purposes, a demigod."

"A demon demigod you mean." Maya raised an eyebrow

Nik nodded. "A demon demigod. That's pretty accurate."

"Where do you think he went?" I asked, thinking about Kas and how he'd disappeared into thin air after she'd injured him. She still felt bad about hurting him. And she'd wrestled with her guilt too- why hadn't she killed him like she was supposed to? Was it because he'd managed to make her sympathize with him? To be honest he'd had a pretty enigmatic personality, one that she'd been slowly drawn to and instead of wanting to kill him she'd wanted to understand him better.

Although she'd expected to get into trouble with Yama for not fulfilling his direction in the end she hadn't. She just decided to consider herself lucky and leave it at that.

"I haven't a clue," said Nik frowning. "And with Kas still out there, we have unfinished business."

"So you guys have absolutely no idea where he went?" Maya asked.

"We have some thoughts. Maybe Naraka."

"Why can't you go and find him and arrest him?"

"We are trying. But so far we've come up with nothing. There have been sightings but as to how trustworthy they are we cannot be certain. He will be found though. That is a promise."

"Do you think he could be the one sending the demons after me?" Maya asked still worried about the demon English teacher.

"I don't think it's likely," he answered and Maya had to agree. Her gut told her that Kas wouldn't be sending his demons after her with the intent of hurting her. So far all the demons that had been on her tail hadn't held back in fighting her. Amber would've readily ripped Maya apart before taking her off to her master. "The demons after you seem much more vicious and I'm not sure Kas would be sending such creatures to find you."

Maya smiled, "Do you think he's really a bad guy?"

Nik frowned, "I really can't say. I know he had his reasons for taking Varuni. And I know he had his reasons for trying to come back to have a life. Maybe he'd done wrong in the past, how can we judge him now?"

Maya thought about Balraj, Kas's sorcerer who'd experimented on her, who'd tortured her trying to take her fire. Maya was sure she wouldn't be able to forgive Kas for that. It's not as if he was totally innocent. It's not as if he hadn't harmed by his actions. Still, Maya hadn't had the heart to kill him when it counted.

Maybe that could be considered a failure. But Maya wasn't going to be keeping one eye on the past. For now she had to figure out what her next step was. What does the hand of Kali do next?

"So, let's talk about blood," said Maya, trying to refocus her attention.

Nik nodded and turned to the row of bloody bottles. The macabre sight made Maya's skin tingle. As she stood and studied them she realized it wasn't just the sight of the blood that was making her feel uncomfortable. It was something about the blood itself.

She shuddered and Nik glanced at her. "What's wrong?"

"I dunno, I just feel weird. All goose bumpy," she said rubbing her arms. Nik smiled. "What's funny?" she asked scowling.

"It's not funny. I'm just happy you can sense it without me telling you to." He had a very satisfied look on his face which Maya assumed was a good thing.

"Okay, so what exactly am I sensing?"

"Your ability to detect demon blood is on high alert because many of those bottles contain the blood of different types of demons," Nik said as he reached forward to grab one of the bottles. "Now, for the next part of the test. You ready?"

"As I'll ever be I suppose," said Maya eying the bottles suspiciously.

"Good," said. Nik as he handed her a small, stoppered vial

filled with bloody sludge. "Now, smell this and tell me what you think of it."

Maya grimaced and took the bottle, holding it carefully, the thought of dropping the vial just as bad as the idea of smelling its contents. She gritted her teeth and brought the bottle closer to her face.

She must have spent too long staring at the bottle because Nik's voice broke through her thoughts, "Maya you really do need to remove the stopper to actually smell the blood." There was a smile in the tone of voice but it didn't make her feel any better.

"I am well aware of that," Maya snapped, glaring at his grinning face. She tugged at the little cork stopper and jimmied it off, bringing the vial close to her nose. It really was a now or never sort of situation. She might as well get it done.

Maya bent to the mouth of the vial, her nostrils positions just an inch from it. She inhaled slowly, tentatively, not wanting to get a lungful of eau de demon. She got the scent of copper, the distinct bloodiness if the odor, but that was all. She realized then that she wasn't even tingling or feeling odd while she smelled the contents of the vial.

She frowned and looked up at Nik's expectant face. "Is something wrong with this blood?"

"Why do you ask?" said Nik, his expression inscrutable.

"I don't smell demon. I just smell blood." Maya shook her head as she spoke, confused. For a few frightening seconds she feared that maybe she was failing at being the hand of Kali.

"Well done," responded Nik, giving her a small round of applause. She frowned at him and he spoke. "It's human blood."

Maya shuddered giving the vial a disgusted glare. "Who did you find to donate this?"

Nik laughed. "You don't worry about its origins, just concentrate on learning the technique and the intricacies of the odors."

"So human blood doesn't give me the heebie-jeebies. That's

comforting," Maya said with a wry smile. She stoppered the vial and moved it over to the far left of the table. "Okay, what's next?"

Nik handed Maya a second vial. The moment the vial touched her skin Maya's body began to tingle with awareness, a sense of discomfort that spread though her limbs and even raised the hair on her scalp. Nik was silent. He waited while she stared the cork. Maya wrinkled her nose as she brought the vial closer then stopped.

"How do you feel?" Nik's soft voice penetrated her foggy thoughts.

Her mind had taken on an almost dreamlike quality, her focus directed exclusively on the vial in her hand. Her palms itched and the back of her throat felt parched. Maya blinked, trying to free herself from the threads of strange power that seemed to be trying to overcome her.

She cleared her throat. "I'm not sure. I feel a bit weird."

"Weird is good." Nik's voice was cool and calming, sending a wash of comfort over her super tight nerves. "Tell me what you feel"

"My palms itch, as if my fire just wants to burst out of it. And my throat is sore, like I need to drink ten glasses of water before I feel any better. And I feel like I'm weak, or drugged." Maya's voice hitched. She couldn't deny she was afraid. These sensations were strange and they had her worried.

"That's exactly what you want to feel. It means your body and mind are reacting to the blood." Nik searched her face. "You have to find a way to handle it, to not let it overcome you."

"Easy for you to say," Maya grumbled.

"I know," he grinned. "I'm sorry. I wish I could be more helpful but all I can do is give you direction. You need to feel your way through it yourself."

Maya nodded, although she was slightly annoyed that she didn't have a real teacher. Not that she didn't appreciated Nik but knowing *he* didn't know how to sense the blood didn't inspire a lot of confidence in her.

She focused on the bottle and brought the open mouth to her nose. She was trying to be brave, decided to just jump in with both feet. Her stomach heaved as she breathed the odor of the blood in and for a moment she was certain she would throw up all over herself. She swallowed hard and concentrated on the smell.

"This is definitely demon but it's not Rakshasa."

"You have always been able to recognize the smell of Rakshasa blood," he said his voice low and encouraging .

Maya nodded. "Yeah, I've been close enough to Rakshasa blood on many an occasion." Maya recalled the pungent odor of rotting meat and incense that she always got when around Rakshasa demons. She knew now that the odor was the smell of their blood. "So what sort of demon is this."

"That vial of blood belongs to a Vitala demon. A Vampire."

CHAPTER 10

Maya's eyes popped wide. "You're kidding me right. For a moment there I thought I heard you say it's vampires blood."

"You heard right." Nik's expression remained neutral.

"So, you're also saying to me that vampires are real?" Maya scoffed.

"I'm real, aren't I?" said Nik, raising his eyebrows. "And so are Rakshasa's. So what's the big deal with vampires being real?"

Maya stared at him, a little unsure how to respond. He was right. So many unbelievable things were really real, how could she now question the existence of vampires. "Um, okay. I see what you mean." Maya bit her lip, her gaze hovering over the bottle of vamp blood. Then she nodded at Nik. "So, what do these vampires look like. Do they have fangs and turn into bats?"

"No, Vitalas are spirits or demons that possess the dead, so most people assume the dead person has come back to life but that is not the case. They use the corpses to get around and can leave the old body for a new one, at will. The only vampiric characteristic of the Vitala is that they have long thin wings and can fly for short distances."

Maya shuddered. More things that go bump in the night. And she had thought the Churel had been bad enough.

"So what's next?" she asked, hoping they would get the whole gross exercise over with as soon as possible.

"Now you need to taste it."

The silence in the garage was an almost tangible thing as Maya stared at Nik, the horror freezing her expression to something she was sure was ghastly.

"What?" she croaked. Blood thundered in her ears and her stomach heaved.

"Taste it." Nik was relentless.

"You're insane. I'm not putting that stuff in my mouth," Maya said, her voice ending in a high-pitched squeak.

Nik watched her, his expression far too patient for Maya's liking. "You have to. There are deeper nuances to the taste of the blood that will enable you to identify the creature if in disguise. It will also amplify your ability to detect the demon. Like with the Ms. Harris demon, you would have smelled her from outside the class if your ability was as strong as it could be. At the height of your strength you would be able to detect a demon within a 500 yard radius. Your ability to detect and track them really does depend on your familiarity with their blood."

Maya gritted her teeth. He was making a good case, everything he said made sense and even the prospect of being so powerful as to detect demons from hundreds of yards away was extremely encouraging, but she was still hesitant. The thought of the Vampire demons blood on her tongue, in her mouth, still made her want to throw up.

For a few moments Nik remained silent, allowing her to think it over. A part of her accepted she would do it in the end. She would not be able to say no to the opportunity to master her powers. That would be stupid. But it didn't mean the idea didn't disgust her.

Maya exhaled, then held her for finger over the mouth of the little bottle before tipping it over. She removed her blood drenched digit, then set the bottle on the table. She stared at the red liquid wetting her fingertip and grimaced.

Then she stuck her tongue out and touched the tip of her finger with it. She didn't want to get any more of the blood in her mouth than she had to. She turned to Nik tongue still sticking out of her mouth.

"Swallow," he said, his eyes twinkling. Maya glared at him. It then occurred to her that glaring while sticking ones tongue out might not be a very intimidating look.

Maya grunted then pulled her tongue into her mouth and tasted the blood. Every cell in her body rebelled and her throat muscles refused to function as she tried to swallow. Bile surged up her throat and she felt a little faint. She gripped the edge of the table and refused to let Nik see her dilemma. At last she forced herself to swallow, and tamped down the urge to throw up as well.

Again she tasted the rot of meat at the back of her tongue, a bitter iron taste too, quite unlike the coppery tinge to normal blood. And something different that made her sure the blood did not belong to a Rakshasa.

Maya nodded.

"Can you tell the difference now?" asked Nik.

"Yes, it's subtle but it's definitely there." She looked at him. "That does not mean I am any less disgusted."

"I'm sorry to do that to you Maya, but it's the only way."

"It's fine. I can handle it," Maya answered, still not certain she believed her words. But the best thing was to get on with it. That meant more smelling and more tasting. "Okay, so who's next?"

Nik reached for another bottle and handed it to Maya who sniffed, shuddered, then proceeded to taste the blood. She had decided the faster she got it over and done with, the better. This time the blood tasted ashy and bitter.

"What demon is this?" Maya asked grimacing.

"That's the Preta demon. They look like corpses, thin skin over bones, with big bellies and long thin necks."

Nick sounded so matter of fact he could have been discussing the weather, instead of demons and demon blood. Maya swallowed hard. The thought that she had just ingested demon blood still making her stomach churned.

"Okay, so what's next," asked Maya, more keen now than ever that she wanted to get the whole thing done. "We've done the human blood. We've done the Vitala blood, and the Rakshasa, and this was the Preta demon. What more do you have for me?"

"Just one more," Nick said as he pointed to the final bottle sitting on the corner of the table. Maya reached for the vial. She couldn't deny that she was relieved that this was the final lot of blood that she had to taste. She opened the stopper, inhaled the scent of the blood and sniffed. She looked at Nik frowning, "This smells like rotten fruit with a tinge of bloody on the side."

Nick laughed. "Taste and let's see if they also taste like rotten fruit."

Maya made a face and turn her attention back to the vial. "Well, here goes nothing." She repeated the process, tipping the vial onto the tip of her forefinger and placing it carefully onto her tongue. And she'd been right, it did taste of fruit. "So what demon is this last one?"

"That is a Pisacha demon. In their natural form that are red-eyed, dark skinned and have bulging bluish veins. They can become invisible at will and can also take on whatever form they chose."

"So there's a very real possibility we have interacted with one at some point?" asked Maya.

"Of course. That is a possibility. And now that you know what their blood smells like you will be able to identify a Pisacha even if it's invisible standing twenty feet away from you. The trick then is to get it be visible. Unless you are able to fight it off just using your sense of smell to guide you."

"I'm beginning to see what you mean," she said turning to face Nik. "The taste of the blood amplifies the ability to smell it. It's as if it trains my nostrils to detect the deeper parts of the blood that can tell exactly what type of demon it is. It's still majorly gross that I have to taste the blood, but I see now why you made me do it."

"I'm glad you have accepted the training in all its grossness," he said giving her a wink. "Now just one more test and you can call it quits for tonight."

"There's more? I thought we were done with all the vials," Maya complained as she watched Nik grab all the vials and push them around on the table, messing with the order so Maya no longer knew which vial was which.

Done, Nik waved a hand at the line of five? Vials and said, "Now for a blind test."

"You're going to blindfold me."

Nik laughed. "No. its just a blind test, in a manner of speaking."

Maya couldn't deny she was relieved. She wasn't sure why but the thought of Nik blindfolding her and making her taste the different blood really, really creeped her out.

"Right, all you have to do is smell the vial now and tell me straight off what demon's blood it contains." Nik paused, then said, "Now turn around and face the other wall and close your eyes."

Maya did as she was told, felt Nik hold her hand and open her fingers to place a vial in her palm. Eyes still shut, she unstoppered the bottle and carefully placed her nose to the opening and sniffed.

The ashy bitter odor identified the blood immediately. Maya grinned. "Preta demon."

She heard Nik say, "Very good," then felt him take the vial away and replace it with another bottle.

One whiff and she knew it was Rakshasa. Nik grunted. "Bear

in mind I may give you the same blood twice just to keep you on your toes." Then he continued to go through the rest of the vials, sometimes trying to trip her up by giving her the same blood one after the other but Maya was right every time.

"Right, " Nik said at last. She opened her eyes and grinned at him. Then he said, "Your ability to detect and identify the demon's blood, right down to species, is stronger that even I expected." He stared at her, a look of pride in his eyes.

"Thanks," Maya said, feeling a tingle of her own pride run through her. And though she knew the power she used was inherently that of the goddess Kali, she also felt a certain level of satisfaction with her ability to learn to use the power well. Thinking of Kali made her wonder about Nik himself and she asked, "Do you have a similar power?"

Nik paused in his task of placing the vials onto a piece of velvet and tying them in place with little pieces of string attached to the fabric. "I do have the power to detect demons but certainly nothing as strong as yours. Among the gods their powers and abilities differ. Mother Kali is the only god with such specific demon related powers." Maya had to take a moment to digest that. The fact that she was more powerful at something than Nik stunned her. He continued to speak and she had to force herself to pay attention. "And remember, your fire power is also stronger than mine."

Maya was even more stunned. "You are joking right?" She stared at him. "You are the one that showed me how to heal myself, and how to fight so I would defeat Kas. How can I be more powerful than you?"

"Because you are." Nik said simply. "I've been teaching you what I know and every time you master the technique within minutes. And the power behind it – that's not something I can compare myself to. I can fight with the fire, yes. But you have more power in your fire than anyone I know. Except for Kali of course." He smiled wryly.

Maya thought about the goddess and the last time Kali had visited her. She'd bequeathed Maya with these powers but she was hardly around to teach her how to use them, let alone master them. It seemed the responsibility for all Maya's training had fallen squarely on Nik's shoulders. Not that she was complaining. She quite liked Nik as her trainer. But Maya had to wonder. Why had she be given these powers? Were they for her to use to do good in general or were they to use specifically for god-requested missions.

Ever since she'd left Patala, Maya had had the funny feeling that she was going to be called back soon on another near impossible mission.

Or maybe she was just being paranoid.

CHAPTER 11

Maya and Nik walked to school in a comfortable silence, the early morning sunshine drizzlingly weakly onto their bared skin. He'd come by to fetch her, appearing on her doorstep as she locked up to leave. She stared up at his face, absorbing the lines of his cheekbones, his dark eyes, wanting to run her fingers along his dark dark eyebrows - his real eyebrows. She blinked, a newborn bird opening and shutting its eyes so desperately slowly. She could see the real Nik beneath the slathered on glamor he'd assumed for his job here in XXX.

She swallowed hard. Why could she suddenly see through Nik's glamor?

Sunlight glinted off the bridge of his nose. Nik was back to his old disguise, with a different shape to his nose and much, much lighter skin. Maya looked forward to hearing what Joss would say.

Tepid sunlight dancing on the soft brushed hair on the top of his head. The soft undercut he'd chosen was nice, a neutral style that gave him that sexy mysterious look. "Nice do." She grinned as he glanced at her, his eyes confused. "Is it just glamor or are we seeing the real thing?"

His confusion dissipated and he grinned. "Ah yes. It's Mother's idea. It's just glamor. She seemed to think I needed a change. So here I am trying it on for size."

"Maybe she was right," Maya winked. "It looks good."

She smiled as he lifted his hand to the short cut sides near his ears. "So you like it enough for me to have it cut?" When she nodded, feeling strange that he needed her opinion, he said, "Good. I'll have it cut as soon as I get the chance."

Then he was asking her how she'd slept. Stupid smalltalk when faced with revelations like this, but she answered and ended up bringing him up to speed on the Churel. He merely nodded at the news, his expression serious but not in the least surprised.

"It's expected for your parents to run into these kinds of dangers. I hardly think that would have been the first time, Maya. You shouldn't worry about them so much. After this incident they're probably already better prepared for the next case."

Maya lifted her shoulder in a noncommittal shrug. It was pretty much what her mom and dad had both told her. He dad was feeling much better and was up and about, readying himself for his next case. But she still felt responsible. They were her parents after all.

"Either way, I think I'll still go with them whenever I can. Who knows, I can probably be useful." She tried to sound blase but she couldn't hide the note of worry in her voice.

She stole a glance at Nik as she pushed her long black hair behind her ear. She'd missed him and she was so relieved he'd returned. But nonetheless it bugged her. She wondered if she was being too selfish, too dependent on him. They hadn't had much of a chance to talk after the whole blood sucking training. He'd left Sabala with Maya and went off to do his thing and Maya, although she had been dying to know what he was doing, had restrained herself from asking any nosy questions.

One ought not to question the son of the god of the underworld.

At least that's what was expected, wasn't it?

They escaped the morning sunshine and entered the hallways of the school. A gasp of Chanel No 5 and they were accosted by a happily grinning Joss.

"Nik," she said whooped so loudly that a few curious heads turned in our direction. Then she lowered her voice to almost a whisper and said, "My favorite demigod has come to town."

The demigod grinned as Joss grabbed hold of him and squashed him in a welcoming hug. "Hello Joss." Nik laughed and returned the squeeze.

Joss held him away and studied him head to foot. "Looking good, Nik. I do so love the whole paleface look you have going on." Joss waved at Nik's face and smiled. She meant every word.

Maya smothered a laugh and pushed the two of them ahead of her. "Let's get moving." Neither of them protested. Joss merely linked arms with Nik, the waterfall of her blonde hair swaying as she asked him loads of forward questions about where he'd been and why he'd been gone so long.

Concern scratched at Maya and she was about to scold her overzealous friend and tell her not to interrogate Nik when Joss spoke. "That wasn't very nice you know," she chided him, poking a green painted finger into his bicep. Joss's fingernails were always well painted though these days she made one important concession for their training - her nails were now always trimmed short. No more talons. "You had us worried."

"I'm sorry." Nik rubbed his arm and had the grace to look a little sheepish. Maya decided she liked Joss giving him the third degree after all. "I really was busy. I didn't realize how long I'd been."

Joss shook her head, clicking her tongue sadly, the tapping

sound echoing around them like an annoyed woodpecker. "I'm sure you know what a cell phone is?" She raised her eyebrows at him.

"I know. I'm sorry." He raised his hands in surrender, then threw an arm around each of the girls and gave Maya a spine-tingling smile. "How about I make it up to you girls? Let me take you out to dinner. Tomorrow night."

Maya opened her mouth to protest. Where would Nik get the money for dinner and eating out since his parents weren't exactly human, working a full time paying job. But Joss cut in and said, "That sound totally perfect to me. You two pick me up at six?" She gave Maya a 'don't you dare say no' glare.

Nik nodded and reluctantly Maya did the same. What was the point in protesting now anyway? The plans were already made and though a small part of her was annoyed that she'd had pretty much no say in the arrangements, she had to admit she like the idea of dinner with Nik.

Nik and Joss. Yes. Definitely something to look forward to.

After grabbing their books from their lockers Nik and Maya headed to English. The class hummed with pre-lesson chatter.

Sandalwood teased her nostrils.

A whisper of blood

The volume dive bombed the moment the door swung open to admit Ms. Harris. Maya had to hide her nod of satisfaction – today she'd smelled the Rakshasa before she'd even entered the class. Beside her Nik gave her an inquiring look and she nodded happily.

Again the demon was careful not to let on that it was Maya she was interested in. And Maya and Nik remained calm and behaved normally. Maya relaxed when Ms. Harris gave no indication that she'd recognized Nik either. His glamor must be working full time. Only when she felt the tension leave her shoulders did she realize she'd been worried about his cover being blow at all.

Maya focused on the demon at the front of the class. Now that she'd tasted the blood it seemed her power of smell had been amplified. The only thing that Maya now feared was she wouldn't be able to hold onto her breakfast because of the pungent odor of the demon that filled the classroom, becoming stronger and stronger by the minute.

She glanced over at Nik whose expression confirmed he was paying close attention to the demon. Worry darkened his eyes and filled the shadows of his profile. The class dragged on interminably and Maya had to force herself to pay attention. The demon had the nasty habit of springing questions on the students when they least expected.

At the end of the lesson, Nik did his obligatory visit to the teacher, explaining he'd been away and asking if he'd missed anything. Maya didn't wait for him. She wasn't eager to tip the Rakshasa off that Nik was with her so she walked straight out of the room.

Anyone who kept Maya company was fair game where the demons were concerned. The thought brought Maya to a standstill in the middle of that hallway. She stood there in silence, frozen stiff, her heart thudding.

Ria had been missing from class again.

"What's wrong?" Joss's voice penetrated Maya's surging fear. "You look like you've seen a ghost. And considering it's you that may be true." Joss grinned.

Maya ignored her and asked, "Have you seen Ria?"

Joss's grin evaporated and she shook her head. "No." She glanced up and down the hallway, as if Ria would suddenly appear just because they wanted her to be at school. "That's bad isn't it?" she asked, her voice simmering with worry.

Maya nodded as Nik caught up with them and they headed to the next class. He shook his head, his jaw held tight. "What is a first class Rakshasi doing at your school? Who would send such a powerful, high level demon to do such a menial task as babysitting?" He spoke so softly that only the two girls would be able to hear him.

"First class demon?"

"Rakshasi?"

Both the girls spoke simultaneously. Nik cleared his throat and pulled his bag higher on his shoulder. "A Rakshasi is what the female demons are often called. Nobody bothers theses days to make the distinction unless we are talking about higher level demons - it just means the difference between the levels of power. The females are often more powerful."

"And Ms. Harris is a high level superdemon?" asked Maya, her mind only half on the conversation. A trill of fear slid through her gut. "What does that mean for us?"

"It means trouble. She's very powerful. She'd nothing like Amber or even Kas for that matter. If you had to fight her you'd have to be in top shape." he trailed off as soon as he saw the girl's expressions he frowned. "What's wrong?"

The girl's hesitated not wanting to take away from the enormity of their demon saturation but Ria was just as important to them, if not more. They shared a worried glance.

"Ria," said both girls at the same time.

"Oh. I take it she isn't at school?"

They both shook their heads. Then Maya asked, "Is there any way you can find out what happened and why she's not coming to school?"

Nik looked at Maya, as if contemplating the possibility, but then he shook his head. "Apart from making myself invisible and entering her house to search for her, no."

"That's a brilliant idea," said Joss, nodding vigorously, her blue eyes gleaming as she glanced over at Nik.

Nik looked at Maya and she nodded as well. "I agree. Brilliant."

Nik grimaced "Me and my big mouth."

"We have to know she's okay. What if another Rakshasa has

her?" asked Maya, fear darkening her eyes. She clenched her fists, feeling her nail dig into the soft skin of her palms.

"Okay, I'll do it." Nik sighed, but something told Maya he himself was concerned about Ria, that he would have checked even if we hadn't asked. "Let's just hope we can get through the day without any dramatics."

CHAPTER 12

The TV was on in the family room but neither one of the girls paid it the slightest attention. Joss sat in the armchair wiggling her foot and staring at the window that opened onto the street.

Maya paced the same stretch of floor over and over.

Sabala sat just inside the room door, his eyes following Maya as she moved back and forth.

Nothing changed until Nik walked into the room.

He stopped beside Maya and Joss gasped. "How did you get in?" she asked. Then her features tightened, "Oh, I forgot for a moment."

Maya faced him. "What did you find out?"

Nik shook his head, his brow creased by a frown, "Not much. Just that she isn't in the house. And neither is Viren. Her room is empty. As if she hasn't been there for a while. It's not helpful I know but I'd have to stay there for days with the hope of catching some piece of information that would tell me where she is."

"Can't we bug them? Or hack their phones? What about checking Viren's accounts for plane tickets or something." Joss moved to the edge of her chair and stared at Nik expectantly.

Maya snorted. "Don't be ridiculous Joss."

But Nik was staring at Joss nodding his head and rubbing his chin, his mind already turning over their options. "Not so ridiculous really. We need to just get in touch with the right people but it can be done."

"Can it?" Maya asked, very glad she was wrong in her assumption. "Then do it as soon as you can. Please, Nik. What if she is in danger?"

"I will, Maya." Nik pulled her into his arms and squeezed her tight. "I promise I'll do whatever I can to find her, okay."

Maya nodded, blinking back her tears. She squeezed him back feeling a million times better. Nik kept his promises and she took comfort in that.

AFTER THE GRIND of the long school day and the stress of both the Ms. Harris demon and the missing Ria, Maya looked forward to a nice dinner with her parents and Joss. Nik ended up joining the family for dinner and Maya cringed as her dad regaled them with the details of his close encounter with the Churel.

Even though Joss knew what had happened her eyes popped as Dev spoke. Maya rolled her own eyes at he dads theatrics. He had a flair for the dramatic, entertaining everyone as they ate her mom's delicious chicken fettuccine.

"Well, Dad. I told you before and I'll tell you again. I am coming with you on your next case," she said firmly, sticking her fork into her pasta.

"Sure you can," he said, nodding as if considering allowing her along. "But if you're expecting to be there to protect us its going to be near impossible for you to be at every single one, you know."

"I can try," Maya responded after swallowing a mouthful of creamy chicken.

"We won't stop you, but really Maya," said her mom, "you shouldn't be thinking of protecting us. We've been doing this long enough. Since you were in nappies, actually." Her mom winked.

Maya was annoyed enough to ignore the teasing. "So what happened with the Churel? How did she manage to trick you so well?" she demanded.

Dev's face grew serious as he faced his daughter. "She fooled us from the start. The family rang yesterday and we drove over to have a word with the mother-in-law of the churel. It seems that she'd tricked the old woman and put a spell on her, keeping her locked in an attic room while taking on her form. From the moment she opened the door we'd been interacting with the churel."

Maya looked at Nik. "Why did I not pick up on her then?" Suddenly she didn't feel so interested in food.

"I'm not sure. Maybe the protection on the house was too strong. Were they burning incense?"

Maya frowned and sat back, her meal forgotten. "Yes, incense and frankincense and camphor. And come to think of it I did feel something. Just a strange sense that something was wrong. Like I felt it in my bones but couldn't be sure what was setting the feeling off. I just thought it was because I didn't like funerals."

Nik's forehead wrinkled. "That is probably the case. You may have gotten the sense of her then, but your power wasn't as strong as it is now. You're slowly learning to understand the new senses that are coming to life."

"So now I'd tell immediately if a churel is around?" Maya asked.

"What's different now?" asked Joss, her fork having stopped in mid-air, her eyes flitting from Maya to Nik.

"What's different now is that my power of smell is super enhanced. I can smell demons from a good distance away. I could smell Ms. Harris while she was still in the hallway, before she entered the class."

"Wow. That's pretty cool." Joss's eyebrows waggled, showing how impressed she was. "So how did you get that power?"

Maya grimaced, picking up her fork and stabbing at the pieces of chicken that remained, cooling in the cream sauce. "You so do not want to know."

"Now we all want to know," said her dad as he wiped his mouth and threw down his napkin.

"Not at the dinner table you don't." Maya shook her head and didn't stop shaking it even when faced with a table full of people demanding her answer.

"Come on Maya, spill." Joss poked her in the arm with her fork.

Nik was laughing at Maya's dilemma and she glared at him. He was certainly of no help.

"Fine. But don't say you were not warned." Maya glanced around the table at her parents and Joss. "Nik returned from Patala with a collection of bottles. I had to smell and taste the contents of those bottles and now I'm able to identify the demons by their smell even from a good distance."

"And what was in the bottles, Maya," Joss asked slowly, her gaze never moving from Maya's face. But her look of horror told Maya she had a pretty good idea already.

"Blood samples of a few of the most common demons." Maya grinned.

"Ewww," said Joss glaring at Nik." You made her taste blood? What is wrong with you? That's disgusting."

Maya looked across the table at her parents. Both sat back looking surprised and a little shocked but interestingly enough not disgusted.

"There are only a certain number of ways that I know how to help Maya hone her skills. I know this particular method sounds disgusting-"

"Sounds?" asked Joss, looking like she was about to hurl. She held her hand in front of her mouth, the delicate movement only amplifying the nauseated look on Joss's face.

Nik continued, "-sounds disgusting, but my choices were very limited. And Maya survived the exercise all the better for it."

He looked at Maya, his expression saying her was hoping for some backup. She grinned, "It's totally okay Joss. I'm fine with it. To be honest it was disgusting while it lasted but I'm glad I did it. It's like the process awakened something inside me, some ability to sense demons. I'm much more powerful now and hopefully that will help me in whatever it is I am meant to do to earn my place as the Hand of Kali." A peek at her parents told her they were both happy with her choices and decisions. "And of course it will help me be more useful on your next case."

Dev sighed. "You're not going to let this go, are you?"

"Nope."

"Fine. Come with, but don't go looking for trouble," he said, resigned.

"I won't. My nose will tell me if trouble is coming." He nodded although he didn't look too happy. Maya didn't care. As long as they didn't go anywhere without her. Then she turned to Joss," Are you coming with?"

Joss laughed. "Sure. But what would all those old people think when Dev and Leela Rao pitch up for a demon removal, or whatever you call it, with a little white chick in tow."

Maya burst out laughing. Joss certainly had a way of saying things. "Okay, I see your point."

Dev laughed. "She certainly does have a point. I do think we may lose some business if we did that."

Maya snorted. "It's not as if you earn anything from it."

"True. But we don't need their money." Then Dev pushed away from the table and rose. "I've got a bit of work to do."

Dinner broke up not long after that and Nik offered to drop Joss at home. Maya waved them off before closing the door and locking it. She turned to head upstairs, hearing the click clack of claws on the wood floor. Sabala had remained in the living room while they had had dinner. Seems he didn't enjoy being around when people were eating. *That was good,* thought Maya. She liked it that way.

Right now, Sabala behaved in a very dog-like fashioned and followed Maya upstairs

Just like a good guard dog should.

CHAPTER 13

The next day at school went by faster as Maya tried to concentrate on learning. Being forced to go to school also meant she actually had to study. It seemed pretty ridiculous but she figured if one day she lost all her Kali powers she'd have something else to fall back on for the future.

The thought brought her up short. Was that a possibility? Could her powers be revoked at any point? She considered that for a moment and supposed a goddess like Kali could take her power away whenever she wished. It made Maya think a little more about ensuring that never happened.

Nik, Joss and Maya went through their day with only one blip.

Ms. Harris.

Maya and Nik took their seats as calmly as possible although Maya's heart was going a mile a minute. Every time she entered the demon's class she expected something awful to happen. But the lesson seemed to go uneventfully until their marked essays on Shakespeare's Othello were handed out. Maya had to hold her breath as the demon dropped the paper on her desk and walked down the row.

Maya spent a moment staring at her assignment in fury. Blood thundered through her head as she tried to absorb the grade. She'd expected her regular, run of the mill A grade, but the demon had given Maya an F. A large, angry one ringed in red. The vicious period beside the F was pressed deep into the paper and ink had spread out in jagged feathers. And as much as Maya couldn't really care less about school, the grade pissed her off-it was the principle of it. She knew her Shakespeare to know that her paper deserved an A. What was the demon trying to do?

She held on so tightly to the paper that it shook in her hand, evidence of her simmering fury. From the corner of her eye she saw Nik's curious glance but ignored him. Trying to slow down her breath, she called calm in much the same way that she called her fire, only making herself feel better when she promised herself she was going to kill this particular demon with her bare hands.

With her fury tempered she gazed around the class, her eyes sweeping over Ms. Harris. The demon sat at her desk, her head down, seemingly oblivious to Maya's fury. But Maya was sure she was just sitting there, counting down the seconds waiting for her reaction. Maya considered the Rakshasa's actions and figured the demon wanted her to react, maybe lash out at her. She was simply trying to provoke Maya, trying to give the demon a reason to get Maya alone.

Maya was furious but she couldn't do anything other than what she would do with a normal teacher. She tamped down her fury until the end of class, wishing she could just ignore it and just go home. She couldn't. She picked up her books and walked up the aisle toward the demon's desk, trying to keep her blood pressure at a decent rate.

"Excuse me, Ms. Harris," Maya asked, pasting a bland smile on her face.

The demon looked up and for a stomach-twisting second

Maya saw a swirl of deep amber in her eyes. It was gone so fast Maya could easily have thought she'd imagined it but she knew what she had seen. If she had ever been in any doubt as to the true nature of Ms Harris, she was now no longer under any misconceptions.

"How can I help you, Miss Rao?" the creature asked, keeping her tone so cool her words might as well have dripped icicles.

"I'd like to ask about my grade," Maya began, then hesitated for a moment. She decided not to go in looking for a fight. "I worked really hard on the assignment and I'm sure I deserved more than an F."

All the demon did was stare at Maya, her brown eyes now flat, the end of her mouth curling with dislike. Then she shook her long black hair, which today she'd worn hanging hallway down her back, and said, "Maya Rao, let me give you a little piece of advice." She paused and scanned the classroom which had emptied as fast as a classroom would empty at the end of the day. No witnesses. Then she turned her attention back to Maya and met her gaze before saying, "You reap what you sow."

Maya stared at her. What a strange thing to say.

If Maya were a normal human being.

The demon was certainly stoking the Fire. Maya swallowed hard, but kept her cool. She forced a frown onto her face, then said, "Huh?" feigning confusion, and all the while reminding herself *'Act like she's a normal teacher'*. Then she gave the demon a weak smile, shrugged and left the classroom. Maya stalked off hoping she'd left the creature with the assumption that though she was angry about her grade she hadn't been tipped off as to what the teacher Ms. Harris really was.

Outside the class Nik leaned against the wall close to the door. "That's a bit of a weird statement," he said frowning.

"Yeah, not to mention the special effects." Maya was grumpy.

"Special effects?" Nik leaned closer as they headed to lunch.

"Yeah, swirling amber-colored eyes. It was there only for a second but really that was long enough for me to know for sure what she is. If I had any doubts that is. Which I don't because I can smell her a mile away." Maya paused, then whispered, "Speaking of which she's headed our way. Maybe a few yards behind us."

Maya wanted to hold her breath as the demon drew closer. For a moment her heart beat at a thunderous rate. They both had their backs to the demon, with no real reason to turn around. But she walked around them, giving Nik a small smile as she passed. A smile that said she was a woman and she thought he was cute. This demon was playing her role very well. At least she hadn't broken through Nil's glamour.

Yet.

Maya growled as soon as the Rakshasa was out of earshot.

"What's the matter Maya?" Nik said with a teasing smile as they watched the her disappear around the corner. "Jealous are we?"

"Sure," Maya scoffed. "Until she rips your insides out and makes a meal of you."

Nik put an arm around Maya's shoulders. "But seriously, this whole thing has me worried, a high level Rakshasi? I'm going to have to tell my father about this. He might have some info on who could be sending them now that we know what type of demons they are."

"How long will you be gone?" Maya frowned, not looking forward to another extended absence. Then she stiffened her spine. She had to quit being a possessive brat.

"Probably only a few hours." He smiled. "And I have plans for us tonight."

"Yeah, that dinner you promised?" She raised her eyebrows.

"Well, that too." When Maya glanced at him, her dark eyes inquiring, Nik responded, "I'm taking you on a demon hunt. We need to test your blood detecting abilities and also put your fire training to proper test."

"Good plan," said Maya, already looking forward to doing something practical with her training.

MAYA BARELY WAITED for Nik to drive up in front of the house before she was out the door. She had to admit she couldn't decide which she was looking forward to more - dinner with Nik or demon-hunting with Nik. Either way she aimed to enjoy the *'with Nik'* part as much as possible. He grinned as Maya plopped onto the passenger seat behind him and shut the door.

"Joss just texted to ask where we were," said Maya, rolling her eyes. Joss's middle name should be *impatient*. If it weren't already taken by Maya, that is. She slipped the phone into her pocket before pulling the seatbelt around her.

"Why?" Nik frowned as he put the car in gear and headed off down the street. "I'm not even late. In fact, I think I'm ten minutes early."

Maya grinned. "Maybe she's just looking forward to the evening out," she suggested. "Or maybe she's worried you'd disappear on us again." She offered the jibe with a smile so he'd know she was just teasing.

Like a pro he ignored in and asked, "Were you looking forward to it as much as Joss?" The look in his eye asked more than just the question.

"Of course. Who doesn't like Italian?" Maya answered, not ready to delve into relationship stuff right now. Instead she chose to tease him and enjoyed the way he grinned back, his smiles make butterflies skate along the insides of the stomach.

Right on cue they pulled up in front of Joss's place where Maya was amused to find her quirky friend pacing the front porch, arms folded, her purse at the ready. As soon as she spotted the car she flew towards it, a ridiculous grin on her face.

"You made it," she yelled as she threw herself in to the back seat and slammed the door so hard that both Maya and Nik winced and shared a wry smile.

"Yup. I made it. Were you ever in any doubt?" Nik asked as he drove off.

"Nope. None at all," Joss replied and winked at him in the rear view mirror, blowing him a kiss. Her nails sparkled pink.

Maya just shook her head. A few minutes later they pulled up in front of Ginelli's restaurant. It was a popular local haunt for the kids since they probably made *the* best pizza in the world. And they tolerated kids doing homework at the tables. The owners liked the idea of homework actually getting done and the kids liked the environment.

They went in and found a booth. The girls slid inside and Nik took a seat beside Maya. They ordered and were chatting about everything and nothing when Maya felt a chill run up and down her spine. Nik must have sensed it too - unless he was too attuned to Maya's moods for his own good - because he threw her a questioning glance.

"What's wrong?"

"No idea," she answered, desperate to scan the restaurant to look for what had caused the feeling. Instead she looked at the table and pretended that everything was normal.

"What does it feel like?" Nik asked while Joss pretended to scan the menu again.

"Like there's a demon in the vicinity." Maya pasted a smile on her face. "And its nearby."

Just then Ms. Harris walked past their table and Maya relaxed. The devil she knew.

"What's she doing here?" Joss grumbled giving Ms. Harris back a vicious stare.

"Whatever it is, let's hope she leaves soon. I don't think I can eat with that stink filling up my nose." Maya grimaced.

"You're going to have to try. Not eating could tip them off."

"Blegh," was all Maya could say in response.

They watched the Rakshasi find a table at the other end of the restaurant and exchanged curious stares as the demon scanned her menu, a successful pretense at being human.

Maya sniffed. "I doubt she's here just to grab a meal. What do demons eat anyway?"

Nik snorted.

"So," asked Joss staring at Nik. "What do demons eat?"

"They eat what we eat. Except for the real nasties. They eat little girls for breakfast lunch and dinner."

"Yeah I just bet they do," said Joss folding her arms. She continued to glare at Nik.

The smile disappeared from his face. "I wish I could say I was joking but it's been known to happen. Most demonic forms have a penchant for human flesh and blood, and some Rakshasas are certainly guilty of that. Although as I told you before not all of them are like that. Some are perfectly normal, just as normal as the next human in fact."

"If you are trying to make me sympathize with them then you are sorely mistaken. There is no way I'd feel sorry for them." Joss sat back, studying her pink nails.

"That's not what I'm trying to do," he said. Then he paused. "Well maybe that's kind of what I'm trying to say. That not all of them are bad to the bone."

"Oh, you mean like Priya?" Maya asked, a hint of a sneer to her words. She couldn't help it. Just the hint of a memory of the vengeful Rakshasa was enough to make Maya's fire rise to the surface.

Nik had the grace to flush. "Priya wasn't your normal Rakshasa."

"Oh yeah, betraying you and Yama was certainly not normal." Maya smiled sweetly.

"Plus she had the hots for you," Joss chimed in with a grin.

Amused at Joss's cheek, Maya glanced at Nik who frowned at the two girls. "Don't look so confused. You can't seriously tell me you had no idea she liked you."

"Well, no. I really never knew she felt that way." Nik scratched his head, and Maya and Joss grinned at each other. But Maya couldn't put all her attention on the banter at their table. Her gaze flitted to a certain table within her line of vision. She sat with her right side to Maya - it would certainly be easy to know when the demon looked over at their table. Had she seen them at all? Was she as oblivious to Maya and her friends as she seemed.

Maya was about to ask Nik what he thought when the demon looked up at someone who strolled toward her table. Maya gasped softly and both Nik and Joss glanced at her simultaneously.

"Someone's just walked up to her table." Maya hunch down in her seat automatically before she remembers she had to act normal. "Crap. It's another demon."

"What, do we have? An infestation or something?" asked Joss, crossing her arms in disgust.

"Right. This is a major worry for me. I'll go back to Patala later tonight to see what I can find out." Nik's voice deepened with just the right touch of worry that it made Maya's blood chill.

"Do you think she saw us?" Maya asked.

"I don't know. Doesn't look like she's aware of us at all." Nik said as the group watched the demon as she sat straight-backed pretending to be Ms. Harris the English teacher. Her dark hair held away from her face with a barrette, black rimmed glasses perched on her nose, the movements of her hands neat and precise. She certainly played the part well. Her companion leaned toward her and spoke in subdued tones, his expression blank, robotic. "And they certainly don't look like they're on a date. She's too businesslike. My guess is he's working for her."

"That could mean she may have more worker demons around," said Maya annoyed.

Joss snorted. "Like I said … in-fes-tation." Joss took a sip of her drink and nodded at Nik. "Do me a favor, Nik. Bring us back a can of Demoncide, please."

I laughed, still keeping my voice down. Best to not draw her attention our way if she hadn't seen us already.

Nik just grinned as our food arrived and we swapped around bowls of chicken fettuccine, Spaghetti bolognese, and Chicken Parmigiana while keeping one eye on the table of demons up ahead. A waitress brought a pizza to their table and we watched them devour it quite humanly, quite neatly.

Joss cleared her throat. "I really was expecting to see them eat like ravenous beasts, dripping sauce and cheese all over the place. How disappointing."

"They are behaving very human. Too human for my liking." I tilted me head at Nik. "Is this how they managed to blend into human society? I remember you mentioned a while ago that there are many of them living among us quite innocently going about their lives."

Nik nodded. "Not all of them are bad. This Rakshasi though, she'd got bad news written all over her."

The demons didn't take long to polish off their pizza and before long they rose and left, with not a hint of whether either had noticed Maya and her friends.

"Phew. Thanks goodness they're gone, now I can enjoy my meal," said Joss, making a face.

Maya let out a breath, as if she'd been holding it the entire evening. Maya laughed. "It's not like you can smell them the way I do."

"Maybe I can't smell them but the sight of them does give me the creeps and that gives me a stomach ache. Now they've left I can eat in peace," said Joss, forking Bolognese into her mouth.

Maya relaxed only when the odor of spices and raw meat had totally disappeared. Then only could she be certain the demon was no longer anywhere in their vicinity. And like Joss, then only could she enjoy her food.

Her mind was still on the demon teacher when they dropped Joss off at home. They waited until she waved and ducked inside the darkened house. Seems her parents weren't home. No surprises there.

CHAPTER 14

Maya and Nik stood at the edge of the local park which was usually filled with joggers and walkers and kids and moms in the daylight. They had left the car in the small parking lot a few yards away, and walked to the edge of the grassy park that bordered the tree-filled reserve. Night transformed the place into something creepy that screamed stay-away-unless-you-want-trouble. Even the lamps lighting the pathways that weaved in and out of the park flickered as if threatening to remove their safety any minute.

Maya rubbed her hands together and glanced up at Nik. "Now what?"

"Use your nose, Fido," Nik answered with such a cheeky grin she almost forgave him for the dog quip. Almost.

"You didn't just call me Fido did you?" she asked, her voice ending in a squeak.

Nik nodded. "Guilty as charged. You are the one with the super powered nose aren't you? Now use it." He nodded his head at the expanse of shadowed trees and grass in front of them. Maya just grunted then payed closer attention to the area around them.

"Fine. But I will find a way to make you pay for that." She threw him one last glare.

"I will look forward to it," was all he said.

Maya glanced at Nik, hiding her smile. He always had a way of making her happy even when she was angry or annoyed.

She turned her attention onto the park and relaxed. Then breathed deeply. A light rain had fallen and Maya could smell the dustiness of the pathway, the scent of peonies in flowerbed to her right. The green of the grass around her.

"Relax,"said Nik beside her. "Try again and this time remember the smell and taste of the different blood types."

She rolled her shoulders and breathed in and out. Then she smelled again, drawing on the memory of the blood in the vials. Then she smelled a familiar odor. Human blood. And Maya flinched. With the power to detect the blood also came the power to hear heartbeats.

"What's wrong?" Nik asked softly. "What do you smell?"

"It's not what I smell. It's what I can hear."

"Hear?" he asked, his eyebrows raised.

Maya nodded. "I can hear this tattoo of heartbeats from all around the park, like soft background music." Maya tilted her head a little to hear them better and yes, she could still hear the thud-thud of human heartbeats. Then she looked at Nik. "What does a demon heartbeat sound like?"

"You'll know it when you hear it. It's not like a human heartbeat so will recognize the difference almost immediately."

"Okay. So what next? Do we take a walk? Walk and sniff?" said Maya making a face.

"I agree, let's walk a bit, and you can keep trying to pick up on anything around us." Nik moved forward and Maya hurried to keep up.

She concentrated on smelling and trying to detect anything unusual in the air. After ten minutes of strolling the outer pathways of the park, Maya clicked her tongue in disgust. "This is just a huge waste of time."

"Patience, Maya. I know for a fact we have a demon lurking around here at night. We've had reports of a couple of crackheads complaining they've woken up in the park the next day with strange injuries." Nik fell silent.

"Okay. I guess you're not going to elaborate because I'm supposed to identify the demon first?" asked Maya.Nik nodded and Maya snorted, turning her attention to the park again.

She took a deep breath and came to a sudden stop.

"Got something?" asked Nik.

"I think so." Maya inhaled again, trying to grasp onto the scent. She scowled as she concentrated harder. There, a hint of meat. "I think its a Rakshasa. I can smell that meat odor." Maya paused then coughed. "No, is a more intensely rotted meat odor. It's a Vitala."

She faced Nik who was nodding his expression serious, worried. "Yes. It's definitely a vampire demon and you've just confirmed what I suspected."

"You mean you didn't know for sure?"

"How could I unless someone sighted the demon, or unless I got uncomfortably close. And from the reports the police have received, nobody has actually seen them. All they have are gouges in their flesh the next day. And of course A strange case of a lot of missing blood, as if they've been drained."

Maya shuddered. "Okay, so it's a Vitala. Are we going to find it? Now?"

"We have come prepared. And we really shouldn't leave the demon running around here any longer than necessary. Who knows when they'll get sloppy or greedy and start killing people. So far they've been feeding off the drug addicts that pass through the park. The longer they remain, the more demanding their needs will get and we can't let it get that far. The risks of someone beginning to investigate will be too high." In the darkness of the evening Nik sounded deadly serious and Maya agreed with every reason he put forward to catch and kill this creature.

"Right, let's get on with it," she said, digging around in her backpack for her Madus. These were the ones from Patala that Nik had given her before her last mission. She dipped the tips into the bottle of Naga poison that had come with it and tucked the bottle safely back into her bag. Then she moved off the side-walk and hid the backpack beneath the dense brush. She moved back to the path and readied herself, swiping the weapons back and forth, and around her. "What about a weapon for you?" she eyed Nik.

"I have my weapon," he said as a short, wide-bladed sword slid from his oversized jacket sleeve.

"Nice." Maya grinned and nodded as they strode further into the shadows of the trees in the middle of the park. "You know, I've been wondering if we shouldn't start making guns to kill these demons. A little Naga poison in a bullet, fill a Glock with rounds of poisoned bullets and we'll be fit for battle."

"That is a good idea. I shall put a proposal to my father and tell you his thoughts." Maya did a double-take at Nik. She'd been teasing and hadn't expected to have him take her seriously but now that she thought about the idea of one day packing a weapon loaded with the ability to kill demons made her feel happy and confident.

The shadows closed around them and every little sound made Maya jump.

"Relax and try to filter all the other sounds out." Nik offered from beside her, his eyes on the path, on the bushes and trees. His eyes were all amber and glowing, similar to how they looked the day she'd first seen it happen and assumed he was really a Rakshasa himself. She recalled how angry and upset she'd been.

"What's with your eyes?" she asked. "You have some kind of glowing night-vision thing going on?"

Nik just nodded. It was enough to remind Maya to shut up

and concentrate on tracking the demons. She breathed in and out steadily. Filtering the smells through, listening for heartbeats. As they walked toward the darkest part of the park, where the branches of the trees entwined overhead to form a canopy so thick that only the heavy rains were able to find a way to trickle through, Maya paused. She thought she smelled something. An odor of rotten meat again. This time much stronger than the scent from outside of the trees.

Maya looked over at Nik and whispered, "We're close."

"How close?" he asked, his voice emotionless.

"Not close enough to hear a heartbeat," Maya answered feeling a little put out at Nik's tone. But she really should get a grip and concentrate on the job. Nik was taking this seriously and so should she. "I'll let you know as soon as I'm that close."

Maya turned her attention to the trees around them, concentrating harder on the odor of the Vitala blood. The scent was much stronger now filling her nostrils to puke point. And she was beginning to detect the softest flutter of heartbeats. A light thrum that put the vampire about twenty yards away.

C H A P T E R 15

"Nik," Maya whispered. When he looked at her she pointed in the direction of the Vitala's location. She hunkered down, mimicking Nik, then duckwalked closer to the stand of trees.

Through the brush they saw a small clearing, the center of which was occupied by a small oak whose branches were too short to reach the surrounding trees. This gave the clearing a clear view of the night sky. The demon paced the ground in front of the tree.

Nik nodded and he and Maya pushed the branches aside and entered the clearing, weapons at the ready. The Vitala turned, speaking before it set eyes on them. "What took you-" Then he stopped speaking, and hissed at the two of them.

Maya was taken aback for a moment. The creature looked pretty much like a human, even his attire of jeans and a hoodie would allow him to pass for the next guy on the street. But when he hissed he sounded totally inhuman, and the rows of sharp teeth he revealed sent the appropriate amount of chills up and down Maya's spine.

"Okay, handsome. How about you give up and make this easy on yourself?" she offered, knowing already that he'd never take it.

He ran at her and Maya lunged with the Madus, swiping left and right and catching him on each of his arms, satisfied that the poison would begin to do its work soon enough. He screeched and held only his arms, staring at her in fury. Then he grunted and ran at her again, as if he'd channeled his fury onto her. He swiped hard at her hand, sending the one Madu flying into the trees.

Maya grunted, and took it as a sign that it was time to bring out the big guns. She accessed her fire and pulled at it, channeling it fast from her solar plexus, through her veins and into her free palm. Her palm tingled expectantly. She'd had plenty of time to perfect the art of calling her fire. Now she sent a blast of flame straight at the Vitala.

]But the fire never hit the vampire.

Maya was knocked off her feet by a flying body. She rolled over and scrambled to get up again. Another Vitala. This time a female. The vampire got to her feet, brushed back a wave of red-brown hair and faced Maya, her unexpectedly attractive features twisted in a vicious grin. She glared at Maya with almond shaped, blue greed eyes. *No fair,* Maya thought. *Too pretty for a blood sucking demo*n.

Off to the side, the male groaned, having been flung against the tree trunk by the force of the flames. The acrid smell of burnt flesh permeated the air. Maya nodded, satisfied.

The female screeched just as loudly as the male had, launched herself onto Maya. Behind the Vitala, Nik stood at the ready but unable to attack for fear of hurting Maya. He kept an eye on the male who was now hobbling on his feet watching the melee. Maya and the female vampire fell to the ground, rolling over twice before Maya got a foot under the demon's abdomen and shoved her away. At the same time she slashed hard at the creatures neck with the vicious dagger-tip of the remaining Madu.

It was enough.

The dagger sliced straight through the vampire's jugular, spraying hot blood all over Maya. The Vitala was as good as dead. As the female hit the ground Maya got the scent of the male.

Violently angry, and nearing her fast.

Although Nik called out, Maya was ready for the Vitala. She bounced from one foot to another, tossing her Madu back and forth between her hands. He so didn't scare her anymore. Every time he moved toward her she slashed our at him. He growled, angry that he was unable to gain on her. Frustrated, he made a mad dash into the bushes behind the oak and the clearing fell silent.

"Where'd he go?" yelled Nik.

"Not far," said Maya quietly. She looked up into the branches of the oak and grinned. The leaves shook and her eyes met the Vitala's. He'd thought he'd hidden himself well enough but not far enough away from Maya's nose. "You've preyed on enough innocent people. Your number's up, dude."

He didn't answer, as if his silence hid him among the leaves. But even if he was unaware that Maya had seen, him, had smelled him, it made not difference. She was still intent on killing him. She aimed a stream of fire at the trunk of the oak, keeping it steady until it began to flare with flame. Then Maya moved to the lower branches, training strong pulses of fire at the leaves. She move relentlessly until the entire tree was in flames, burning so bright she had to step a few paces away.

And while the fire raged the demon screamed. He couldn't leave the tree, couldn't jump for fear of getting caught. And now the tree was going to mean his death as surely as it had offereed an escape.

Maya and Nik backed away further from the conflagration. "The fire department will be here soon. We'd better get out of here," said Nik waving the smoke from his face.

"My Madu," yelled Maya rushing to the trees. The smoke

scraped at her throat as she rummaged around on the ground, almost whooping for joy when she found the missing weapon. She felt the luxurious heat of the tree against the cold of the night. Nik grasped her hand and they ran, not stopping until they came to the bush where she'd hidden her backpack.

She reached for the strapped and grabbed hold, about to pull when felt Nik shove her into the bush. Then she was nose to nose with him hiding under the leaves as police and firemen raced past.

"We can't run," said Nik, eyes on the path.

"Then, transport us out of her now." Maya said, shocking on a cough.

"Okay." Nik scowled scanning the path through the trees as he held out his hand.

He was too late.

"Hey." The voice sounded to their left. Two separate pathways came pretty close together with just the small bush and a few wide-leaved plants between them. Maya shoved the Madus into her bag and scrambled to Nik. She shoved him against the wide tree trunk at his back and grabbed his hands, looping them behind her. Then she planted her lips onto Nik's and wound her hands around his neck. Just in time, as the leaves parted and a policeman stared at them, not even bothering to wipe the sleazy smile from his lips.

"You two better get outta here. There's a fire up ahead and you might want to take your little party to a more private place." He was still grinning as he held the leaves aside for them. They pushed off the tree, brushing the dirt off their clothes. Maya didn't dare to look at Nik's face. She grabbed her rucksack and threw it over her shoulders hurrying up the pathway, keeping her face down to mimic embarrassment. She was far from embarrassed though. The whole episode had been rather thrilling.

Once they were out in the grassy bank where they'd first stood, a few yards from Nik's car, Maya stopped walking. She might as well face the music. When she turned to face Nik as he walked up behind her, she stopped and closed her mouth. She'd been about to apologize but when she saw the grin on his face she stopped.

"Smart move there, Maya." He nodded approvingly.

"Really?" she asked him, folding her arms. She wasn't sure how to feel now. A soft flush crept along her cheeks.

Nik walked up to her and bent close. So close all she had to do was tip her head forward to touch her lips to his. But she didn't move. She kept her eyes down, afraid what she would see in his eyes after she'd accosted him. Despite his approval she wasn't sure about his reaction.

Nik cupped the back of her head and titled her face up forcing her eyes to meet his. He smiled then looked at her mouth. She took a breath and then he kissed her. A soft, tender kiss that deepened as she leaned in toward him.

Then she remembered the blood.

"Oh gross."

"Gross?" Nik looked affronted.

Maya giggled as she saw his hurt expression. "No. Not you," she said pointing to the blood on her face. "This."

"It's just a little blood."

"It's just a little gross," she responded glad the hoodie had hidden her blood-wrenched face and chest.

"But you tasted the blood of the Vitala just the other day." Poor Nik. So confused.

"It's still gross." She grabbed him by the arm. "You won't understand. I need to get home and shower. This is way too disgusting."

Nik shook his head and went around to open the car, mumbling something about women and how crazy they were no matter which plane they lived on and how he didn't think he'd ever understand them.

Maya just smiled.

CHAPTER 16

*M*aya sat at the kitchen table doing her homework while her mom rolled out rotis. A very suburban evening for a very non-suburban family.

Not to mention the totally non-suburban four-eyed hellhound lying on the floor beside her.

Maya stared at the blackened burn mark she'd made not so long ago. Her mom had refused to sand it away and re-varnish it. Even when Maya offered to do it herself she'd still refused, saying she wanted the reminder of how power in a human is far from godly and that the bearer of that power has a great responsibility. All Maya saw was evidence of how stupid and childish she'd been.

"Hey strangers," said Claudia as she breezed into the kitchen, a huge grin hiding the tired lines tracking deep into the soft skin beneath her eyes. She dropped her bags and came around to give Maya a tight squeeze. Sabala rose and trotted around Claudia, stopping only when she gingerly patted him on the top of his head, her eye wide as she stared at Maya, fascinated at the hellhounds welcome.

Maya grinned. "Where have you been?" she asked, dead curious.

"One Churel, one Vitala, two simple ghost haunting and one case of bad indigestion incorrectly diagnosed as witchcraft." Claudia counted each one off on her fingers then collapsed into the nearest stool.

"Wow. I didn't realize you guys did international demon hunting." Things were certainly getting interesting. She glanced at her mom who poured a tall glass of ice cold juice then set it in front of Claudia.

"We go where we're called. But these last few month have felt like there are more incidents that are legitimate than not." Claudia rubbed her forehead and wrapped her hands around the cool glass.

More curious than ever, Maya asked, "Does that happen often? I mean, with the situation being not legit."

Claudia shrugged, the shadows under her eyes more prominent in the kitchen's bright fluorescent light. "Sometimes it really is something as simple as indigestion. But there has been the odd case where the cause is a little murderous even when it's not demon related. I once had a wife try to kill her husband with arsenic. And a mother making her kid sick feeding him extra salt all the time." Claudia sighed and ran her fingers through her hair.

"You look like you need a rest," said Maya's mom. "Drink that and go get some sleep. The guest room is ready for you. Dev or I will take the next run."

Claudia looked up, relief smoothing the frown on her forehead. "Are you sure?" When Leela nodded, she sighed. "Thanks, I do need a rest. I'm so jet-lagged my body has no idea what's up or down." She drained her glass and stood up, kneading the muscles at her neck. Maya felt sorry for her. Claudia's fatigue was obvious to anyone who looked at her. She winked at Maya, then bent to her laptop bag to withdraw three files. "These are all the details on those cases." She dropped the files on the kitchen table and bent to pick up her bags.

Maya watched as Claudia left the kitchen giving Sabala a fairly wide berth, and headed upstairs. "Why didn't you tell me you guys worked internationally?" she asked her mom.

Leela shrugged as she stirred the contents of the pot on the stove. "It never came up." Then she looked over her shoulder at Maya. "But I do think it's time you got a little more active. If you want to, that is."

Maya didn't have to think twice. "Of course I want to." She grinned. "I think it's pretty cool jetting all over the world killing demons and saving people."

"Mmh. I thought you didn't like the idea of being a Kali follower," said Leela as she raised an eyebrow and smiled at Maya.

Maya made a face. "Yeah, how long are you going to hold that against me?"

Her mom laughed. "As long as I'm able."

As their laughter died Dev, walked into the kitchen, his forehead crumpled by a dark frown, looking like he'd lost something. He didn't even want to know what they were laughing about and usually he would let them rest until they spilled.

His daughter and wife both spoke together, "What's wrong?"

Leela moved the pot off the stove and switched the burner off, before turning to her husband. She and Maya both stared at him, waiting.

Dev sighed, rubbing his fingers through is hair. "The call just came through. We have another case. A father in Tucson is looking for help with what he thinks is a possession."

"It will have to be one of us. I'm backing Claudia up, she just got home and is sleeping off her jet lag."

Dev nodded. "That's fine, I'll do it." Then he looked at Maya. "I'll take Maya with me. Time she got to see more of what we do."

Maya's mom nodded although she frowned. "What's wrong, Mom?"

"Nothing," she said, shaking her head. "Just be careful. With those demons after you, you just never know which one of our call-outs is actually a trap."

Maya nodded and turned to her father who waved her off. "You'd better get packing. And essentials only. We need to get out of here fast. And we'll be driving all night."

Maya frowned, instantly disliking the thought of being cramped in a car for eight hours when a plane would do just fine. "Aren't we flying?"

"No. We have a bag full of goodies that airport security would find a little too strange." Dev grinned.

"Oh. But how did Claudia travel to Europe with her stuff?"

"She didn't. We have a base in London and one in Greece, where we keep stocks of everything we might need. Most of the hunters stop there first, then drive on."

"That sounds a heck of a lot cooler than I'd ever thought," said Maya quite unimpressed, if not totally disappointed at her own lack of air travel.

Her father grinned and shooed her off. "Get going. I'm leaving in thirty minutes."

Maya nodded and hurried up the stairs, with Sabala close on her heels. She smiled as her Mom yelled for to take a shower because she wouldn't have any idea how long it would be before she had the next one.

Maya shuddered at the thought.

HALF AN HOUR later they were packed and already heading onto the Interstate. Maya glanced at her dad. "You okay with him coming?" she asked giving the hell hound in the back seat a vicious glare. Sabala remained unperturbed, giving her a bland glance with his liquid eyes.

He'd made endless circles around her feet, and almost tripped her up when she'd tried to stop him from getting into the car. There was no controlling the giant-sized dog so in the end the bothersome creature won and now took pride of place in the back seat of the rental.

Her dad shrugged. "He's meant to help protect you right?" Maya nodded, feeling a slight flush of shame at her dad's implication. "Then he's just doing his job, you know."

A peek in the rear view mirror told her that Sabala was still sitting on the seat, his head perked up behind her as he looked out the window. She could see the slight shimmer of his glamor and was satisfied that he'd listened. Without his glamor she'd refused to take him anywhere, preferring to steer clear of creating mass mayhem on the streets when people get an eyeful of a the four-eyed five-foot canine. Even genetic modification would be stretching it as a valid explanation.

Maya titled her head in her dad's direction, eager to move on to a more palatable subject. "So tell me more about this case. How much do you have to go on?"

Dev cleared his throat as his flashed his indicator and changed lanes. "Not all that much. It's one of the problems we experience too often. It's unavoidable really, especially since most people don't know what they're dealing with. Too often the case is just a normal illness like food poisoning. Or a psychological one. That on stymies far too many priests and shamans."

Maya frowned. "So who pays for the wasted trips?" Dev flicked a glance at Maya. "No. Wait. Who pays for all the travel and expenses involved. I know we aren't rolling in money." Maya raised her eyebrow and stared at her dad, waiting for an answer.

"We don't pay from our pockets. It's quite organized really."

As Maya stared at her father so many things clicked into place and she gasped softly. "KALIMA Technologies. You don't work for a software company do you?"

Dev chuckled. "I sometimes do. It pays to actually create software every now and then so the company doesn't scream 'dummy corporation'." He laughed.

"So what is Mom's role in KALIMA?"

"Housewife, of course. Not everyone can physically work for the company. And there are employees who have no idea what we really stand for."

"So those employees do real work and keep the company going while you guys work off-site."

"Exactly."

"I have to admit you have it very well organized. So where does the money come from?"

"Various contributors. Wealthy people we have helped in the past. People who have contributed long before we ever came into the picture. Government organizations who are aware but would rather we dealt with the weird and unexplainable on our own. And of course, temples and religious organizations that believe in our cause."

"Wow. I didn't know it was so far-reaching." Then she fell silent.

"What's wrong?" When she didn't reply he said, "Thinking about all those times you dissed the 'Kali followers'?"

Maya folded her arms and looked out of the window. Her cheeks were red and she didn't want her Dad to see the livid proof of her embarrassment. "Something like that," she said.

"Don't worry about it. There are a lot of people who start out in total denial and they eventually come around."

Maya grunted. Desperate to change the topic she said, "So you haven't told me what you know about this case."

Dev looked at her again and nodded before turning his gaze back to the road ahead. "The girl in this case is very ill. She seems to be wasting away even though her diet hasn't changed. And she isn't bulimic."

"How do they know she isn't. Bulimics generally don't advertise when they are about to stick their finger down their throats," Maya asked, her tone dry. She knew all too well about bulimia, having seen Joss go through the very same thing the previous year.

"Well, let's just say these parents are very hands on. They don't leave the girl alone at all. Not since they noticed her illness. They've ruled out anorexia, bulimia and any possible health related issue. She isn't on any drugs that would have a weight loss side effect either."

"So, of course they assume the cause is paranormal."

"Yes. But what we need to figure out is what or who is causing her illness."

"Any ideas?"

"None that I want to put my money on right now. I need to examine her first."

"Could it be a type of Churel? One that preys on girls?" asked Maya.

Dev nodded. "Maybe. Or it could be a Vitala or even a ghost."

The rest of the journey was spent discussing the different demons that Dev had encountered and who were likely to cause the wasting away of one poor suffering girl. Maya was glad too that Sabala didn't reek the way most dogs did. The car would have been filled with doggie odor by now had her hell hound been a regular pooch. She supposed there were some advantages to Sabala after all.

They arrived in Tucson in the early hours of the morning, just as the sun was peeking over the distant horizon. Dev pulled into a motel and booked a room for them while Maya texted Joss as she waited in the car. She got a text back from Joss almost immediately.

Why didn't you take me with you?

Maya hadn't realized Joss would want to come, nor did she think her dad would have allowed it, so that's what she texted back to her annoyed friend.

Still. You could have told me. Maybe if I asked your dad nicely he would have agreed. I need the practice too you know.

Maya grinned at Joss's petulant response but she did have a point. She replied, *Okay, I'll talk to my dad about bringing you in on the next mission.*

She pocketed her phone as Dev opened his door and started the engine. He drove around the building and found a spot in front of the room he'd booked. Maya and Dev grabbed their bags and headed inside the motel room, leaving it open and extra few seconds for Sabala to click his way inside. He found a place beside the door and below the window where he took up guard. Maya ignored him although she couldn't help but admit she felt a tad bit safer with him watching the two possible entrances.

Maya glanced around their room and was glad she didn't need to shudder. The place was pristine, bright blue carpet, white walls and two double beds covered with blue and white striped bedspreads. The pictures on the walls were prints of white buildings on a hillside looking down at the deep blue oceans of Greece. Santorini or Mykonos, Maya guessed.

She loved the colors they'd chosen and was glad the motel was not dark and dingy. She flung her bag on the bed and rifled through it for fresh clothes. As she headed into the bathroom to brush her teeth and shower, she glanced over at her dad. He was already powering up his laptop, the dark frown on his face indicating the flavor of his mood.

CHAPTER 17

Refreshed after a quick shower, Maya and her dad got drive-through breakfasts and headed to the address of the ailing child. Sabala sat in the back, oddly disinterested in food. Maya made a mental note to check with Nik if she was meant to feed the dog anything in particular.

They drew up in front of a small Santa Fe style home complete with flat roof and sloping salmon pink walls. Maya followed her dad to the front door, swallowing nervously as she went. What would these people think to see a teenage girl accompanying the man who came to save their child?

"Can he come inside?"

Dev nodded. "As long as he walks on air."

Maya glanced at the dog who lifted a padded foot. She watched as he retracted his iron sharp claws. "Fine," she said to Sabala. "One sound out of you and your ass is back in the car."

The dog bowed his head to Maya and took his place at her side.

Dev knocked at the door and when it opened it revealed a very short, very bald man in wiry glasses. He squinted as Dev reached out to shake his hand. "I'm Dev Rao. I'm here about your daughter." The man tilted his head up and surveyed Dev suspiciously, then took his hand, giving it a quick shake, letting go of it so fast it was a wonder he didn't go rushing off to disinfect his hand.

"Thank you for coming so soon," the man said as he ushered them inside, but Maya could tell her was merely being polite. Sabala slipped inside soundlessly, keeping close to Maya.

Dev hadn't introduced Maya and it seemed the man wasn't interested in her identity as he didn't even bother to look at her. *Fine*, Maya thought. *Children are meant to be seen and not heard. I get it.*

They were shown into a sunken lounge, and thought they took the step into the living space but Dev didn't sit. Maya schooled her features at her dad's rudeness but neither Dev nor the man seemed to care.

"I'm Sam Nath. My daughter Gita is the one you've come about." He gave Dev another cursory glance then nodded and began to walk off. "If you'll wait a moment I'll go call her."

Maya said nothing as she sat and waited, her eyes on Mr. Nath's back as he disappeared down the long stone passage. Sabala sat back on his haunches not two feet away from her. Too close as far as she was concerned . The hell-hound really needed a lesson on personal space.

Despite her dad's presence, the silence of the room lay upon her like a scratchy blanket and she wasn't sure how to ease her discomfort. The heat of the day filtered into the room, doing battle against the struggling air conditioning, and mostly winning.

She glanced at her father. What was he thinking? How was he prepared to tackle this situation? She didn't have to wonder too long as only moments later the sound of footsteps echoed back up the passage.

Mr. Nath came towards them, his shoulders slightly hunched thought his eyes remained round and sharp. He reminded Maya of a vulture. His body hid his daughter from view until the very last moment. When he stood aside to introduce her, Maya swallowed hard. The girl was emaciated. Her collarbones jutted out at the neckline of her T-shirt, the short sleeves of which did nothing to hide arms that were just skin and bone. Her skin was a dull pale, marked by jagged trails of blue veins.

Maya was glad that she didn't have to speak because she was sure that she wouldn't have been able to say a word. The girl gave Dev and her father a cursory glance, her pale brown eyes far too large for her face.

"This is my daughter. Gita, they will be asking you some questions. Make sure you answer. All of them." Mr. Nath's tone was far too impersonal for Maya's liking, and from the slight stiffening of her dad's spine she saw he wasn't too impressed either. Considering the condition the girl was in, surely she deserved to be treated with a little kindness. It was almost as if Mr. Nath blamed his daughter for her illness. At that moment Maya wasn't sure that she liked him too much. But her like or dislike for her dad's client was irrelevant.

Dev rose and held out his arm. "Hello, Gita. My dear, please come and sit next to me so that we can talk."

She gave a slight nod, the movement sharp and jerky. She hesitated for a moment, glanced quickly at her father, then walked the few feet to the couch and sat down slowly. She seemed so fragile, as if the slightest breeze would break her into pieces.

"So, can you please tell me exactly how you feel?" said Dev, his brows furrowed as he took in the state of the girl's body. "I know this is difficult for you, so please take your time."

She cleared her throat. "I'm very weak, sometimes dizzy. I eat as much as I've usually eaten but it seems I can't eat enough to stop getting thinner." The girl's eyes were glassy. She stared at Maya's dad, her expression almost blank.

"Can you tell me how long this has been happening? Go back as far as you can remember."

Gita nodded. "About two months now. It's that long since I started losing weight. I even tried eating more. Even those meal replacement shakes. But they don't help."

"And you really haven't changed anything about your eating habits, besides possible eating more than normal?" Dev leaned forward and Maya got the feeling that he was hoping the girl would admit something. But Gita didn't. She just shook her head in agreement. "Okay, so the next thing I want to ask is if there's been any significant changes in your daily life. Have you changed schools, changed friends, just anything that would signify a difference in what you used to do before this began to happen to you?"

The girl shook her head. The silence was punctuation by the ragged hiss of the conditioner and the scratchy inhale-exhale of Mr. Nath's heavy breathing.

Dev turned to the father, concern coloring his face. "Mr. Nath. There's one more thing I have to ask. I just want to apologize in advance. It's a difficult question to ask and even more difficult to answer, but I do have to."

Mr. Nath stared at Dev, eyes narrowing as he tried to fathom what the question would be. At last his eyebrows moved and he seemed to come to some decision because he gave a small nod and averted his gaze.

"Now, Gita. I need you to be very honest with me. Can you tell me if you have either begun to smoke or to take any form of drugs in the last two months."

"What are you trying to say," Mr. Nath growled taking two steps forward before stopping in his tracks. He glanced suspiciously at his daughter.

Sabala got to his feet and I glared at him to stand down. He watch Nath for a moment or two then decided he wasn't really a threat and sat back onto his haunches.

He would've said more but Dev held up his palm. "I'm really sorry but it's is one thing that we need to rule out before we can go any further. If it is drug related, and I'm not saying it is, then we will know there's a solution. If it is not drug-related, then we can go ahead and consider a more sinister reason. Again, I'm sorry to ask the question, but it is something that we have to know." As he spoke, Dev kept his tone even, unemotional, making Maya marvel at her dad's ability to converse with people who are so tense and skittish. There was not a hint of accusation or criticism in his voice. Which was likely what convinced Mr. Nath. He glared at his daughter and nodded, giving her permission to admit or deny.

But the girl stared at Dev, and shook her head again. "I don't take drugs and I don't smoke." Her eyes darted to her father, then back at Dev. "And even if I wanted to, I wouldn't be able to. My brother goes to the same school, and he keeps an eye on me."

Dev nodded. "Thank you. I'd like you to think again about any changes in your habits over the last two months. I know you said no, but it's possible you may have forgotten something that you think is very minor, but that might be significant to us to help you treat this problem. Anything like the route you take to school where you sit at lunchtime. Anything."

The girl's head jerked up and her eyes widened. "There is one thing that I've changed. Sorry, I didn't really think that it was that important, but they were painting the cafeteria and we had to find somewhere else to sit to eat our lunch. So we started eating outside on the edge of the fields, under the trees. It was too hot to sit anywhere else."

"Are you still sitting under those trees," Dev asked and the girl nodded.

"Can you take us to the school? I need to see the tree up close."

Mr. Nath nodded. "We can take you, but what do you think just looking at the tree will tell you?" His question brimmed over with skepticism and even his wrinkled brow revealed his disbelief.

Maya's dad remained unruffled. "Looking at it may give me nothing. We may need to perform the ritual on the off-chance that it could succeed."

"So I'm assuming you have an idea of what might have caused this?" The man's question held more than just a hint of a challenge but again Dev merely ignored his tone and just offered him a sharp nod.

"I suspect the tree under which you're daughter has been sitting could be the source of her illness. There is every chance that it is haunted by a Bhoot."

The man's face paled and Gita looked stricken. Maya just felt stupid. What the hell was a Bhoot? She kept her features in check as Dev got to his feet and said, "Well, no time like the present."

CHAPTER 18

"You want to go now?" Mr. Nath seemed to hesitate, his neck remaining stiff and unforgiving.

"I'd suggest we move as swiftly as possible. In the interests of the health of your daughter." To Maya it seemed there was an unspoken challenge in her father's words. One which Mr. Nath seemed to shrink from. Instead his gaze settled on Maya for a brief moment. She kept her expression clear even as she acknowledged the disdain on his face. Heat rose in her cheeks but fortunately he had already turned his gaze and now concentrated on her father.

"Fine. We can go. The sooner we get this mess sorted the better. I suppose a Bhoot is better than black magic."

Dev raised his eyebrows. "Is there any reason you would think someone would resort to black magic and more especially target a member of your family? Do you have any enemies?"

Mr. Nath hesitated, his eyes going a shade darker. He seemed to regret the mention of black magic but now it was clear he had no choice but to explain. "Of course, I have enemies," he answered, his tone belligerent, defensive and more than a little arrogant. "I'm a very wealthy man. And you know what it's like having money when everyone else around you is poor. Everyone and his brother wants a handout and when you say no they don't exactly appreciate it. They just assume you're selfish and miserly." The look on his face made it clear that he didn't that Dev and Maya would understand his position. Again, Maya felt her fury rise and this time heat tingled in her palms. With a start she tamped it down, wondering why her fire had risen unbidden. And so quickly. She hadn't even concentrated to call it to her.

Dev cleared his throat and his words broke through the heat simmering in Maya's head. "It is possible this could be a curse of some kind but I would like to rule out the Bhoot first. If that doesn't work then we can explore other options."

Mr. Nath nodded. "Fine. I suppose you know what you are doing." Before Maya's dad could respond he turned on his heel and headed to the entrance hall. As he went he called over his shoulder, "Let's get this done then."

Maya's hands closed into fists at her sides. It didn't seem to take much for the man to rub her the wrong way. Her dad touched her arm and they followed Mr Nath out and headed to their car, Sabala close on Maya's heels. Nath pressed his remote and the garage door rattled as it drew up to reveal a gleaming black Chrysler. The only thing missing was the chauffeur. Nath got in and gunned the engine as his daughter left the house and climbed into the beast of a car.

"She's afraid of him," said Maya as they watched the Chrysler glide forward, out of the garage and past them to the driveway. Dev turned the rental's air conditioner on full blast but it didn't seem to do much except spit out lukewarm condensation that collected on the plastic vents. In the back seat the hell-hound seemed indifferent to the heat; no panting like a normal dog. Score two for Deadland Doggie.

"Yeah, that's no surprise. The family dynamic doesn't seem to be very healthy."

"I didn't see a wife."

"She was there." When Maya's eyebrows rose Dev said, "Someone was in the kitchen. Cooking, I presume. Either mother or grandmother."

"Seems he likes his women not seen and not heard," said Maya dryly.

Dev laughed. "Exactly. He's a domineering man. Should the Bhoot not be the reason the girl is ill then I wouldn't be surprised to find either jealousy or dislike as the reason for and attempt at black magic."

Maya cleared her throat as they followed Nath onto the main road and drove some distance back in the direction of the city, "Forgive my ignorance but what exactly is a Bhoot.?"

Dev raised his eyebrows and glanced over at Maya. "A Bhoot is a ghost."

"Oh," said Maya averting her eyes. She felt more than a little stupid having not known something as simple as what a Bhoot was.

"No need to feel bad, honey. There are a lot of things your Mom and I haven't passed on to you for various reasons."

Maya snorted. "Yeah, mostly because I wasn't interested in hearing them."

Dev laughed, the sound rough and soothing to Maya's hurt. "Yes. That too. But mostly because we knew that when the time came you would have a huge load to bear. You were a little rebel to begin with so it wasn't so easy to indoctrinate you. You asked too many questions, argued too many points to death. We figured it would be an uphill battle to train a Kali Hunter who wasn't ready to believe in Kali. So we did everything else we thought would help."

What he said made a lot of sense. Not that Maya had stopped rebelling. It seemed she'd never appreciated the real value of her parents until the day Kali's power came streaming out of her hands.

Not that Maya would change anything. She liked the way

things were with her family and counted herself Lucky especially when she thought of Ria. She hadn't seen Ria in weeks and with Nik unable to find her in her own home who knew what her future husband had done with her.

Dev pulled up in the parking space beside Nath and they got out with Sabala in tow. The girl took a little longer and Maya hesitated only for the first moment before giving Nath a dark glare and heading over to help the girl alight. The child's knees wobbled and it was clear to anyone watching that she was incredible weak.

After a moment she managed to take a few steps and was able to walk slowly without assistance.

They followed as she led then along the side of the main school building toward the fields at the rear. The set of game fields were bordered by a line of old trees, set around fifty feet apart. The trees were large, branches hanging thick with leaves, reaching far for good shade cover for the students. Maya could see what had drawn the girl and her friends to those trees.

Gita walked slowly ahead of them, turning their little group into a slow procession. At last she drew to a stop beneath a old Ash tree. Sabala made a circuit around the tree the stared up into the branches. He remained steading, clearly not comfortable enough to sit. She looked over her shoulder at Dev. "This is the tree." He nodded as he stopped beside her and studied the tree.

"Can you tell if a Bhoot is there?"

Dev shook his head, a look of frustration flitting across his face. Maya had to hide a smile. Her father certainly didn't have much time for Mr. Nath. "Not really. They don't leave any significant traces of their presence, apart from their effect on the people they possess."

"Possess? Are you saying she is possessed?" Mr. Nath's voice rose as he pointed a thumb in his daughter's direction. Sabala gave him a narrow eyed stare, four times over.

"No, that's not what I am saying," Maya's dad responded, this time unable to keep the annoyance from his voice. "If there is a Bhoot here, it will feed on the spirit of one of the people who frequent this area. Sometimes the ghost can feed on the energies of more than one person but that depends on the age of the ghost and on its need for strength. From your daughter's symptoms it's fairly safe to assume that the Bhoot is feeding on her spirit, drawing her life source from her. And since in the end this is all a matter of assumption so we can have a place to start, I can't be certain that is the case. Why don't we try one thing at a time? It's the best way I know how to do my job." He ended with a note in his voice that may have crossed the line of civility a little and Maya glanced at Mr. Nath, concerned he would take offense. He said nothing, just clenched his jaw and stared up into the overhanging branches.

Maya noticed her dad didn't seem to care, having already returned his attention to the tree. He made one circuit around the thick trunk, then shook his head slightly. "Okay, I can't see any outward signs. There isn't anything more I can expect to see so you can go back home for now. I'll be by later with a preparation."

Mr. Nath said nothing, just gave Dev a sharp nod and turned on his heel. He walked off without a backward glance, and without making sure his daughter was at his side.

Gita drew alongside Maya. "I'm sorry about my dad. He can be a little difficult at time. And it's all been quite stressful for him." Maya raised an eyebrow. Stressful for him? Here was another female making excuses for the male in her family. For a moment Ria's face shimmered over Gita's and Maya had to hold in a shudder.

Maya snorted. "As stressful as it has been for you, I'm sure."

Gita gave Maya a startled glance, then looked away and smiled as she walked across the field after the slowly disappearing figure of her father.

CHAPTER 19

Maya watched the Gita disappear around the corner of the building then turned to face her dad, "So we got nothing."

He shook his head and pursed his lips. "Nothing concrete but the newspapers might give us a little more information."

"That's a good idea," she said as they all walked back to the car. The sun streamed down from the pale blue Arizona sky, unrelenting and merciless. Maya felt her scalp tingle with the heat and wondered how people live in this kind of constant, soul-sucking weather.

In the car Dev turned on the air conditioner and flipped his laptop open, while Sabala got comfortable in the back seat. He'd hardly been any trouble at all and Maya was beginning to think she'd overreacted about him tagging along.

She peered over at the monitor. "You're checking now?" Maya asked, surprised to see him flip his computer open like your neighborhood geek.

"No time like the present," he said as his fingers flew over the keyboard.

When he frowned she asked, "What's wrong?"

"The newspaper. You have to have a paid subscription to search their archives."

"And?"

Maya couldn't see what he was getting at until he spoke. "I don't like having to pay for a 3 month subscription just to research one detail."

"Unavoidable?"

"Unfortunately," he answered with a sigh and reached for his wallet. Credit card details given, he was soon searching the paper's back issues. He turned the laptop so she could see. "Bingo. A number of suicides around the area, two on the school premises."

"Really?" Maya shuddered to think of what people at her school would say about Byron's disappearance and Amber's gory mid-hall murder in a few years time.

Dev nodded. "One suicide by drug overdose over a breakup. The other was a hanging. Says here he was a straight-A student using Ritalin to pull all-nighters. He got busted by the principal and probably couldn't handle the repercussions. No note. Kids found him when they arrived at school in the morning."

A strange cold filled Maya's veins and she rubbed her arms, a feeble effort to bring back the warmth. "Some kids are under a lot of pressure. Maybe he couldn't handle disappointing his family?"

Her dad looked up, concern clear in his dark eyes. "Ritalin abuse. Are there any kids at your school using it?"

Maya didn't even think, she just answered. "Sure there are. Some of the advanced Math and scholarship kids use. It's common and some don't seem to have any issues with people knowing about it."

"Anyone try to sell to you?" There he went, probing, but Maya found she didn't mind at all.

"Sure." Maya nodded, then sighed as she leaned back into the leather seat. "But it's so stupid. Why go to such lengths? Energy drinks I can understand, but over the counter keep-you-awake pills, Ritalin, drugs. I just don't understand how they think it will help."

"It's most like the pressure from their parent and their teachers. You don't really know what's going on in a person's head, their personal pain. A parent's pressure can be difficult to endure. Abuse of any form can aggravate a simple attempt to keep up to a lifestyle that courts death, without the person even realizing how far things have gone."

"And when they realize it it's already too late," said Maya sadly.

"That's right kid." Dev ruffled Maya's hair and laughed as she whined at him to stop.

Then he went back to being serious again, tapping a finger against the screen of his laptop.

"We know it's a hanging, and it's probably that very tree. Do you want to check and verify which tree?" asked Maya.

"Doing that right now. I think I saw an article that had a photograph of the spot with bouquets of flowers and candles beneath the tree," he said already tapping away, a concentrated frown marring his forehead.

"When did this happen?" Maya asked, staring out at the school which shimmered like a mirage in front of them.

"Six years ago."

"So enough time has passed for most of the kids to have forgotten about it. Nobody in their right mind would have dared sit under the tree if they knew." Maya shuddered, knowing nobody she knew would ever sit under that tree if they knew what had happened there. Death had a way of demarcating lines between itself and the living.

"Exactly."

"So what now?"

"Now we get the materials together for a preparation."

"What do they do with it? Tie it around her neck like an

amulet?" Dev paused and stared at Maya. She laughed. "An amulet? Really?"

Yes. An Amulet. It's one way to ward the Bhoot off and to remove its possession. It's easy enough to tell Gita to stay away from the tree, but in all likelihood he will follow her. By now he has a taste for her life's essences so it won't take much for him to find her wherever she is. The best way to help her is to make her invisible to him and if that's not possible then having something on her person that would keep him away can be the thing that saves her."

"So what will work? Holy Ashes?" asked Maya trying to recall the possible options.

Dev nodded again. "Ashes, water. Turmeric; they hate turmeric. And of course metal. I'll make the amulet as soon as I get back to the motel."

"And what about the spirit? Can we do anything for him?" asked Maya, now concerned with the ghost of the boy. He must have gone through a horrible time for him to reach that point where he decided it was over for him. What could they do to help a soul so tormented?

Dev sighed. "That's going to be difficult. If he was buried we use a similar warding to the one for a Churel, but it's not guaranteed. I can use metal nails in the tree and around the school. That might prevent him from draining someone else life-force in the future. The mantras may be worth a try."

"Okay. Why don't we get them the amulet and come back here tonight and say some nice words for him?"

"As you wish," Dev said giving Maya a wink. "I'm surprised you care about his wellbeing this much."

"He deserves peace as much as the next guy. He was probably just a poor confused kid who made the wrong choice." Maya shrugged, glad she had people to talk to if she ever was in such an awful position.

"You are right. So that's what we'll do." He shut the laptop and started the car. As they drove back to the motel Maya stared out the window at the streets of Tucson as they flitted by. She couldn't get her head around how much of the world was still unseen. How many people walked down the street never knowing who walked beside them, what walked beside them.

Sometimes ignorance was bliss but Maya wasn't sure she ever wanted to be that blind again.

BACK IN THE motel room Dev set about preparing the amulet and Maya and Sabala watched as he filled a small plastic tube with water and tipped in a sprinkle of turmeric and white holy ash. He sealed the tube with a small screw-top lid, twisting it until it was tight. Then he rifled around in his drawer for three metal nails; small ones, plain and simple hardware store nails. He removed a small black square that Maya saw was actually a tiny bag, just large enough for the vial and the nails to fit comfortably. He pushed them into the bag then folded the edge over and pulled out a needle and black cotton.

"What are you doing?" Maya asked. She gave a short laugh and stared at him.

"I have to seal the edges. Can't have the potions falling out of the bag. This has to work and keep working for a long while." His gaze remained on his handiwork.

Maya narrowed her eyes at him. He knew exactly why she'd asked. He was hopeless with a needle and thread but it seems he persevered when the situation required it. But she couldn't stand to see him sticking his tongue out as he poked the needle into the fabric.

"Just give it here." She held out her hand waving it impatiently.

He handed it to her so fast she was sure he'd have whiplash. "Thought you'd never ask," he said with relief. Maya laughed and took the bag, quickly sewing the open edge closed. "You have any idea how long that would have taken me?"

"Yes, actually I do."

Dev sighed as he leaned back in is chair and threaded his fingers behind his neck. "I always say sewing is a woman's work."

Maya raised one eyebrow. "Watch what you say. I'm the one with the needle." Her dad just grinned as she gave the sealed bag back to him.

"Right, I'll take this to the Nath's and leave them with the instructions. Want to come?"

Maya shook her head. "No I need to finish my reading for English. I don't want to fail the demon's second essay assignment."

"No, you certainly wouldn't want to do that." Dev winked as he headed out the door.

Maya shut it behind and grabbed her bag. She climbed onto the bed and flipped to the bookmarked page. *Romeo and Juliet.* Scintillating reading. But she was determined to treat the essay as if a real teacher were setting it. One wrong move and she'd mess everything up.

Don't act normal. Be normal.

LATER THAT AFTERNOON they checked out of the motel and headed to the school field. They left the car, carrying her dad's bag full of hunter gadgets, accompanied by the ever silent, ever sedate hell-hound.

The fields looked different at night; all reaching shadows and ominous angles. At the tree they both paused, staring at the shadow-laden branches above them as if expecting the ghost to glide down and greet them. But nothing happened. Dev relaxed, then stepped right up to the trunk and craned his head as if searching for something within the tree.

"Got it," he said triumphantly.

"What are you looking for?" asked Maya.

"A small space where the branches meet the large trunk. Somewhere to hide their little hex bag.

"Hand me three nails and the hammer." Maya did as he requested and watched as he pounded in the large black nails, sisters to the ones they'd driven into the grave of the Churel. His movements were easy and sure, as if he'd done it a hundred times before.

Then, with a small trowel, he dug a little hole in the ground between a couple of entwining tree roots. Inside it, he placed a tiny marigold whose head drooped over in a sad arch, parched from the heat, as if bowing to the power of the suns rays even when no visible sights of the the existed. Also in the hole went frankincense and another nail. Sabala trotted over, sniffed the contents of the hole then returned to stand at the edge of the shade.

Dev gave him an odd look then set the rock hard tree sap alight and got to his feet. While the smoke wafted up from the hole he spoke a series of mantras. Once he was done he covered hole with a scoop of soil, snuffing out the burning frankincense in the same movement. He pressed the soil hard, ensuring it was firmly packed, then stood up.

"It's done. The best I can do. Let's just hope he finds his peace." Dev sighed and gazed up into the branches as if he could see the ghost and communicate with him. Maya knew exactly how helpless her dad felt.

The scent of frankincense wafted on a breeze like a pale emaciated ghost, undulating through the air and then disappearing on the black night air. She didn't feel any different or any better now that the rites were completed. Funny how she'd assumed she'd feel that something had changed in some way.

As they all walked back to the car Maya remained deep in

thought until she heard the trunk slam shut. She jerked her head up and met her father's eyes.

"Are you okay?" he asked, his eyes darkening with worry as he searched her face for the answer.

She nodded but she couldn't bring herself to smile. She got into the car and she sighed. "I'm not sure how I feel about all of this. I do know I feel impotent."

"Just because you have powers doesn't mean you have the ability to solve all the problems of this world," Dev said as he shut his door and they buckled up while Sabala seated himself, spreading his long legs across the entire back seat. Good thing he didn't shed either. Score 3 for the hound.

Dev drove out of the lot and turned back toward the city. The stars were pinpricks of bright white in the black sky, and on the horizon a seas of multicolored gems glittered, urging them forward.

"I know that but I still feel helpless. What's all these powers for when I can't use them? Smelling demon blood? How is that supposed to help anything?" She stared listlessly out the window, seeing neither traffic nor people nor bright lights.

"It helps to be able to defend yourself against those who will want you for their own evil reasons. A power like your's come with-"

"Yeah, I know. A power like mine comes with great responsibility. I know. I had my own personal run-in with Balraj, the overeager sorcerer remember." Dev said nothing while Maya shuddered at the memory of Balraj's torture not so long ago. He'd cut her, bled her and tried to extract her fire power. The pain had been excruciating and unbearable to the extent that there'd been moments when Maya had prayed for death to release her from her suffering.

"But you got through it didn't you?" asked her dad. He glanced at her and all she could see was his understanding and his attempt at making her feel better.

She nodded. "Yeah. I got through it but I lost Kas." She still hated the fact that she hadn't killed or at least captured the demon prince Narakasura. But it all happened so fast. Not to mention that she'd sort of empathized with him at the time.

"You can't blame yourself for that."

"Yes, I can," she insisted, the profound ache that simmered inside her soul agreed that she could. "I can because I know deep down that I didn't want to kill him. I hesitated and that's what cost me his capture."

"Can you pinpoint why?" When she glanced at her dad he seemed serious, although she wasn't sure where he was going with his line of question.

Maya nodded as she turned away to look out the window at the miles of desert and tumbleweed that skittered by. "It's because I liked him. It was as if I understood him on a certain level. And killing him just seemed wrong."

"Even though he sent demons to attack you. Even when he made his sorcerer try to take your power away?" her dad asked and she could sense he was controlling his anger. Both her parents had been horrified to hear of Maya's experiences in Swargaloka at the hands of Balraj, and Dev had been justly furious. Even pacing the living room floor hadn't alleviated his anger and it had taken days before he was able to accept the Kas hadn't been relieved of his head.

"Yes. Even then. It seemed there was something driving him." She looked at her father. "What if he was just a pawn and someone bigger and more powerful is behind all this?"

"Is that what you think?"

"It's what my gut is saying. It just didn't seem to fit. The way he spoke to me, the things he said."

"Did he come on to you?" Anger rippled through Dev's voice.

"No, Dad." Maya cracked out a strangled laugh at the question and at her dad's fury. "He didn't. It wasn't like that at all. It was more like we clicked as two people who could be friends. And I find it hard to accept that I felt that way about a horrible mass-murdering demon king."

"I know it's hard but what if that is the reality? That he is guilty?"

Maya sighed, swirling incessantly in a sea of uncertainty. "If that is the case then I guess I can't trust my gut anymore. And I'd have to accept I'm the reason we didn't catch him." Maya glared angrily ahead at the blacktop as they sped endlessly toward it.

"You know that this is something you might never end up confirming. Not unless he turns up someplace again," said her dad and Maya disliked that he was likely right.

"Yeah, well. If he does I'm certainly not going to be hugs and balloons. The bast-" Maya cleared her throat and flicked a chagrined glance at her dad. "The guy did stick me with a dagger."

Dev ignored Maya's almost-swearword. "Not too nice of a guy if he stabbed you in the back is he?"

"More like the side, but I accept your point." Maybe she should be less flippant considering the level of her dad's seething fury.

"But you still don't think he's all that bad of a guy?" There was that edge in his voice again. The one that made her wonder if this conversation should never have begun in the first place.

"Nope."

"I guess everything is a journey of understanding." He was trying to be understanding, despite his distrust of Kas. She could tell, and she'd never admired her dad more that that moment. "Maybe, if you do ever encounter him again, you can approach the situation with more of an objective eye, given that he did try to kill you in the end." She could tell he wasn't convinced by her sympathetic stance, and he probably never would be.

Maya nodded, but she still wasn't so sure. Yes, it stung that Kas had stabbed her but she'd gotten the feeling that he'd been desperate. And desperate people do desperate things. In the end he'd looked like he'd regretted hurting her. Then she sighed. "And in the end I could be totally wrong and he is just an evil son- . . . er . . . evil demon."

"That may be. But you also could be right. So just stay alert and aware at all times." It was the best and only advice she was going to take regarding Kas and she was glad her dad seemed to understand that. She wasn't sure how she would respond if he came on hard and strong insisting she was wrong about Kas. She glanced again at him but his face didn't give anything away.

Soon they turned onto the Interstate and headed west. Homeward bound. Maya used the rest of the ride to finish reading XXXX, figuring she was better off getting that English assignment out of the way.

"Maya, wake up." Dev shook Maya's shoulder and she opened gritty eyes to the view of their garage door.

She lifted her head, felt something wet on her shoulder and her cheek, then flushed beet red. Drool. Like a freaking baby. Drool soaking through her teeshirt and pasted all across her cheek.

Great.

Her dad must have had a bellyful of laughs. She'd fallen asleep between sentences, somewhere in the last two hours of the trip and her dad hadn't awakened her. It looked like night with the sky all blue black and barely a star in it, but the crisp air floating into the car said it was very early in the morning. Too early.

Annoyed, she dragged herself and her bag inside the house feeling as though she'd been hit by a Mack truck. Her muscles were sore, her butt ached and her eyes felt like a boatload of sea-sand had been poured into each one. She was so tired she almost slammed the door in Sabala's face, having forgotten he was even there at all.

Maya headed straight to bedroom making a face. She had

about as much chance of skipping school as she did of being crowned Miss America. She sighed, climbed the stairs and fell face down onto the bed.

A soft clacking sound alerted her to Sabala's presence. Thank goodness the creature hadn't progressed to the licking stage of their relationship. That would have totally marked the end of things between them. No licking.

Score 4 for the pooch.

THE NEXT DAY went by uneventfully and Maya was again at the kitchen table, this time poring over her Math homework. She figured she might as well get into the habit of getting work done when she can. The trip to Tucson had given her a bit of time related education.

On the road and on the case, time open often not as available as you'd think and using those pockets of minutes she had to get things done made too much sense for Maya to ignore it.

Her mom was busy peering into the oven where a small leg of lamb was slow-roasting. Her day had been uneventful with Nik gone and Joss chattering as usual. She'd arrived home been immediately roped into peeling onions and potatoes for the creamy gratin she loved. She'd gotten the meal prep out the way fast enough and was now folded over her books, swinging her leg under the table.

Leela moved toward the edge of the table, arms on her hips. Maya felt her watching and glanced up in case her mom wanted something but all she got was a smile.

"What?" she asked giving her head a little shake.

"Nothing. Can't a woman look at her daughter?"

Maya opened her mouth to say no the frowned. "I suppose. But if looks could kill..."

They both giggled and then Maya's mom said, "To be honest

I'm trying to get used to seeing you so comfortable around the deities and all the things you need to do, both good and bad. Especially when you were the one who refused to believe in them." Leela shook her head and laughed softly.

"You won't let me forget that will you?" Maya asked, exasperated.

"Not really," said her mom and they both burst out laughing.

Maya narrowed her eyes on her mom's face, suspicious now that the topic came up. "I take it Dad told you about my worries about Kas?"

Leela pushed away from the table and headed to the stove to check on the boiling potatoes. "Of course. I'm sure you knew he would."

"It's called Skype, dear."

Maya snorted. She opened her mouth to respond but her attention was drawn to the kitchen doorway. Sabala, who'd taken a seat beside the doorway, raised his head from his paws and gave a soft whine as the air shimmered,. Wisps of shadow whirled, spiraling around a figure that slowly formed before them.

Maya tensed, pulling her fire to her fingertips, ready to slam fireballs at the intruder. Slowly the spinning threads of darkness shifted into a familiar face and Maya relaxed.

"Hello, Maya," said the goddess Chayya, her dark almond shaped eyes glittering with amusement as she took in Maya's wary stance and open palm. "I do hope you do not plan on incinerating me."

Maya laughed and relaxed, shaking the fire from her hand. "Of course not." She grinned at the goddess whose dark hair fell in soft waves to her slim waist. "How have you been? It's been a while."

Chayya smiled serenely and inclined her head. "I am very well. I hear you have been improving in your ability to control your powers."

News certainly got around. Not that Maya minded too much if it was Chayya. Maya shrugged. "I'm getting there."

The smile evaporated from Chayya's face for a moment. "You have made amazing progress. Do not deny yourself the credit for your hard work." Maya gave a shy smile as her cheeks flamed. Before she could figure out how to respond, the goddess continued. "I apologize. I am unable to stay long. I have something for you."

With a flourish, a scroll appeared in her hand. She held her palm out to Maya, who took the scroll, frowning at the goddess. "What's this?"

Chayya nodded at the rolled up paper. "Open it. The letter is for you. From Lord Shiva."

Maya went cold, and suddenly her throat became dry and scratchy as she tried to swallow. "Lord Shiva?" she asked, her hand now trembling a little. She'd been summoned by a god before but had not yet had the privilege of communicating with the most important and most powerful god of all. Lord Shiva was to Hindu's what Zeus was to Greeks. A message from the god of gods is no small matter.

Her hands shook as she cracked the golden seal. She placed the paper on the table and smoothed out the rolled parchment. The message was written in Sanskrit and Maya's stomach clenched tight. She couldn't read the language, had never learned to.

Now what?

She looked up at her mom who had craned her neck to get a glimpse of the message. "Do you know how to read it?" Maya asked. Leela shook her head, disappointment clearly etched on her face. "I thought you and Dad knew how to read Sanskrit?"

Before even as her mom opened her mouth to answer, Chayya broke in. "All you need to do is concentrate, Maya."

Maya threw a skeptical glance at Chayya but in the face of the goddesses encouraging expression, Maya decided she had little to lose by following her instructions. She ran a hand over the parchment and studied the words, written in dark blue ink on yellowing paper. Moments later she frowned and shook her head, glancing up at Chayya. "Nothing's happening."

"Patience, child." The goddess spoke kindly, not a hint of annoyance in her tone. She seemed eternally serene and her emotions gave Maya strength.

She nodded and returned her gaze to the parchment. Not so long ago she would have laughed at the prospect of staring at a foreign language in the hopes that it would eventually make a lick of sense. That was way back when gods and goddesses were not as real to her as her parents, when hell-hounds were creatures of myth and Kali was merely an awfully hideous figment of her imagination and not the kind generous and stung goddess she now knew her to be.

Maya forced herself to relax and concentrate on the curves of the letters. As she blinked she thought she saw a flicker of light shimmer over the parchment. Then her eyes went wide as each letter began to shine, letting of rays of light as if the parchment was held up before a blazing sun.

Then even as she blinked she thought she saw the letters begin to move. But when she concentrated harder she realized they hadn't budged at all. She let out a breath, surprised that she had been holding it in all this time. The world seemed to have stilled around her. She blinked at the bright letters and was about to shade her eyes when she gasped.

The letters made sense to her now, as strange as it sounded. It was as if the light that shone from them held the meaning. She couldn't explain how she understood a language she had never learned but she knew what the parchment said.

"What is it Maya?"

Her mother's voice penetrated her concentration, forcing her to look up. "I can read it," she whispered, the shiver in her voice clearly revealing her inner conflict.

Leela moved to Maya's side and bent to examine the letter. She looked at Maya, frowning. "How can you understand it? What does it say?"

"I don't know, it's more like I can sense the meaning than actually read it." Maya nodded to herself. She couldn't have put it any better. Then she stiffened as the message became clearer. She glanced at her mom, knowing that her next words may come as a shock.

"It's a summons to Mount Kailas."

CHAPTER 21

Silence hung in the room for a few moments, heavy and uncomfortable as Maya and her mom stared at each other. Leela's face was pale as she cleared her throat and asked, "Are you sure that's what it says?"

Maya nodded. She understood totally why her mother was asking the question. Lord Shiva and Mount Kailas. Both were unimaginable to Maya. Going from a non-believer to mixing and mingling with the gods was a transition in itself. "I'm sure."

Chayya had remained quiet all this time and seemed to not want to interfere with the family reaction. How did you make small talk with a goddess? Not like you could say 'how's things?' and expect an answer. So in the end she just thanked Chayya for bringing her the message.

The goddess smiled and her beautiful face lit up. "It is my pleasure Maya. And I did want to also check on how you are doing? I have heard that you have had some Rakshasa trouble at school?" Maya nodded and ran gave Chayya brief run-down on her demon-teacher. "Best be very careful Maya. But I think you can handle whatever they try."

"Hopefully I can," said Maya, pasting a weak impersonation of a smile on her face. She wasn't about to tell Chayya that she wasn't exactly looking forward to going head to head with a high-level Rakshasi, especially not one as powerful as the teacher-demon.

But Chayya must have senses Maya lack of self-esteem because she shook her head. "You must learn to believe in yourself, Maya. That is the first step to success." Maya swallowed, unsure how to respond. She settled for a wooden nod. The goddess seemed satisfied with her response and inclined her head.

Then Maya glanced back at the scroll and asked, "How do I get to Mount Kailas? Can you take me?"

The brief spurt of happiness that Maya had felt died a quick death when Chayya shook her head. "Not yet." The Goddess gave Maya a teasing grin. "First we need to get you ready. It isn't every day a human girl gets an audience with the god of gods."

"Oh." Relief filtered through Maya. But she hesitated, "I think we can fix than easily enough. I've got plenty of clothes to choose from."

"Not those I hope?" Chayya winked as she traced her fingers across Sabala's head. Somehow the hell-hound had moved from his post to the goddess's side without Maya noticing.

Maya laughed as she gave her jeans and black U2 teeshirt a glance. "No. Definitely not these. And if I don't have anything appropriate I'm sure Mom has something."

But Chayya was shaking her head. "I have a better, quicker option. Come with me." Maya raised her eyebrows but didn't refuse the goddesses request.

She stepped forward giving her mother one last glance over her shoulder before Chayya whisked Maya away in a swirling tornado of black shadows, to the tune of Sabala's disappointed whine.

∼

THEY REAPPEARED in what looked like a small living room, complete with couches and a serving table laden with scones, tea and finger sandwiches.

"Where are we?" Maya asked, half afraid her voice would set of alarm bells. She stood staring at the shimmering glass chandelier hanging from the center of the ceiling.

"The private viewing room at Noorjahan Couture." Spoken as if SE spent every other day at the shop in Hollywood.

Maya swallowed hard and it felt like her throat twisted in on itself.

World famous clothing designer Sandra Valente owned Noorjahan Couture and the shop was located on Rodeo Drive.

And Chayya had brought her here? Maya was in total awe. At last she managed to speak, hoping she didn't sound like she was in shock. "What are we doing here? I can't afford anything from this designer. Not in a million years. Well ,maybe one of the beads on her designs but a dress? Never. Ever." A pause to breathe.

"It is a good thing then that I am, how do you say it? Good for it?" Chayya asked with a raised eyebrow.

"Yeah, that would be how you say it," responded Maya, her eyes still traveling the room as Chayya swept through the thick velvet curtains drawn across the entrance. Within moments she returned with a tall, attractive woman, her shoulder length hair perfectly highlighted.

Maya stiffened. Chayya had brought the designer with her. And Maya was so in awe she was sure she was about to faint. She was annoyed with herself though. She didn't normally go gaga over people. Gods maybe, but not people.

"Maya, this is Sandra. She's promised to find something suitable for you." Chayya smiled and so did Sandra. And suddenly Maya felt calmer. The designer certainly didn't have the arrogance or haughtiness she'd expected, and Maya wondered if she knew who Chayya was. Maya glanced at the goddess but it was too late to ask as Sandra asked her to turn around on the spot. Maya obeyed, did a twirl and as she returned to face the designer all she saw was the woman's back as she disappeared between the curtains.

Maya felt slightly deflated but the Goddess of Shadows seemed very much at ease. "Does she know who you are?" Maya whispered to Chayya.

Chayya turned. "I am one of her wealthiest customers. That is all she need know. Of course, I do use the name Chayya Malhotra."

Maya smiled. She suspected the goddess was incognito and was glad she hadn't blurted out anything weird. Before she could ask any more questions the curtains were thrust open and two girls, perfectly made up and dressed in hand beaded skirts and blouses in blue and pink pastels, that would have been good enough for Maya as far as she was concerned.

She watched as they lay the sealed bags on the couch and left. Sandra leaned forward and unzipped the first one. As soon as Maya saw it she knew she didn't care what else the designer had brought. This garment was the one.

The skirt and blouse was made with the finest gold fabric. Thousands of tiny diamantes and gold beads covered every inch of the material. The skirt was bordered by a strip of blood red fabric, this time heavily beaded with only gold beads of varying sizes. Sandra dusted out the length of red fabric that would be draped over Maya's shoulder. It matched the border so beautifully Maya couldn't wait to put the garment on.

"Right, off you go, young lady. The changing room is behind the glass. Just press it to open."

Maya walked toward the large mirror on the left wall and pressed the left edge feeling a little foolish. When the door popped open she sighed with relief. Very snazzy, she thought as she entered the large, mirrored room and hung the garment one of a series of cast iron hooks on the wall. She undressed and slipped into the gold skirt and blouse, then left the changing room when she realized she'd left the scarf behind.

She entered the room to a chorus of oohs and ahs as Sandra and Chayya showered praise on her.

"Gosh it's not me. It's this outfit. It's just gorgeous." She stared at herself in the mirror.

"Don't be silly," said Sandra frowning as she folded the swathe of red fabric with deft fingers, then dusted it out before tucking one end into the waist of Maya's skirt. "The garment only accentuates a girl's beauty." She fussed a little, walking the long fabric around Maya and draping it around her body. Finally she threw it over Maya's shoulder and pinned it in place.

Then she turned Maya to the mirror. "Now that is gorgeous," she said with a happy grin.

"Absolutely." Agreed Maya. The vision reflected in the mirror was truly beautiful- a garment fit for the King of Gods. "I love it."

Sandra turned to the next garment and lifted a peach creation from the bag but Maya was already shaking her head. "No. I think this one is just perfect."

"Well, aren't you just easy to please. But I do understand what you mean. With that black hair and dark curved eyebrows of yours, and your skin tone, the red and gold is just perfect." Sandra stood beside Maya and nodded. Maya retreated to the dressing room to change back into her infinitely humble jeans and tee. She was just leaving the room when she heard Sandra say, "Right, I'll have it delivered to you, Chayya or to Maya's address."

"Can we take it with us? We need it in the next few of hours," Chayya answered as if she did these drop in and grab deals all the time.

Sandra's expression showed her surprise only for the briefest moment. Then she smiled again and patted Chayya's shoulder as if they were long-time friends. "Of course. I'll have it bagged and I'll just put that on your account?"

Chayya nodded and the delighted designer swept out with the

garment. Maya was already beginning to miss the luxurious soft-ness and the rich weight of the outfit on her body. She chuckled to herself thinking back to a time when she'd hated the mere thought of wearing anything Indian.

THEY ARRIVED BACK at Maya's house where she headed straight upstairs with her new outfit. Sabala, who'd waited in her room, got to his feet when she walked in and laid the garment out on her bed. She scratched his forehead briefly before heading into the shower. She was grimy from the day and wanted to freshen up before meeting Lord Shiva. She cleaned up, applied some light makeup and donned her new garment. Slipping on a pair of low heeled gold strappy sandals she headed downstairs with the hell-hound in tow and entered the kitchen to find Chayya and her mom deep in discussion.

They both looked up as she walked inside, and both their faces contained the same smiling admiration. "Maya, you look gorgeous," said her mom, her voice breaking. God, she hoped her mom wasn't about to do something crazy like cry on her.

"She looks perfect for meeting a god," said Chayya.

Maya frowned. "But why do I have to get dressed up to see Lord Shiva? I didn't need to stand on ceremony with you or with Lord Yama."

"Lord Shiva is the creator, the preserver and the destroyer. He is the last god you ever want to enrage. It would pay for you to put your best foot forward at all times. And Shiva can sometimes be unpredictable." Chayya shrugged. "You can understand he has a lot on his shoulders."

"Okay," Maya responded, smoothing the red fabric draped across her abdomen. A ripple of nervousness filtered through her as she contemplated the meeting. Then she straightened her spine. "Are we leaving yet?"

Chayya laughed. "It is good to see you eager to meet with the God of Gods."

Maya cleared her throat. "It's more the fact that I am eager to get this over and done with."

The goddess smiled at her honesty and inclined her head in a small bow. "A good enough reason. Let us be going then."

Sabala clicked closer and Maya eyed the hellhound. "What about the pooch."

"He goes back to Patala until you return. You may be a while."

Maya raised her eyebrows but said nothing as Chayya clicked her fingers and her demon dog disappeared.

Then Chayya held out a hand.

$\mathcal{M}$aya held on to Chayya's hand and the room disintegrated around them. They arrived within a swirling mass of black and grey shadows, the ground beneath their feet firm and rocky. When Maya exhaled and a cloud of white left her mouth she gasped. Glancing around she realized she stood on a large rock that stuck out of a sea of snow.

Her entire body convulsed with shivers and her teeth chattered. She certainly hadn't dressed for mid-winter and hoped the rest of the journey wouldn't be spent shivering her tail feathers off. "Where are we? Is this the place?"

Chayya shook her head. "We are almost there. I wanted to show you something."

"And you couldn't show me this someplace warm?" Maya could barely get the words out without her teeth crashing against each other.

"I'm sorry. It will take but a moment." Chayya smiled and put an arm around Maya, turning a little. The sun was high and bright but not at all warm. The goddess waved at the the view and said, "Look."

Maya stared ahead of her and for a moment she was confused.

All she saw was what looked like a small valley flanked by two mountains. The shadowed valley opened up to a snow covered flat-faced mountain and Maya gawked in amazement, her near-frozen state forgotten. "Wow. That is beautiful."

"Welcome to Mount Kailas, Maya Rao," Chayya said, giving Maya a little bow, awkward while also holding Maya's shoulders, but a bow nevertheless.

"Are you serious? That's the mountain we are going to?" When Chayya nodded Maya was even more confused. "But there's nothing on top. It's just a huge pointy-topped mountain that looks more like an iceberg than an actually mountaintop."

"I assure you it is very much a mountain. Kailas is made entirely of solid rock. What you see is the north-face which is sheer and unclimbable although the south side is slightly more curved."

Maya shook her head in awe. "But I still don't see how the top of that mountain could hold anything larger than a tent let alone a palace or a kingdom."

"One should not always trust only what we see." The goddess said then held out her hand.

Maya took it wordlessly and they disintegrated into undulating strips of shadow.

They reappeared on the edge of the mountain facing the valley she'd seen moments again and for a moment she was disoriented but the change in direction. When she realized she was standing at the top of Mount Kailas she looked down instinctively. She stood a foot from the edge and was able to see straight down the side of the mountain. From this vantage point the cliff face wasn't as smooth and flat as it looked from the ground. Rocky outcroppings jutted out here and there, little shelves filled with piles and piles of snow.

Maya took a deep breath and stepped away from the edge. She wasn't afraid of the height of the mountain. What got to her was the scale of it and the reality that she now stood in a place of myth.

Maya glanced around and found Chayya standing silently at her side. The goddess had changed her sari in the time it took for them to re-materialize. Now, a silver, diamante studded sari draped itself around her body. Even her eyes seemed duskier, shimmering with silver sparkle hidden in the dark shadows of her lids.

"Wow. You look awesome."

"Thank you, Maya. I did not want to appear inadequately robed. Especially not with that beautiful creation you are wearing."

"Not very likely," said Maya, still very much on awe of Chayya, her personality and her looks. She cleared her throat. "Right, so where exactly are we meant to be going?" she asked turning on her heel, expecting to see a few yards of rock. Instead she gasped and didn't breathe for a long moment as she stared at the picture before her.

She and Chayya stood on the edge of a grassy field, a stone pathway cutting it in equal halves. Trees grew in the distance, providing cover from the biting wind and the further they walked the warmer Maya began to feel. Something moved among the wild trees, a flash of orange that sent a cold shiver running up Maya's spine. She slowed to a stop and watched a regal Bengal tiger as it stared back at her, its large glassy eyes never leaving her face.

Just when she thought it was about to bound toward her the animal lifted its magnificent head in a strangely human nod, then turned to stalk off into the dense tree-line. Before it disappeared it looked back over its shoulder at Maya, as if to check she'd gotten the message that he approved of her presence.

Maya sighed and returned her attention to the building ahead of them. Maya had thought the white marble palace of Swarga-loka was beautiful. It had nothing on this incredible vision that was the abode of the God of Gods. Before them rose a palace that gleamed in the sunlight, that shimmered as if made from snow and ice.

The turrets and spires, windows and trellis facades all gleamed pure white and all Maya could do was stare in wonder.

"Beautiful isn't it?" asked Chayya noticing her silence.

"It's beyond description." Maya sighed. "Is it made of ice?"

"Yes. Legend has it that the palace rose from the ice and snow atop Mount Kailas, forming itself into an abode fit for the Great God."

Maya frowned, wondering at the mechanics of the building. "Doesn't the sunlight melt the ice? And it must be freezing inside it. How do they manage?"

"The palace is ice. Pure in its creation. Nothing can destroy purity. Thus the building stands in the warmth of the sunlight, as it has for thousands of years."

"I see," said Maya as she blinked against the sparkle of sunlight against the highest rounded spire. Of course, there would be a magical, mystical answer. Maya should have been prepared to accept things as they were, not as she wanted them to be.

"Come. We must get moving. There is a way to go yet." Chayya walked off and Maya had no choice but to stop gawking and follow.

A low stone wall blocked their path, probably only as high as Maya's shoulder. A set of cast iron gates protected the only way through the wall that Maya could see. As they moved closer the gates began to open as if someone unseen commanded they be allowed inside.

And what an inside it was.

A veritable forest of lush green trees grew within the walls and Maya felt like she'd just walked into a tropical jungle. Soon they passed through the thick tree line which opened out into a large garden. Marble fountains dotted the green lawn, water springing high into the air, sparkling in the sunlight as they fell from the hands of marble nymphs and stone apsaras.

A marble pathway guided them to a set of steps leading up to a gigantic pair of glass doors. Maya blinked unsure if she was looking at glass or diamond. Only when she felt warm fingers press up against her chin did she realize she was staring with her mouth hanging open

"You will catch flies."

"Surely not here." Maya laughed softly. "I can't see flies existing in a place as exquisite and godly as this."

"Lord Shiva is the creator, the Preserver and the Destroyer. He is the beginning and the end of life. What are flies if not a small part of the Lord's universe?" asked Chayya, her face serene.

Maya did a double-take. "I hadn't though of it that way." She nodded as they headed across the threshold, passing whisper close to the shimmering doors. "Is that glass?"

"It is quartz."

"I thought diamond would be more suited," said Maya craning her neck to see if she could make out the top of the doors.

"And where in the world would you find a diamond the size of these doors?" Chayya waved her hand at the twenty foot high doors.

"I guess you have a point there."

They entered a large room that had Maya's jaw dropping again. Numerous chaise lounges were scattered around the room, elegantly finished in cream fabric, with swirling paisley patterns done in golden thread. The arms were curved and comfortable enough to take a nap on. Cushions of every shade of gold and red were thrown artfully upon the beautiful couches. Gigantic hand-woven carpets covered the floor, depicting Indian hunting scenes that dated back thousands of years. Small, artifact filled tables ran along the walls and beside the seats, brass decanters and cups gleaming in the sunlight.

Along one wall was a balcony of sorts. A stone platform, one large step in height and five feet to the window, gave out onto the garden. It was fashioned much like a bay window, complete with made to fit pads for seating and scattered with luxurious gold patterned cushions. Six slim, carved pillars divided the palatial window seat reminding Maya that this was no ordinary home.

"We can sit here while we wait to be seen."

"How do they know we're here?" asked Maya as she stared at the fresco's painted on the walls. Dancing nymphs, apsaras and men cavorted on bright green meadows and white crested seasides and lonely mountaintops. A number of strange animals were included, creatures Maya had never seen or heard of.

"They know. Nobody enters Kailas without an invitation."

"What would have happened if we came up the mountain without an invitation?"

Chayya smiled. "The mountain is well protected agings intruders."

Maya didn't like the goddesses cryptic answer. "Don't tell me intruders are killed?" Maya flushed at the thought and was relieved when Chayya shook her head.

"No. They are transported straight back down the mountain and no doubt suffer weeks of wondering if they had only imagined their success. Besides, it is near impossible now to get a permit from the Chinese government to scale the mountain."

"You mean they actually stop people on pilgrimage?" Maya frowned at the thought.

"No. They discourage the climbers. They seek to protect the mountain and to maintain the respect of it for religious reasons."

"I hardly see the Chinese as religious." Prejudiced much, thought Maya, wanting to bite her tongue.

"Remember to always look beyond what you see, Maya. The choices of the government may not always be so easily explained away. Perhaps they care about the safety of the potential climber because Kailas is almost certainly a deadly climb. Perhaps they seek to ensure a religious place is not overrun by hundreds of uncaring tourist climbers whose desire is merely to conquer the mountain."

"With no respect to the religions who hold this place close to their hearts." Maya nodded, finally understanding what the goddess was trying to say. She flushed, hoping her prejudice had not reduced her in Chayya's eyes. She knew she'd try to be a little less judgmental next time. She smoothed her skirt down and walked to the stepped balcony. Beside her, gigantic cushions invited her to sprawl upon them and relax in a royal fashion but her attention was on the scene beyond the window.

Peacocks strutted in the manicured gardens and in the distance, where the manicured lawn met the wild jungle she saw the flicker of black and orange stripes. The tiger still lurked, reminding her she was the outsider.

She sucked in a breath and shook her head. She was currently standing on a mountaintop that was fabled to be the home of Lord Shiva. Fabled? Ha. The very word was laughable.

The fable is now the myth and the myth is the reality.

$\mathcal{A}$ sound behind Maya caught her attention and she turned to see a man approach Chayya. He was dressed in a long, brocade coat in tan with fine red paisley print. He wore a small red turban and a viciously curved knife hung from his belt. He looked like he belonged in another one of those well-illustrated stories she'd grown up with.

He smiled from behind a thick handle-bar mustache and bowed, leaving as quietly as he came. Chayya rose and dusted her sari out. "It is time," she said holding out her hand. "Come. We must not keep him waiting."

"Will he get angry if we take too long?"

"No. But it will be impolite." Chayya's voice held a tinge of dryness and Maya glanced at her wondering if she was annoyed with her. But the goddess seemed unaffected as she glided down the passage in the wake of the turbaned man.

They passed through a series of halls dotted with elegant marbled pillars until at last they reached a second set of gigantic doors. Inside, the doorway led into a enormous hall, where cream and white marble flagstones covered the floor. The room was divided into three by two rows of colossal columns that reached up to ceilings inlaid with gold scroll work.

Maya and the goddess of shadows walked down the avenue of columns until they reached the golden dais at the end. On it were a pair of tiger-skin covered low chairs. Quite unexpected as a throne for the god of gods.

As they stepped toward the dais a figure began to form upon one of the stools and within the blink of an eye Maya was face-to-face with Lord Shiva, Creator, Preserver, Destroyer.

The God of all things.

She shivered a little and her knees shook but thankfully she remained standing and didn't embarrass herself by toppling onto her face before the Eternal God.

She took in the physical form of Shiva. In reality, his skin was not as blue as some had claimed. He was a luxurious, golden complexion, but beneath the beautiful browned skin there was a blue glow. That was the best that Maya could describe it. It wasn't as if his skin was just blue. It seemed to glow with a deep blue phosphorescence. And the effect was incredible beautiful.

He wore a headdress of dreadlocks, wound neatly atop his crown, encircled by gleaming brown holy beads, much like the multitude of paintings and carvings she'd seen. But his ebony hair was luxurious and silky, far from the drab Rastafarian hairdos she'd come across in her lifetime.

Strangely enough there wasn't a snake in sight. Thankfully.

The god of gods was dressed in a long coat, mandarin-collared and fashioned from shimmering oyster silk, patterned in gold and black paisley print. Beneath the coat he wore a pair of baggy black silk pants. His feet were covered in soft, hand-woven leather slippers. She'd almost expected to see them turned up at the toe like many of the Sultans of old but was silently thankful they weren't.

His garb was beautiful but simple, and unlike anything that Maya had expected, although she suspected rivers flowing from his head would certainly cause a bit of a flooding issue within the hall. And the river Ganges no doubt preferred to be in the ground where she belonged.

Shiva sat with his feet crossed at the ankles and inclined his head to Chayya, his black eyes glittering like obsidian. "Goddess Chayya. Welcome to my home." His voice was golden and beautiful and echoed around the room like a soft bell, heavy and rich and almost sultry.

"Thank you, my Lord. It is a beautiful place and I am honored to be here." When Shiva bent his head again Chayya turned to Maya. "My Lord, this is Maya Rao."

Lord Shiva tilted his head in Maya's direction and she felt the full force of his perusal. A strange wave of energy pulsated from the god, not unpleasant, just unusual. "Welcome, Maya Rao. I am grateful that you accepted my invitation."

Maya blinked, her lashed closing and opening so fast she could have doubted she'd moved them at all. Invitation? She swallowed as she stared at the blue-tinged skin on the god's beautiful face. From her recollection of what the gold-inscribed scroll had said, she was pretty sure it had read more along the lines of a summons than an invitation. Not that she was about to say as much to the god.

Instead she nodded. "I am honored that you chose me, my lord." Belatedly she realized that as the god of gods he could probably read her mind and she flushed at the thought.

But if he had availed himself to her thoughts, Lord Shiva seemed unaffected. He spoke in smooth tones, "You have not long come into the powers given to you by Mother Kali, and you have shown the qualities of a true warrior. And your skills are quite unique in that you possess godly power but you are only human." He paused a moment as Maya considered the words 'only human', finding that oddly, she was not offended. "I understand you have been learning to control the skills Mother Kali has given you."

"Yes, my Lord. Nikhil has been helping me." Her cheeks grew warm at the mention of Nikhil but she scolded herself silently. Shiva probably already knew everything that was in her heart. She may as well be standing her naked. She certainly had nothing to hide, nor could she hide anything even if she wanted to.

Lord Shiva smiled and Maya could have sworn his eyes twinkled with mischief. "Ah, yes. The son of Yama. I have no doubt that he will be an asset to you." Maya flushed then hoped the god hadn't noticed. She wasn't sure how to respond to Lord Shiva's comment regarding Nik so she chose to remain silent. "Well, I suppose I had better get to the point. We have no time to waste in the matter." He got to his feet and stepped off the dais. As he walked Maya noticed his hall was also blessed with the wide window seating, only here it spanned the entire length of one wall of the majestic hall.

At the window he paused and looked back at Maya for a moment before turning to the window to examine the stunning view. "We need you to retrieve Gandiv, the bow of Rama, and to bring it back to its true home."

 ilence fell heavily in the huge hall as the sound of Maya's thundering heart filled her ears. "Oh," was all she managed to say. The bow of Rama truly belonged to Lord Shiva and he was asking her to find it and return it to him. She cleared her throat as she realized she owed him a proper response. Something more than a tiny 'oh'. "Yes, my lord, I will do ask you ask."

"Do not worry, Maya. You will have sufficient assistance to perform your task. The bow has spend too many years in the hands of humanity and nothing good has come of it. It is time Gandiv came home to rest. Men have fought over that bow, avatars have wielded it, but it is time it achieved the peace it deserves." He stepped off the balcony step and came to stand before Maya.

She held in a shiver of apprehension as a gentle resonance flowed off his body and eased into her personal space. It felt almost like the wings of a butterfly, light and feathery, kissing the skin of her cheek. Maya raised her eyes and looked at the god's face. He was smiling, the expression beatific, godly. "You need not be nervous, Maya. Just do your job and make us all happy."

She nodded but he'd already turned away and didn't see her as he walked back to sit upon his simple throne. Maya glanced at Chayya, raising her eyebrows, uncertain of her next move. Should she leave or should she stay until he verbally dismisses her.

But she needn't have worried. Lord Shiva said, "Mother Chayya, take Maya to visit with Narada. He has knowledge of the whereabouts of Gandiv and he will help you find it." Chayya nodded and bowed. Maya followed suit. Again she wasn't sure if she should say something. Thank you for thinking she was worthy, maybe? Or thank you for the privilege? She should say something.

"You need not say anything, Maya Rao. It is my job to know your heart and your soul." Maya would have flinched with shock but she managed to retain some control over her shocked reaction. She should not be surprised. She'd suspected he could read her thoughts.

Instead she forced a smile to her wooden lips and bowed. She could not have spoken even if her life had depended on it. Not without revealing her shock. He continued, "Now go with Mother Chayya. And my blessings are with you. May you find the strength to overcome your obstacles - of both mind and body. May you have the wisdom to choose the method of your battles, and may you have fortitude in the face of failure. We are depending you, Maya Rao. Go with my blessings."

Maya straightened from her bow, the words Lord Shiva had spoken still resonating in her mind and in her heart. She felt a little shell-shocked as she followed Chayya out of the hall. When she glanced back over her shoulder she saw that the god of gods had already disappeared leaving the beautiful, cavernous hall, beautiful, cavernous and empty.

As they stepped over the threshold and passed the gigantic crystal doors Maya let out a sigh of relief. The fresh mountain air slammed into her, giving her something else to think about other than her audience with the god of gods. She shivered, drawing the shawl of the outfit closer around her shoulders to ward off against the sudden chill. She didn't recall feeling cold when she'd arrived but then adrenalin had probably surged through her in anticipation of her meeting, warding her body against the thin air and the cold that spoke of fresh snow and icy peaks.

They paused on the steps and Maya glanced over at Chayya. "Are we leaving now?"

Chayya nodded. "Yes."

"Straight to the sage?"

The goddess shook her head. "No. You must go home first and prepare. Gather your things and let Nik know where you are going. He would likely want to accompany you given he has a few special skills that you may need. I will speak to Narada and tell him to expect your visit."

"Okay then, home it is." Maya sighed as they set off, retracing their steps through the garden, and past a cheeky peacock that tipped his brilliant blue head at them as if asking why they had the audacity to pass without offering their whole-hearted admiration. The bird rustle its feathers then began to follow them, keeping a healthy distance. Peacocks from Patala to Mount Kailas. Seemed no place is belong the reach of the arrogant yet uniquely beautiful birds.

Maya sighed. "Tell me. I'm just a human girl. Why can't the gods do these kinds of special things themselves. Surely it's not hard for a god to appear wherever it is they are holding the bow and take it."

"What you say is true. But despite the powers of the gods most try to follow the rules. They will not involve themselves directly with humans, or travel within the human plan unless it is of paramount importance."

"Unless of course they are an avatar." said Maya dryly.

Chayya smiled. "That is correct. But there are no avatars at the moment."

"Why not? There have been for ages. Why not now?"

"Because the age of Kali Yuga is coming to an end." When Maya frowned the goddess continued, "Within the age of Kali Yuga, man will descend into darkness. Faith will flee the souls of man, selfishness and vanity, power and rage will reign. What use do humans have with an avatar when there are so few left to believe?"

"Won't the existence of an avatar make people believe?" Maya was convinced it would.

"And how with the unbeliever be converted when all his eyes see is a mere man?" Chayya face darkened, the Shadow of worry blanketing her features. Maya knew what she meant. Even with proof it would not be enough. "What use would there of a Jesus who walks the earth when so few people will look to him and believe, when so few have the humility to accept the word of another."

Maya sighed again, feeling the tingle of the icy air in her lungs. "It is the age of entitlement."

"That is the truth of it." Chayya nodded.

"My Dad always says that. He used to say it often when I was rebellious. But then he stopped and I always wondered why."

"Entitlement is a different animal to rebellion. Even Lord Krishna was rebellious. Every soul needs to find itself and you are no less worthy of a time of self-exploration Maya, than any other human."

Maya flushed at the goddesses words. Not that it was anything to have pride in, but she liked that Chayya felt she was worthy. She cleared her throat as they reached the edge of the mountaintop. "So home it is."

Chayya held out her hand and Maya grabbed hold of her bangled forearm. The last thing she saw before they blinked out of existence was the flash of gemstones on the goddesses bracelets.

CHAPTER 25

Chayya deposited Maya in the front hall.

"I do have to go back immediately," she said with a quick apology for not staying to speak to Maya's parents. "Take this. Use it to call me if you have need of me."

Maya looked at the small brass container that sat gleaming in the middle of her palm. "How do I use it?"

"Open the lid and release the Shadow. Think of it as a distress call. Or maybe an emergency text message?" Chayya winked and then the goddess disappeared in a flash of black and grey shadows. Maya studied the engraved brass container, staring hard at the hinged lid that was now tightly shut. It wasn't heavy but Maya shook her head. A shadow wasn't likely to be heavy. Then she smiled at the goddesses comment.

Emergency text indeed.

Maya pocketed the small container and headed into the kitchen. It lay empty and silent and Maya wondered where everyone was. She tugged her phone out of the tiny beaded bag she'd taken with her and raised her eyebrows. It was three in the morning.

No surprises that nobody was around. Not even the pooch.

She headed for the stairs and grimaced. The balls of her feet were throbbing and she held onto the banister and balanced on one foot at a time to open the straps on her golden sandals. At last, barefooted and comfortable, Maya climbed the stairs, enjoying the feel of the cool wood beneath her fevered feet.

Reaching her door she stopped in disgust. She needed help to get out of the blouse she was wearing. Half a dozen hook-and-eyes traveled down her back and she'd never been very good at gymnastics. Unless she planned on sleeping in the hand worked garment she had to get help. She hesitated as she glanced at her parents door. She'd disturb them only as a last resort. Crossing her fingers she headed to the spare bedroom and tapped softly on the door.

Please let Claudia be home.

When Claude didn't answer, Maya opened the door slowly and poked her head into the darkened room. Weak light from the streetlight seeped in through the thin drapes, giving everything in the room a creepy, horror movie feel.

Including Claudia's face.

Her features were hooded and unrecognizable in a macabre, chill down the spine way. She sat stock still on the bed in her lacy nightdress, aiming the barrel of a gun at Maya's head.

Maya froze in the doorway, her mouth hanging open. She didn't dare move a muscle, just watched Claudia reach slowly for the bedside lamp with her free hand. A soft flick of the switch and butter-yellow light flooded the room.

And they both sighed with relief.

"Maya. What the hell are you doing creeping around in the middle of the god-damned night?" Claudia hissed the words as if she too were not inclined to disturb Maya's sleeping parents. She failed to hide her shock as she relaxed her stiffened arms and placed the gun carefully on the bedside table without taking her eyes off Maya.

"What the hell are you doing packing a pistol?" Maya

responded, the shock in her voice equal, if not greater, having just had the gun pointed at her. "Please tell me that thing isn't loaded."

Claudia raised an eyebrow. "Pfft. An unloaded gun is the same thing as condom with a hole in it the size of Chicago. Absolutely no protection. At. All." Then Claudia stiffened as she stared up at Maya in horror. The words were out. She couldn't take them back now. Her face reddened.

They both stared at each other for a moment then burst out laughing. "Omigod, Claude, I cannot believe you just said that!"

"Don't tell your mother." She grinned. "So what can I bribe you with."

"Well, first you can get me naked."

"Seriously, Maya? You chose three in the morning, face to face with a Glock, to come out?"

Maya choked with laughter. "Sorry, no, that is so not what I meant." She snorted as she turned around and showed her back to Claudia. "I need out of this prison if I even hope to get a good night's sleep. Hooks, eyes. Do your thing."

As Claudia undid the blouse Maya admired the shimmering, multicolored gleam of the diamantes in the lamplight. She couldn't deny the garment was stunningly beautiful and she felt a tug of sadness knowing she'd have to return it to Chayya when she saw the goddess next.

Claudia sighed as Maya slid the heavily beaded blouse off her shoulders. "That is an incredibly beautiful outfit Maya."

Maya nodded and echoed the sigh. "Fit for an audience with The Big Cheese himself."

"Shouldn't that be Big Panneer." Claudia giggled.

"Or Big Kalari?' offered Maya as she sank onto the bed. She preferred Kalari, the rich cheese, lightly fried with a warm, gooey center. She'd always disliked the rubbery, crumbly texture of

Panneer. Her stomach grumbled, reminding her that she'd set out to with Chayya without having eaten anything. And she was starving.

"That does not sound good." Claudia eye Maya's bare stomach with a grin. "Why don't you shower and change into your pj's and I'll make dinner warm for you."

Maya nodded gratefully and headed back to her room. A shower sounded amazing especially with the chill of the Himalayan mountain air still in her bones. She completely forgot the probability of disturbing her parents with the sound of running water. She stood under the hot stream and sighed. Not every girl comes home to tell the tale of meeting the god of all things. She turned off the shower and stared at the faucet. How odd to do such mundane things as showering and changing and eating when compared to visiting the tops of mountains that most people knew didn't even exist.

Changed into pink and white striped pj's, and sat on the bed to slip on her favorite bunny slippers. With softness of the bed beneath her, Maya felt a surge of fatigue wash over her, a tsunami of tiredness that carried her along unresisting. Her eyelids drooped and she looked at the blankets. All she wanted was to curl up under the covers but her stomach gurgled again, reminding her that Claudia would be downstairs making something warm for her to eat. She shoved off the bed and hurried downstairs.

When she entered the kitchen she laughed out loud.

Her parents were sitting at the kitchen table in their pajamas, sipping steaming mugs of something. Probably hot chocolate, knowing her mom. Maya went in for the hugs and when Claudia kicked a chair away from the table Maya sat in it sending a worried glance in her direction. "I'm sitting, okay. But please feel free to beat me with anything you may have on hand, as long as it's cooked and hot."

Claudia laughed as she placed a plate heaped with juicy slices of roast lamb, soft potatoes drenched in a creamy sauce and the dreaded Brussels sprouts. But she was so hungry she didn't even mind the bright green vegetables. At least her mom didn't cook them to death like Ria's mom did.

As she shoveled the first forkful into her mouth and enjoyed the delicious goodness of roasted meat and potato gratin, Dev set his mug down and looked at Maya. "How did it go?" he asked softly.

"Dev," Leela admonished, glaring at him. "Leave the child alone. At least let her eat before you start interrogating her." Her mom gave a soft huff. But when Maya opened her mouth to respond, her mom turned the heat of her glare on Maya herself. "Maya Rao. Don't talk with your mouth full. What have I been teaching you all your life?"

Maya cringed. Dutifully, she swallowed, then turned her attention back to her food as Claudia hesitantly launched into an account of her most recent trip to a small town in the Ukraine. Maya's eyes popped when Claudia outlined a horrific case of a cannibalistic killer that an entire town had assumed was the work of a demon. The man - or monster - killed four children before Claudia had arrived to investigate. A good thing the police investigated Claudia's anonymous tip or they would never have found the real live human killer.

"Why the hell would anyone do such a thing?" Maya was careful to swallow her food before she spoke.

"Well, in this particular man's case, he'd grown up in a time of extreme poverty," said Dev. "It wasn't unusual at the time for children to be scolded and warned against people who lurked in the streets waiting to abduct them and eat them." A sad look coursed across her dad's face. "The worst of it was those warnings were more often truth than fairy tale."

"Sheesh, Old Man Grimm. Thanks for the bedtime story. I'll be sure to sleep like a baby now."

Everyone burst out laughing and Maya soon wiped her plate

clean and gratefully accepted the mug of hot chocolate Claudia handed to her.

"Feeling better now?" Her mom asked as Claudia pulled a chair close.

Maya nodded and forced a smile on her tired face. "Like a whole new warrior." After a moment's silence she told them everything, from her arrival at the foot of the mountain and the incredible view looking up at Mount Kailas, to the meeting with Lord Shiva. Everyone at the table listened in reverent silence.

"Too bad you didn't take your camera," said Claudia as she sat back in her chair. "Would have loved some pictures."

Maya slapped the warm wood of the table to a chorus of laughter. "Damn. I knew I was forgetting something. Maybe next time."

Her father sobered for a moment. "So you have to find Gandiv? How soon do you leave?" The words seem to remove all humor from the gathering.

"Tomorrow morning. Or as soon as I can get a hold of Nik. Apparently he might prove useful," she said with a raised eyebrow.

Maya watched as her mother eyed her dad, a teasing look in her eye. "They do have their uses," she said as she watched her husband.

For a moment Dev remained oblivious as he drained his mug. When he sat it on the table he realized all three women were watching him, wide grins on their face. "Hey. Watch it. I still wear the pants in this house."

"Yeah. Whatever helps you sleep at night," three voices said in unison. Maya sat back and watched the friendly argument - three friends teasing each other, so comfortable with each other than no insult ever made a mark.

She smiled and then she sighed.

Back to work tomorrow, back to the job of being the Hand of Kali.

CHAPTER 26

The first thing she did when she got up - after brushing her teeth of course - was to text both Nik and Joss. Then she waited for one or both of them to arrive as she showered and threw clothes into a bag. She chose sensible shoes, trainers and boots. Jeans and jumpers. A few cotton kurtis - embroidered tops that came all the way to the knees. This time she certainly didn't plan on fighting in a beaded skirt and blouse. She paused when she looked at the Valente hanging in her closet. Then she shook her head and chose two other outfits, fancy enough for dinner or a wedding, and folded them neatly before placing them inside her bag. It wouldn't hurt to be careful.

She was going to India after all.

A knock on her bedroom door announced her first visitor. Joss entered. "What's so urgent that you couldn't talk to me in school about it?" She glared pointedly at her watch that said seven-thirty in the morning. "And what was so damned important that you made me wake up an hour early for?"

"I'm leaving for India today."

"What?" Color drained from Joss's face as she sank to the bed beside Maya's open bag. "Why?"

"There's something I need to do. I've been to see Lord Shiva and this is something he's instructed me to do. Kinda have no choice really." Joss was too silent and when Maya glanced back at her she realized why. Her friend's mouth hung open and she stared goggle-eyed at Maya.

"Did I hear you say Lord Shiva." She asked in a whisper. Maya nodded and described everything to her friend, leaving nothing out. "So you really met him?"

Maya nodded. "And believe me it was an experience to remember."

"I bet."

"What's wrong?" asked Maya. Joss had been uncharacteristically quiet through Maya's monologue.

"Nothing. Just that this is pretty incredible. I know I shouldn't be amazed consider we went to Patala and met Yama and then to Swargaloka and met Varuni. So meeting a god shouldn't be amazing or anything you know. But darn it I'm amazed. I feel like Dorothy in Wonderland."

"I know what you mean. It's still amazing. But seriously I think we've reached the ceiling in terms of amazement. After meeting him I don't think there's a single thing that can top it." Maya sat beside her friend and nudged her. "So are you coming with me or what?"

"You are kidding right?" Joss glared at her. "If you set foot outside of this country without me . . . Believe me I know people. I can put a hit out on you like that." She snapped her fingers and looked so outraged that all Maya could do was laugh.

"I don't doubt it, but let's keep the hit men on stand-by for now. They may coming in handy, you just never know."

"Okay," she said, her face as deadly serious as any of the hit men she had on speed dial. Then she giggled. "I suppose I should pack. And I'd need my passport."

Maya nodded. "Get it just in case but I'm not so sure we'll be traveling tin class."

"Ah yes. So where is Scotty then? He'll need to beam us there so shouldn't he be appearing in our midst sometime soon?"

"Who is Scotty?" asked Nik as he walked into the room.

The girls grinned, Maya forgetting her annoyance at Nik for taking so long to arrive and for not even bothering to respond to her text. "You seriously telling me you don't know who Scotty is?" asked Joss incredulously.

When Nik shook his head they choked and spluttered and eventually Maya managed to say, "Space: the final frontier?" she shook her head, waggling her eyebrows at him. When he just stared at her, a blank look in his eye she continued, "These are the voyages of the starship *Enterprise?*" He still stood there, looking confused and Maya sighed. "When we return you, Mr Demigod, are going to get an education."

"An education in what?" He frowned.

"An education in a classic piece of cinematic history that has shaped our society for the better. We will turn you into a Trekkie or die trying." Maya raised her hand and Joss followed suit. Both were serious as they made the requisite sign, fingers on their right hands parted in the middle to form a 'V'. Then they said, "Live long and prosper." Before dissolving into a fit of giggles.

Nik raised his hand and tried to emulate the Vulcan greeting, failing miserable as his fingers refused to obey. Then he snorted in disgust. "What is going on with the two of you?"

"It's a Vulcan greeting," answered Joss, clearly wanting to put him out of his misery.

"What is a Vulcan? As far as I know there is no culture in existence called Vulcan. I'm confused." And he certainly looked it.

"Never mind. You'll know when you get your education." Maya waved the topic away and said, "For now all you need to know is we need to get to India and pronto." Maya replayed the events for Nik and was glad when he didn't look incredulous. In fact he seemed unaffected by the news. Too unaffected. She frowned as she stared at him. "You already knew?"

"How could you tell that just by looking at him?" Joss asked confused, but they ignored her.

"Yes, I knew. Only some of it, though. My father was informed about Shiva's intention to request this of you."

Maya's eyes narrowed as she looked at him. "So, when exactly did you know about this?"

"Not until last night when Chayya came to fetch you."

"You were in Patala?" asked Maya. Then she stiffened. She had no right asking him these sorts of demanding questions. When Nik nodded all she did was give him a smile. She tried to inject as much warmth into as possible and she could only hope he hadn't heard the harshness in her question. The last thing she wanted to be was a fishwife when she wasn't even a wife. She suppressed a shudder at the thought, then threw her shoulders back. "Right. When is convenient for you to leave? I'm packed. Joss is heading home to do the same."

"Joss is coming?" he asked.

"Joss is here. And yes, Joss is coming." Joss raised her voice and pouted. Nik looked at her and grinned.

"Okay you want a lift home to get that packing done fast?"

When she nodded eagerly he held out his arm and she slid her hand into the crook of his elbow and said, "Beam me up, Scotty." Nik gave her a quizzical look and then they both disappeared while Maya smiled and shook her head at the disappearing shades of watery light.

She finished her packing and walked downstairs to leave her bag in the hall. Her parents were in the study and she walked right in. No time to stand on ceremony. Her mom glanced up from where she stood at her husband's shoulder, both frowning and staring at the screen, the glow of the monitor reflected on their faces. "Leaving so soon, honey?"

Maya nodded. "I'm all packed and Nik just took Joss home to pack too."

"Joss is coming?"

Maya laughed and instinctively looked behind her in case Joss was standing there. "Yup. She'd have a triplet set of cows if I leave her behind."

Dev snorted as he pushed his glassed up his nose and looked at his daughter over the top of his laptop screen. "You be careful, young lady. Don't take any chances and be careful."

"Don't worry, Dad. The last thing I need is to die on the job. I don't think Lord Shiva would consider that a good enough excuse."

He laughed but her Mom didn't look too happy. "And don't get mad Mom I'm not being disrespectful. The dude is powerful and he reads minds."

"Don't you think if the dude can read minds then he'd know you just referred to him as a dude?" Leela raised an eyebrow at her daughter and Maya knew it was too late. Mom was mad. And Maya was getting the I-raised-you-better glare.

"Sorry, Mom," Maya said, then rushed to her parents, gathering them together and squeezing tight. "You guys behave while I'm gone, okay? And Mom, don't let old Grimm here get anywhere near any Churel's."

Leela nodded. "Don't worry, I'll keep a close eye on him."

"You do that. His taste in women is getting a little dodgy." Dev just watched them and shook his head with a small smile curving his lips. "Are you two done?"

"No. Not really," they both answered together.

"Okay, adults. I'm ready to go. Better head out to the hall. Not sure what Scotty has planned in terms of our travel arrangements."

"Scotty?" asked her mom.

"Mom," Maya admonished, raising her voice a little. "Not you too," she said shaking her head.

"Oh. Sorry. Blank moment," she said then straightened, giving Maya the Vulcan salute before saying "Live long and prosper."

Maya laughed and left them in the study.

It was a good thing she was born to Trekkie parents. Wouldn't have been a comfortable life if they hadn't been geeks like her.

As she entered the front hall she heard footsteps coming up behind her. Glancing over her shoulder she saw her mom hurrying toward her with a card in her hand. "Here. Take this." She handed Maya an American Express card and said, "There's enough on it to pay for your room and for food and other incidentals. Ring if you need me to load up more."

Maya raised her eyebrows. "Hunter money?"

Leela nodded. "As much as you need."

"Okay." She said tapping the card onto the palm of her hand. "I should be okay but I'll let you know if I need more."

"You might not need to worry too much. Your dad and I will fly over in the next day or so. We just need to clear up a few things."

"Mom, you don't have to come with me."

Maya stared at her Mom, exasperated but Leela shook her head. "No, it's not what you think. We may not be able to help you but we thought it was a good time to go up to compound. See a few people. Catch up." She shrugged but Maya got the sense that she was trying to brush off the importance of their trip.

"Okay, text me when you guys arrive." Then she hesitated. "They do have cell coverage and wifi there don't they?"

Leela laughed. "Maya, you're going to India, not Patala. And like the US they have very capable cell coverage and wifi in the cities. And just like the US out in the sticks the coverage gets sketchier." She shook her head and drew Maya into a quick hug. "Be careful, honey."

"Yes, Mom," Maya replied and smiled as her mother headed back to the study.

Before she could begin to think about the trip the air beside her shimmered and Nik and Joss appeared. Joss dropped her rucksack beside Maya's backpack and put her hands on her hips. "Right, let's do this."

Maya raised an eyebrow and glanced at Nik. "So how exactly are we going to do this?"

"I'll take you directly to the hotel and we can check in. Then I'll return for Joss. We shouldn't be too long." Both Maya and Joss nodded.

"Oh, what about Sabala?" Maya asked. She actually missed her hellhound.

Nik shook his head. " He stays in Patala until you return home."

Maya nodded as Nik bent to grab Maya's bag and then held out his hand. Maya took it and felt a surge of heat as he threaded his fingers with hers. No formal crook of the elbow for her. And Joss's waggling eyebrows confirmed she'd taken note too. Maya glared at her friend but it didn't last long as she and Nik dissipated into shimmering light.

The next moment they appeared in a marbled hallway. Nik tugged on Maya's hand and she allowed him to lead her down the short corridor and turned into a plush hotel reception area. The space was enormous and Maya craned her neck to see hanging planter boxes on every balcony overlooking the reception. The balconies went up at least twenty floors and Maya stared speechless.

"What is this hotel?" she whispered, feeling decidedly out of place in the luxurious building.

"The Oberoi in Mumbai." Nik led her to the concierge desk that comprised of a small table flanked by two comfortable armchairs. A glass vase of bright red tulips matched the girl's lips and her sash. *Not what you'd expect from your standard hotel,* Maya thought. The concierge smiled up at them as Nik seated himself and Maya followed suit. The girl's dark eyes slid over Nik, and Maya stiffened. Nik, on the other hand, didn't seem to notice her perusal. He just leaned forward and said, "We have a booking. Two rooms under the name Nikhil Malhotra."

Malhotra again? thought Maya. Must be the go-to name for deities these days.

The girl nodded, pursing her red lips as she leaned forward and typed into a computer console hidden from view by a red screen. She glanced up and smiled, "Welcome to the Oberoi, Mr. Malhotra." She looked at Maya, her smile of greeting genuine enough, then said, "Let me call the Luggage Concierge to help you with your things."

Nik shook his head, "No there is no need. We've traveled light."

"Very well then, you have two Premier Ocean View rooms. Please enjoy your stay," she said still pleasant as she slid two card keys across the table and turned her attention back to her computer as Nik grabbed the keys and got to his feet. Maya followed him as he headed for the bank of elevators.

Two floors up they left the elevator in silence, walking quickly to the first room, the plush carpeting swallowing the sound of their footsteps. Nick swiped the card key against the panel and opened the room for Maya. As the door shut behind them Nik dropped Maya's bag on the bed and said, "I'll be back."

Maya giggled. "Thanks Arnie," then sighed with pleasure at the sight of the room. The bed was simple yet elegant, two bright red cushions and a long grey sash across the foot of the bed. Comfy armchairs and the requisite wall panel TV. Not to mention the floor to ceiling window that had a view of the ocean that made it look like the room was floating on water. Maya went to window and stared out at the expanse of water. That would be the Arabian Sea, if her memory of Indian geography was still intact.

The moon lingered low in the sky and cast a pearly glow on the cresting waves of the ocean. For a moment it was disconcerting to see night outside the window until she remembered the time difference.

When she turned to look for the bathroom she choked with

shock and pleasure. The bathroom was walled off from the room by a glass window and a heavy handled glass door. Directly in front of the glass panel sat a deep tub ideal for endless hours of soaking. Along one wall more glass sectioned of a giant sized shower and a toilet.

Stunning.

That was the only word Maya could think of to describe the luxury of the room.

Then she remembered that Nik hadn't mentioned payment. She reminded herself to give Nik her Amex to pay for the room. Then she sat on the small ledge beside the window and lost herself staring at the rolling black waves.

CHAPTER 27

ik didn't take long to reappear with Joss. He deposited her in the room then left the key on the table. "I'm going make a quick trip home for clothing and toiletries. I'll see you two for dinner?"

"Um, yeah. I think we missed breakfast but dinner sounds good," said Maya as Nik waved and disappeared.

When Maya turned to Joss she burst out laughing at the expression of amazement on her friend's face. This from someone who's holidayed all over the world with uber-rich parents. "Amazing right?" Maya asked.

"It's fabulous. We never came to Mumbai or I'd have wanted to stay here for sure," she said, her voice husky with reverence as she dropped her bag on the floor and tiptoed to the window. "Not as lovely as the rooms in Patala but still amazing in it's own right."

"Where are you parents? Did you tell them you were coming with me?" asked Maya.

Joss nodded, still facing the water. "Yeah, they're in Bahrain. Dad's meeting with this prince who's an oil tycoon or something. I said I was coming with you and your parents. They left me in your mum and dad's care anyway." Joss's voice was light and unaffected but Maya knew her parent's lack of interest hurt her deeply.

For now, Maya waited until Joss turned around and saw the bathroom. The squeal she let out would have awakened the dead.

"Shh. You'll have security come running."

She waved a hand to shush Maya. "Wow. This is incredible." Then she frowned. "Good thing we aren't self conscious. Imagine sharing this room with just a buddy."

"Or a guy." Maya shuddered at the thought.

"So, dinner?" Joss was food-focused.

"Yes. Let's get ready. Who knows how fast Mr. Malhotra moves through time and space."

"Mr. Malhotra?" Joss scrunched her forehead in a frown.

"Yeah, the son of Yama uses a pretty high class alias."

"Well, he has to have a real persona here in this worlds, doesn't he? Wonder what it takes. Or does he have a mysterious bag filled with passports and different currencies."

Maya snorted. "You're confusing your international spies with your demigods. Study harder."

"He is a sort of spy if you think about it. A spy for the gods." Joss nodded as she thought about the description, the happy grin on her face indicating she was satisfied the way she called it.

Maya laughed as she headed into the bathroom. "Bet he'd have something to say about that." Inside the bathroom she turned to face Joss. "Make sure he doesn't come inside the room while I'm in here. Suddenly, I'm not so sure how appropriate glass-doored bathrooms are."

"Jeez. What if you order room service and then head into the shower? Bet the room service guys have seen a fair few naked people." Joss giggled and Maya left her to it, turning on the waterfall shower and getting undressed. She kept her bath towel close at hand just in case but nothing untoward happened and when she walked out of the shower she could see Joss sitting on the bed flipping channels through the lightly steamed window.

"Your turn," Maya said as she rummaged in her bag. When Joss abandoned her channel surfing and headed into the shower Maya glanced at the door. She looked for a chain then realized how ridiculous a security chain would be to use against a guy who could appear wherever he wanted at will. Instead she just changed as quickly as possible, throwing on a long black skirt and cap-sleeved beaded black blouse. She was brushing her hair out when Joss strolled out of the steamed shower wrapped in a huge towel. She followed Maya's actions, hurriedly changing into a pair of black silk Palazzo pants and a white sequined top. She paired it with white heels and moved to the mirror.

Maya stepped into a pair of black strappy sandals and stared with envy at Joss as she skilfully applied her makeup. Joss joked all the time how makeup could transform a person's face like magic but Maya was always unsuccessful. Her own dusky skin had shadows and highlights the seemed to stay in place no matter she did with foundation or concealer. Resigned she approached the mirror and began her own simple routine - a dusting of bronze eyeshadow, black eyeliner, mascara, and lipstick.

Done, she turned to Joss who was staring at her with envy. She sighed. "It's so unfair you know."

"What is?" asked Maya.

"Your skin and your coloring. You don't have to do much to look amazing but I have to stand in front of the mirror for ages painting on this face." Maya stared at her friend about to laugh. "Why are you looking at me like that?"

"I never really thought of it that way. And here I was being envious of your ability to look so amazing."

Just as both girls turned back to the mirror and fluffed out their hair the air shimmered and coalesced slowly into Nik, nicely dressed in black suit pants and a bright white shirt. "Ready ladies?"

"You look yummy," said Joss giving him a wink.

He flushed then regained control of his features, giving her a small bow. "Thank you, ma'am." Then he glanced at Maya. "Ready?"

When she nodded he headed for the door saying, "Don't forget your card key."

Maya grabbed the key and shoved it into her small beaded bag. The poor drawstring sequined handbag did multiple duty, matching anything that Maya wore whether it was to a wedding, a party of to a temple. She'd surely be lost without it. She tucked the credit card inside as well then followed the other two outside, letting the door hiss shut before hurrying to catch up with the elevator.

A short ride and they reached the restaurant floor. As they entered Maya paid little attention to Nik's discussion with the maître d'. The restaurant was unusual with its rich wood floors and gold glass place settings. Expectant waiters dotted the room awaiting the needs of the patrons, spiffy in their starched white shirts and black aprons. The maître d' led them to their table and no sooner had Maya and Joss reached it did two waiters appear to help seat them. All the fussing made Maya slightly uncomfortable but she said nothing, just forced herself to enjoy the luxury. Better to be served by humans than odorific demons.

Soon the menus arrived and they studied the dishes. Maya didn't take long to make a choice. She always went for the seafood. Before long they made their orders and then spent some time enjoying the beauty of the room.

When their food arrived in oddly slanted bowls set beside a dome of rice artfully placed on a banana leaf bed, Maya had to admit she'd never been to restaurant like this before. "The kitchen here is headed by a Michelin starred chef," said Nik and Maya wasn't surprised. The food was certainly both fancy and tasty enough. Neither could she not be impressed that Nik knew what a Michelin starred chef was.

As they were rounding off dinner, and Nik was saying, "We'll head out to see the sage first thing," Maya noticed a young couple sitting in the far corner by the window. The girl's posture and profile niggled at Maya's suspicions. They looked slightly familiar but it only until the girl turned her face toward Maya that she recognized her.

Ria.

Maya's expression must have given away her shock. "Maya? What's the matter?" asked Joss placing a hand over Maya's now icy fingers.

Maya swallowed hard, listening to the deafening patter of her heartbeat. "I know where Ria is and why we couldn't find her at home."

"Where?" Joss asked already turning to scan the room. She stiffened the moment she laid eyes on Ria and her fiance, and her face was pale and expressionless as she turned back to the table. "Fancy seeing them here."

"She's probably trousseau shopping. Unless she's here for the wedding." Maya's voice was dead as she spoke. There was something else she'd seen but she wasn't planning on mentioning it to Joss while Nik was there. She'd wait until they were in the privacy of their room.

While they'd been discussing Ria, Nik had remained oddly silent. Even when they finally rose to leave he seemed deep in thought. But when Maya got to her feet she knew the movement at their table would draw Ria's attention. And she knew there was no way she could avoid going over to greet the couple.

When Maya looked up she met Ria's gaze and both friends stared at each other for a moment. For the briefest time, a smile brightened Ria's face. It seemed she'd forgotten herself because all it took was a glance at Viren for that happy smile to disintegrate like smoke on the wind.

"That does it. I'm going over there." Maya headed for the

couple, watching the guarded expression on her old friend's gaunt face. Ria had lost her little girl chubbiness.

"Me too," said Joss throwing her napkin on the table before following close at Maya's heels.

When the two girls converged on the table Ria had no choice but to stand and submit to hugs. Viren offered is hand and Maya and Joss shook it coolly.

"What are you guys doing in Mumbai? Isn't it just gorgeous?" asked Joss, infusing her voice with the bubbly tones of an airhead. Maya had to school her expression. Good going Joss. Viren would never expect this piece of blonde fluff was onto him.

Viren spoke, cutting Ria off as she was about to answer. "Wedding shopping actually. The wedding is in three weeks. We are marrying at my parents estate in Juhu Beach."

Maya blinked. He'd just named on of the wealthiest residential areas in all of India. "Congratulations. I had no idea it would be this soon," said Maya unable to keep the bite out of her voice.

"My apologies, Maya. We would have invited you had we known you would be in Mumbai. In saying that I must apologize again as we do not have any invitations left. The wedding is fully catered you see."

"That's fine, Viren. We are heading back to California tomorrow so it all works out in the end, right?" She forced a smile on her lips and glanced at Ria who's eyes remained downcast. A strained silence hung over the table and the girls, taking that as their cue, stepped away from the table. Viren rose, his back to his future wife and held out his hand first to Joss who took it with a sultry, pouty smile pasted on her face. She shook his hand rather slowly and rather seductively. While Viren was busy staring at Joss, Maya pulled her card key from her back and held it out to Ria who took it and slipped it down the front of her blouse so fast Maya was unsure it had even happened.

When Viren turned to shake Maya's hand she was looking at him, the picture of innocence. She shook his hand, curbing the urge to wipe it off on the nearest napkin, and followed Joss out of the restaurant to Nik who was waiting patiently outside.

"Good work on the key pass, Maya."

"Yeah. I'm glad he didn't see that. And good job on the googly eyes."

"Thanks. He got my Angelina special," said Joss with a small pout.

"Who's Angelina?" asked Nik frowning.

"Angelina too?" asked Maya as she and Joss exchanged disbelieving glances. "Don't you watch TV?"

Nik shook his head. "I have no time for television. I believe the only time I ever spent watching TV was at your home Maya and little bit when I was really young. The Muppet's, I believe and Sesame Street."

"Phew," said Joss. "Saved by the puppets. We thought you were a goner for sure."

Maya laughed and held onto Nik's arm. "Can we get a card key for Joss? Just in case?"

He nodded and headed to the concierge. After a few moments of discussion, he returned with a key for Joss and they all headed back upstairs. In the the elevator Nik looked at the girls. "What was all that with Ria and her fiance?"

"The guy's a douche and she needs saving that's what," said Joss, an ugly expression on her face. Maya felt pretty much the same.

"She's not happy. It's clear on on her face, how he ignores her. She's not even allowed to speak for herself." Maya's throat closed as she felt tears fill her eyes. She turned to face the door, blinking away the moisture and was thankful that Nik didn't press the issue.

He said goodnight at their door and headed to his room.

CHAPTER 28

Inside the privacy of their room Joss spun to Maya and said, "You don't even have to ask me. I am the queen of makeup and I know what I saw."

"It looked like he tried to choke her," said Maya quietly.

Both girls sat heavily on the bed and looked at each other. Maya just wanted to cry. "I've never felt so helpless before. I have all this power and there isn't a damned thing I can do to help her."

"Maya, it's not your fault you know. Or your responsibility either." When Maya glanced sharply at Joss, she simply shrugged. "It's true. We can try to help her but we aren't responsible for the choices she makes."

"And what if she has no choice? Then what? Whose responsibility is it then to help her?"

Joss looked down at her clenched fingers and said nothing.

"I guess we wait. She has the key. If she wants to speak to us, or needs help all she has to do is use it."

The girls lay back on the bed and stared at the ceiling in silence. They lay there for a long while and when the lock didn't click they eventually sighed and got up. After changing into pajamas and hanging their dresses in the closet they crept under the covers.

"You think she'll come?" asked Joss, her face hidden in her pillow.

"I hope so," said Maya staring at the white expanse of the ceiling.

"You don't need the distraction you know?"

"I know. But Ria is just as important."

"And how does one abused girl compare to the all powerful god of gods?"

"Because she is the one in danger."

"I see your point." Joss said softly.

Soon they were both asleep, with only the faint light from the hallway filtering through into the room from beneath the door.

Maya woke and sat straight up in the bed. Something had disturbed her and she glanced at the short hall that led to the door. A light shone in the hall, growing larger until it streamed into the room past the foot of the bed onto the drawn drapes.

Maya scrambled out of the bed, her hands at the ready when she saw Ria walk tentatively into the room and shut the door behind her.

"Ria!" said Maya in a strained whisper but she needn't have bothered to keep her voice down because Joss was already bounding out of the bed. They both reached the fragile-looking girl at the same time. They would have drawn her into a tight group hug but she stared at each of their faces and burst into tears.

Joss and Maya looked at each other, unsure what to do with their sobbing friend. Maya held her around the shoulders and guided her to bed. Ria sat without protest and reached up to wipe away her tears. A box of tissues appeared in front of her nose and she gave Joss a watery smile.

After Ria dried her eyes and dealt with her nose, Joss pulled up one of the chairs and the girls gathered close together. Maya grasped Ria's hands in hers. "Do you want to talk about it?"

Ria sobbed and then took a deep breath and nodded. Her eyes were misted with tears, underlined by purple smudges now visible on her makeup free skin. Below her chin, the marks on her neck were obvious too. But neither Joss nor Maya commented on them.

They waited for Ria.

"Maya. You were right all along. He couldn't be trusted." She squeezed Maya's hands together so hard that it hurt. Maya winced but she didn't pull away. "I'm so, so sorry for the way I behaved, Maya. I wish I could take it back."

"You don't have to apologize to me, Ria. You know that. And I understand. I really do. You thought he was an escape from your dad," said Maya softly.

Ria snorted and the sound was wet and sad. "Out of the frying pan into the fire. Burned either way you look at it."

"You're not blaming yourself are you?" asked Joss. When Ria glanced at her, giving her a guilty look, Joss said, "Look, you can't pick your family any more than I can pick mine. You shouldn't blame yourself. What you should do it figure out what your next step is."

Ria frowned. "What do you mean? I just came to speak to you two. Did you think I would leave him?" When Joss and Maya exchanged knowing looks she said, "You did think I was going to leave him. Well, let me tell you something. You know nothing about what I'm going through. He's dangerous and angry. I have no chance."

Maya squeezed her hands. "Of course, you have a chance. You just need to take it."

Ria pulled her hands away. "That's where you're wrong. Where will I go? Where will I hide? There's nowhere that I can hide from him." Then she laughed and sound was almost cruel, and definitely self deprecating. "Know a way into the Witness Protection Program?"

Maya wasn't sure what to do. She patted Ria on her back awkwardly and said, "We'll figure this out okay. Give us your mobile number. And mine is still-"

"Don't bother. He doesn't allow me to have a cell."

Maya stared at her friend's face. "How did you manage to get here?"

"He left to visit the casino with his cousins. He does that every night."

"And he leaves you behind alone?" Ria nodded. "How does he know you won't make a run for it?"

"He has my passport. And beside where would I go in a strange country? Who'll help a strange girl who whines about her abusive fiance? He owns me."

Maya touched her arm. "He does not own you. So don't you go believing that for a single second.You hear me?" When Ria nodded Maya bent her head to meet her friend's eyes. "We will figure something out. Just keep the card."

Ria shook her head. "I can't. It's too dangerous. What if he finds it?"

"He won't." Maya smiled. "Take one of you sanitary pads and cut a neat slit in it. Hide the card there. No way he's getting anywhere near the ladies stuff."

Ria giggled. "Maya, you are brilliant. He'd need a hazard suit to go near my stuff and then he'd still probably think twice."

The three girls laughed and then Ria got to her feet. "Thanks, you two. You've made me feel a lot better."

But Maya didn't let her leave so fast. She hugged Ria getting a bit too close to the bruises on her neck. "Be careful okay?" she said looking at Ria's neck.

Ria flushed, the skin of her face and neck reddening, setting the blue and purple of the bruises out in stark contrast to her pink skin. But Maya left it at that, deciding it was better not to interrogate her friend. There would be time enough to find out why the bastard had done that to her.

After tucking the card into her bra, she gave both girls a wave and left. Maya stood in the doorway watching her as she disappeared down the hallway. Back to her prison.

Maya sighed as she closed the door and headed back into bed.

"I'm worried about her, "said Joss. "What if he finds out she left the room?"

"Chances are he'd do worse that try to choke her if he does find out. Let's hope she's super careful." Maya sighed as she plumped up her pillow. Sleep didn't come easy. Maya couldn't figure on being able to sleep when Ria was in such danger. But late into the night, her eyes grew too heavy and she fell into a deep sleep.

CHAPTER 29

Maya got a wake up call the next morning.

One she never remembered requesting. Nik. She smiled as she put the phone down and headed into the shower. Soon both girls were ready. This time Maya had admitted to herself that considering she was visiting a holy man, more appropriate garments were in order. She'd dressed in a simple white salwar kameez.

She was fiddling with the scarf at her shoulder when she noticed the odd look Joss was giving her. "What's wrong?"

"What about me?" asked Joss, hands on her hips.

"What about you?"

Joss waved a hand at her jeans and tee. "Where's my clothes?"

Maya inspected her friend's clothing and nodded. "Did you bring a dress?" Joss glared and her and nodded. "Then the dress will have to do. I only brought this one in case we visited a temple or something. "

As Joss slipped a hot pink knee length dress over her head she asked, "Do you think she's alright?"

"I damn well hope so," said Maya, gritting her teeth. "I'm not sure I'm strong enough to stop myself from burning Viren alive if he so much as touches a hair on Ria's head."

"I'm down with that."

"Of course, you'd be. You won't be the one on the run from the law."

"I'm with you all the way. I run where you run."

Maya laughed and pulled her handbag over her neck. Armed with her Amex, her phone and a few Rupees she was ready to hit the streets of Mumbai. They left their room and walked to Nik's.

"Just be prepared okay?"

"What for?"

"Outside."

"What's wrong with outside."

"You'll know when it hits you." Maya snorted.

Maya was rummaging in her bag for the address Chayya had given her when Nik opened his door and stepped out into the hall with them. The trio hurried downstairs not one of them thinking of breakfast.

They headed across the gigantic reception area and passed a beautiful bright red piano. The instrument looked strange in the middle of the large sparsely furnished area but it seem to work well enough. With the piano distracting Joss, Maya kept an eye on her as they approached the double set of automatic glass doors. The two doors allowed hotel visitors to exit the building without allowing too much of the outside in.

As the heat of the day hit them Maya counted off the seconds on her hand with Nik grinning as she reached one. "Oh. My. God. What the hell is that hideous stink?" Joss shrieked, and held her nose with two fingers. Her face was red as she tried not to breath the scent of Mumbai into her lungs. "That is just wrong."

Maya grinned.

"So that is what you meant." Joss glared at her. "You could have given me a better warning you know."

"I know."

"You are no true friend of mine, Maya Rao."

Maya was still grinning as the bellhop opened the door to a black four-wheel-drive, the hotel's name prominently displayed on the door panels. The driver twisted to look at the girls as they climbed in and grabbed window seats on the right. Maya bristled as he skimmed over them and clearly dismissed them, continuing to seek out a male face. He looked relieved to see Nik and said, "Where can I take you, sir?" he asked a the rolling, sing-song accent.

Nik glanced blandly over at Maya as he climbed in and took a seat beside her. "Miss Rao will give you the address." The driver at least had the grace to flush.

As Maya stifled a grin and read out the street name, careful not to give the driver too much information about where they were headed. One never knew who was watching them right now.

The vehicle rumbled into life and they jerked into the street. Soon they were crawling through Mumbai morning traffic. Nik sat beside her, oddly silent as he repeatedly glanced at his phone, as if he was waiting for a message or a call. Maya didn't bother him too much. He's seemed distracted since they'd arrived in Mumbai.

Drivers were honking their horns with such constant persistence it seemed as though they were all part on a large uncoordinated orchestra. Cars and trucks veered so close to each other that Maya had squeezed her eyes shut a few times when it seemed certain they were destined for a head on collision with an oncoming vehicle. But at the very last second, in what seemed like a dance well known to all Mumbai drivers, they swerved apart and continued on their individual paths, passengers and vehicles all in one piece. Maya could not say the same for her sanity

Maya shook her head as she watched the mayhem of the traffic. She'd heard many times what a pleasure it was to drive on

American roads, where law and road rules actually apply, and that the recklessness of Indian drivers are only due to their utmost belief that God will protect them no matter what. The rites were done, the chants were chanted, and a new driver sets off on a driving future left in the hands of the gods.

Maya snorted.

Last time she checked there were no Traffic Gods in the Hindu Pantheon. She was staring out the window at the huge bright blue truck beside them when Joss gasped. Maya glanced over her shoulder and looked in the direction of her friend's gaze.

Down.

A daredevil on a bicycle zoomed between their vehicle and the blue truck and Maya held her heart in her hand, sure the man would be squashed flat soon enough. But he zoomed through the tiny gap and swooped in front of their car.

"Wow. He's got guts," said Joss, shock clear in her voice.

"Not guts. Faith," said Maya scornfully.

They both watched as the cyclist weaved in front of their car then moved to the right again. Around them horns honked in a strange chorus, then set into a momentary lull. Their driver sped forward, catching up to the cyclist until he was alongside his window. When their driver rolled down his window, Maya expected him to greet the cyclist or talk to him.

Instead he slapped him upside the back of his head, the sound so loud and sharp it traveled inside the car through the open window. The girls turned and watched as the stunned cyclist wobbled on his bicycle a little until he slowed almost to a stop, rubbing the back of his head in a daze.

Maya and Joss stared at each other in silence, then seconds later they both burst out laughing.

"You'd never see that back home, " said Joss.

"For sure, you won't," Maya said glancing at Nik who sat eyes downcast concentrating on his tablet, oblivious to the poor cyclists predicament.

A few minutes later the driver drew up at the side of the road and said, "I can drop you here. I can't go any further or I'll never get out of these roads. Too busy."

"That's fine, thanks," said Maya. "I'm not sure how long we will be but I shouldn't think it would be more than an hour."

The driver nodding in the signature side to side way of most native Indians. "I will wait here then."

They nodded at him as Nik passed jumped off to hold the door open. Outside they were bombarded with heat and smells so thick they were almost palpable. Maya wanted to hold her breath but she knew she needed to get over the odors now or it will continue to pose a problem throughout the trip. Joss didn't look like she faring too well.

"Breathe," whispered Maya.

"No. How can you stand the smell?" she said without breathing.

"You need to get used to it. Then you'll forget about it. If you wanted perfumed malls you should have stayed at home."

Joss glared at her but she looked like she'd accepted what Maya was saying because in the next moment her chest heaved as she let out the stale breath she'd been holding and inhaled the streets of Mumbai. "Fine, but if the stink kills me I'm coming back to haunt you."

"It's a deal," Maya grinned as the trio began to walk down the narrow street. The road was wide enough only for one vehicle yet a few brave drivers were maneuvering their little cars through the tight squeeze.

"So, Nik. You've been pretty quiet. Any advice on how to behave with the sage?" asked Maya.

"Sorry, Maya. I'm waiting for some information from a source. My mind is a little preoccupied." Nik glanced at Maya and gave her a thin smile. "Don't worry about the sage too much.

The key is to just be yourself. He is a simple man, I'm told. If long-lived."

"How old is he?"

"A few hundred years old at least. I don't know his specific age."

Maya was about to answerer when she was shoved aside by a pair of oncoming men, walking as if they owned the sidewalk. And elbow caught her in her side and her first instinct was to blast his ass with a ball of fire. "Maya, control." Nik said in her ear and Maya blinked. How had she been so close to losing it.

"Asshole," Joss shouted, waving a fist at the backs of the men who continued on their journey oblivious of how close they'd come to being barbecued. Maya was turning back to continue down the street when she saw him.

A shudder ran down her spine as the odor of blood wafted acress to her. On this street, filled with the stink of sweat and roadside food mingling with the rank odor of urine and god knows what else, Maya could barely smell the demon's blood. But she'd gotten enough of a whiff to peg him as a Rakshasa.

She linked her hand with Nik's and smiled adoringly up at him. Just as he frowned at her sudden change in behavior, Maya said, "Don't look but we're being followed."

Nik gave a small nod. "Demon?"

"Yup. You know how much I adore them."

"Right. We have to get rid of him. We don't want them to know where we're going."

"I was hoping you'd say that." Maya grinned then pointed at a shop at their left. The strong smell of brass cleaner filled her nostrils and she said, "Hey Joss. Let's go in here. I want to show you something."

Joss followed and as the girls entered the cramped shop Maya whispered an update into her friends ear. Joss stiffened. "My Madu's are inside my bag. Can I get it out without having the whole shop watching the show?"

"Not likely. That's why once we enter we need to split up. I want to draw him deep into the shop." Maya paused in front of a gigantic brass vase that came as high as Maya's shoulder. It was filled with brass spears and tridents almost as tall as she was. She lifted a trident and tested its weight in her hand. "This will do."

"Do we have to split up? I want to see you shish kabob him," Joss complained.

"Behave yourself."

"Whatever. You just want to keep the fun for yourself," said Joss as she rounded on Nik, grabbed his arm and pulled him into a small passage filled with shelves overflowing with brass pots and trays. For a moment Maya was sure that nothing was balanced as well as it looked and it would all come toppling down on the two. Then she figured it wouldn't matter anyway. They were unlikely to be murdered by a stack of pots and platters.

Maya moved further into the shop and from the corner of her eye she could see both Joss and Nik keeping their eyes on her. The scent of rotting meat became stronger as the demon fell for her ruse and followed his inside the shop. He come up behind her thinking she was easy pickings, so when she spun on her heel the trident firmly pressed into his throat, he gurgled with shock.

"Why are you following me?" Maya growled softly. "Who are you working for?"

He just stared at her insolently, clenching his fists at his sides. Did he think he was going to get away from her? *Not much chance of that buster,* she thought.

The trident at his throat didn't seem like much of a deterrent as he stared at her, eyes glowing red and gold. He pressed against the triple tips, uncaring as they broke skin and drew three spots of blood. It was as if her was taunting her, daring her.

Was this loser uninformed or dumb? Did he not know who he'd been following? Or did they know something that she didn't?

When he raised his hands to reach for her neck she decided

enough was enough. She shoved the trident into his throat so hard all three spikes popped out on the other side of his neck. At the same time she didn't waste a single second. She called her fire, balled it up in both her palms sending the heat of the flames into the weapon. The metal pulsed and shivered as fire swam through it, shimmering as it raced up toward the triple points.

The Rakshasa stared down at her in consternation. "Guess you didn't expect that did you?" Neither had Maya. She'd taken the trident as a means of defending herself. She'd never for a moment gone into this planning to imbue the trident with her fire. But she was glad she had.

In the few seconds it took for the fire to enter his body, he realized he was dead or close to it. He struggled, stepping away, trying to flee. But each point of the trident ended in a small triangle, like an arrowhead. Making it rather difficult for him to free himself.

He was stuck.

His eyes widened as fire filled him, as the glow inside him grew brighter and brighter. Even his glaring eyeballs glowed. And then in a puff of breath he disintegrated in a cloud of bronze and gold embers. It never ceased to amaze Maya that these demonic creatures came to such a beautiful end when she put them out of their misery.

The last soot and embers floated to the ground celebrating the end of another Rakshasa.

CHAPTER 30

ik and Joss closed in on Maya. "Good job," said Nik.

"Yeah, that was pretty cool, what you did with the fire in the trident thing." Joss was nodding with approval but Maya didn't feel like celebrating just yet.

"We're being followed and I don't like it."

"I'd take you the sage but there is a possibility he is being watched. If I take you and they have wards set up then all we will do is endanger him by alerting them as to where we are going."

"Fine. What do we do then? What if they are still watching?"

"Wait here. I have a plan." Nik spoke and then a moment later he went invisible.

"That is so freaking cool," said Joss as she stared at the spot Nik had just occupied.

"Yeah," Maya sighed. "Would love that ability. All I got was freaking fire."

"Hey, don't knock fire. You're pretty much hell on legs for all the demons of the world."

Maya laughed. "Since you put it that way."

Nik returned in minutes, something black and long draped

across his arm. Before he held them up Maya knew what they were. Burqas.

"These will be perfect," said Maya. "We could walk right past them and they'd never know."

Nik nodded. "That's the idea." He handed them the garments. The girls set their bags on the floor before slipping the Burqas over their heads. The black dresses covered them head to foot with only a lace grille over their eyes allowing them to see where they were going. They shrugged their bags over their shoulders and filed silently out of the store. Nik stayed behind for a few moments, giving them a head start. He remained invisible, following a few meters away, keeping an eye out from the rear.

Maya kept a firm bead on her surroundings, watching face after face, scanning every person slouching in a corner or half hidden by shadows.

She smelled him before she saw him.

Coming up behind her, the odor of rotten meat seemed to fill the air and Maya stiffened. She had to force herself to put one foot in front of the other. Had to steel herself against warning Joss who was walking just slightly ahead of her.

The demon came abreast of her but she ignored him and walked straight on, not even missing a step. He was scanning the street, looking for her and coming up short. He didn't bother to look at the veiled woman right beside him. Maya continued to walk on. The Rakshasa surged ahead, craning his head, scanning the street and then decided to cross to the other side. He shoved a messenger boy aside, sending him sprawling on the floor, his bags of clothing plopping onto the dirty sidewalk. Maya and Joss neatly sidestepped the fallen boy and though she felt a pang of regret at not stopping to help, she walked on.

She watched the demon disappear into the crowd up ahead and sighed with relief as they reached the address Chayya had given her. She paused in front of a fabric shop, where rolls of brightly colored material stood in barrels marked 'linen', 'muslin', and 'poplin'. She walked slowly through the middle aisle, flanked by large glass counters filled with flat folded fabric. Joss was close at her elbow and Maya met the glance of one of the men at the counter. He stared at her, his eyes flat and uninterested, as if making a sale was the last thing he cared about.

Maya didn't stop to ask him anything. Chayya had said go through the shop and into back room, then up the stairs. Maya did as the goddess had instructed and headed for a doorway covered in long ropes of beads. She pushed it aside and the wooden bead bickered and complained, like a forest full of chattering monkeys. Joss followed closely and then they were in a small, dingy backroom. Canisters of food lay half open and something moved along the back shelf. Something dark and covered in fur. Maya shuddered then pulled Joss along as she hurried up a set of small stairs at the left wall.

One flight up they pushed aside a second curtain of beads and both girls gasped in surprise as they walked into the room. They stepped into a whitewashed room, so clean and bright compared to the dinky room downstairs that it felt like they'd stepped into another world.

The floor was white marble, and dozens of white cushions were strewn across the tiles. The windows were covered with white silk and it blew in a soft breeze. Although the building itself was old, the room seemed timeless.

Both girls threw off their Burqas, eyes studying the room. Something shifted along the wall and Maya glanced at the small man who sat cross legged, his bony legs covered by more white fabric. She'd expected the orange ocher of most holy men and was surprised he'd dressed in white.

The sage lifted his gaze, meeting Maya's eyes with a sparkle, a hint of a smile at his lips. And Maya grinned at him. She'd seen him before. "I know you," she said as he inclined his head giving her a benevolent smile.

"Yes, my child. I know you too."

"How do you know him?" whispered Joss reminding Maya that she was still with her.

"From Swargaloka." Maya glanced at Joss who frowned.

"I don't remember him."

"I saw him on the way to the palace. On one of the city streets." Maya wanted Joss to shut up. Talking about the sage while he sat right in front of them was quite rude. So she turned her attention back to the ancient man, stepped toward him and sat on the floor, folding her legs into a loose yoga position. "Thank you for seeing us," she said, thinking she should perform some kind of formalize. Instead she just placed her palms together in the Namaste greeting.

"It is my pleasure, Maya Rao, to assist the Lord of Creation. And you, too. Your reputation precedes you."

Maya flushed. "Chayya has been to see you."

"Yes and do not worry. She has only good things to say about you, my child." The sage straightened as the beads at the door crackled furiously. Maya glanced over her shoulder and watched Nik walk inside the small white room.

The old man rose to his feet, not a single crack of old bones to be heard. He bowed low before Nik. "Welcome,my Lord."

"There's no need for ceremony, Father."

"Ah, but my lord, it is not ceremony to greet a god as befits him."

"I am but only half a god," said Nik, laughing.

"And half a greeting would no doubt seem strange," returned the sage and everyone laughed. He seated himself again, "I believe you are in search of Gandiv. And I can help you."

"How do you know where it is?" Maya asked, then flushed at the directness of the question. The last thing she needed was to offend the man meant to help them locate the bow.

"Gandiv is holy and all holy objects give off a certain resonance. If you have the power to hear the heavenly sound they give off, you can find all the holy objects in the world."

"Oh, so we're talking heavenly GPS. Interesting," Maya mused, intrigued by the inner workings of various heavenly abilities and powers.

"Exactly. The only problem is that it is easily warded if the person who possesses it knows how."

"Is it warded now?"

"I'm afraid that it is. I do know where it is. Or rather where I last felt its location. But it seems to have disappeared in the last day or so."

"So if you tell us where it is we'll have to search the entire property?"

"Not necessarily." The sage tilted his head and stared at Nik. "Heavenly GPS is much stronger to heavenly creatures."

Maya's gaze snapped to Nik. "Nik can sense the bow?"

The sage nodded. "Even if it is warded, a god can sense the presence of the bow through the protection spell. I'm not certain how it works or how close you need to be, but you will need Nikhil." Then the old man reached for something beside his cushion and handed a small slip of paper to Maya. "This is the address."

"Thank you," Maya said, taking the neatly folded sheet.

"The home is in Juhu Beach and the owner, Raj Thakkur, is an art collector. He is holding a fund raising dinner tonight. I will arrange for invitations to the event to be sent to your hotel room."

"Oh. We'll have to get inside during a party?" asked Maya, now worried. "Won't there be security?"

"The invitations with secure your entry. What you do while inside the building is up to you. So don't do anything to raise suspicion."

"Don't get caught, don't get thrown out," muttered Maya.

"Something like that," answered Narada.

Maya smiled as got to her feet. Joss rose too and the old sage followed suit.

"Be careful, Maya Rao. You have the power so use it. But do not be rash. Pick your battles."

There would have been a time when words like those would have sent Maya bristling but she didn't take offense. Instead she flushed and nodded. When an awkward silence began to stretch Maya said, "Thank you so much. I'm not sure how we can repay you for your help."

"I haven't helped yet. Go and find Gandiv and I will be satisfied that I have helped at all."

Maya put her hands together and bowed to the sage. He repeated the gesture and with that Maya felt they were dismissed. The three turned to leave but when Maya paused at the door to take one last glance at Narada, the room was empty. He'd disappeared. She shrugged as she descended the stairs and followed Joss and Nik through the fabric store and past the sullen store clerks.

CHAPTER 31

Outside they turned and headed back to the hotel car. Once in the vehicle they remained subdued, refraining from talking more because of the presence of the driver than anything.

The drive back was hot and subdued as the air conditioner battled against the overpowering heat inside the car. Sweat tricked down Maya's back. She'd never been so relieved to see and air conditioned hotel in her life.

They all filed into the girl's room and Nik took a chair turning it to face the girls who'd thrown themselves on the bed.

"Room service?" he asked.

"Finally, someone mentions food," said Joss. "It is almost lunchtime you know."

"Yeah," said Maya. "I didn't think you'd be pleased to sample Eau de Mumbai on a full stomach. And I just haven't been hungry. I am now though, so room service sounds lovely."

"Well, let's order and once your meal is done we have training to do," Nik said meeting Maya's eyes.

"Training?"

"Yes. We have a few hours to kill before the party. You need at least one training session to keep you on your toes."

Maya nodded as Joss asked, "What about me?"

Nik pursed his lips. "You can go to the hotel gym. An hours run and a session on the punching bag should keep you limber. I'd take you too but I want to concentrate on Maya's fire."

Joss waved her hands in the air. "That's cool. I can take a hint." When Nik's face twisted with worry Joss laughed. "Hey, I was just kidding. I understand."

Maya grinned and said, "So, about that food?"

They ordered samoosas and a selection of pakoras club sandwiches.

"Oh and Joss, I don't think you should come with us tonight."

"What?" Maya hid a smile as Joss's face grew red.

"Three of us can't go creeping around a strange house by ourselves. And if something happens I can only get one of you out in an emergency. It complicates things with three." Nik looked unhappy but unapologetic.

"Oh, so three's a crowd then?" She looked hurt.

"In this case it is," Maya butted in before Nik got into more trouble. "Nik's right. With just Nik and me he can go stealth and if anyone see me its just one little lost girl. Or Nik can beam me right out of there."

Joss pouted. "I see what you mean but it doesn't mean I have to like it."

A knock on the door signaled the arrival of their food. Nik hurried to let them in while the girls cleared a space on the table below the wall mounted TV. The waiter left the food and was on his way out when Nik stopped him, placing something in his palm. The man grinned, bobbing his head up and down repeatedly saying thanking Nik as he left.

"Did you tip him?" asked Maya as the door clicked shut.

Nik nodded. "Sometimes that extra money counts." Maya

watched Nik as he spoke, liking the effect that he was unafraid to reveal his kind and caring self.

The aroma of fried food wafted toward them and her stomach rumbled. She was famished. "Right. Let's eat."

They descended on the food and very soon all that remained on the silver platters were wadded napkins and the fine slices of plate decoration lettuce. As soon as they were done Nik said, "Get ready. I'll be back in ten minutes."

"Where are we going to train?"

"Somewhere special and somewhere you won't hurt anyone." Nik winked as he headed out the door.

Maya huffed as she scooted off the bed and dragged her bag out of the closet. Inside she found a pair of black sweats, a tee and hoodie. She shoved her feet into her trainers and stood up to face the mirror. She dragged her hair into a ponytail and then looked around. A hair-band danced at her shoulder and she mumbled her gratitude to Joss as she finished tying up her hair.

"Right. Done."

"Wonder what he has planned for you," mused Joss as she picked up the remote to skim the channels. She settled on a movie with English subtitles and was so absorbed that when Nik knocked on the door and Maya let him in, Joss barely noticed.

"So that's what we brought her here for? To watch Bollywood movies?" asked Maya, raising an eyebrow.

Joss waved them off and Maya grinned. Nik reached for her hand and they disintegrated into nothingness.

As they reappeared Maya's feet felt strange, as if she wasn't on solid ground. When she looked down she saw her sneakers half buried in fine golden sand.

"You brought me to the desert?" she asked Nik who stood beside her waiting for her reaction.

"Yes. It's the Thar Desert to be specific."

"Are we still in India?" Maya asked, eyes narrowed.

Nik nodded as he scanned the dunes surrounding them. "These are the Sam Sand Dunes on the outskirts of Jaisalmer." Maya put a hand to her eyes as she looked around. They stood in a valley, the dunes around them rising high enough to hide both Nik and her from prying eyes. Something tapped her upper arm and she took the pair of sunglasses Nik offered. "Thanks. You could have told me."

"I wanted to surprise you."

"I am. It's incredibly beautiful."

"So before we start I want to show you something." Nik held out his hand and Maya took it. Before she could ask any more questions they disappeared, then shuddered back into solidity, this time on solid ground. They were standing at the top of a set of stairs, facing a domed structure made from golden sand. Numerous carved archways held up the rounded roof and inside stood a square pedestal holding up a white carving. As Maya looked out of the structure she saw dozens of similar buildings built on the rise.

"It's beautiful." She sucked in a breath, staring at the golden domes. They shimmered as the sun hit them, giving them an ethereal air. So out of place in the barren desert, yet so much a part of it.

"These are the cenotaphs of the old Rajasthan kings."

"Cenotaphs?" asked Maya, confused. She'd never heard the word before.

"Cenotaph means *empty tomb*. The structure is a monument to the dead king but his remains are not kept here."

"Ah." Maya nodded and stared out at the line of cenotaphs. "Are they all for kings?"

"Many of them are. There used to be a lake here, and gardens built at the waters edge."

"In the middle of a desert?" asked Maya in disbelief.

Nik nodded. "One of the kings built a dam that fed the gardens and the lake. Unfortunately, the river changed course or dried up leaving this place a golden desert."

"That's sad. But it's beautiful," said Maya as she traced the carved pillars, walking from bright sunlight into cool shade. "Kind of hard to believe that it's still here after all these years."

"Let's hope it lasts a long time into the future. It's good to be able to see what the people of the past were able to create. When beauty like this can endure the passage of time, it can also give people hope that they too can achieve something memorable, something remarkable."

Maya eyed Nik. His words were so poetic and she realized she was seeing a side of him that he'd so far kept hidden. It must not be easy to live for so long. He'd been so quiet lately.

She inhaled, decided there was no time like the present. "Are you okay?" She walked toward him, partly to see his face beyond the black lenses of his sunglasses, and partly to be closer to him.

"Sure. I'm fine." He gave her a stiff smile.

"See, now I know you aren't fine." Her lips twisted wryly. "Unfortunately, the fact is I know you too well to believe that. So, tell me what's wrong. You know you can trust me, right?" Maya posed the question, her heart stilling with the fear that he may confirm that he didn't trust her. What would she do if he said no?

Nik sighed and leaned against the pillar at his back. "I'm sorry. I know I've been a bit distant." He stared into the roof of the dome, then removed his glasses and rubbed the bridge of his nose. "I suppose being here is quite appropriate. It's my mother."

Maya sucked in a breath, now more worried than ever. "Is she sick?"

Nik shook his head slowly, shadows of sadness hovering over his features. "No. It's just the passage of time that is taking its toll. I'm trying to convince her to return to Patala to live out the last days of her life but she just laughs and says no way she wants to die in the Underworld. That there is time enough to get there after she dies."

Maya frowned. "Nik. How come she lives here instead of being at your father's side?"

Nik smiled and Maya felt a little foolish, her question more romantic than practical. "They do love each other but it's hard for a human to live in a god's realm. And my father's responsibilities would never allow him to live anywhere but Patala. Mother loves the sea, the sunshine. And she thought an earthly upbringing would be more beneficial to me than being raised in Patala."

"And she was right. You turned out pretty well in the end," said Maya with a grin.

Nik snorted. "Mother did a good job, she raised me without airs and graces, and she made sure I was never arrogant, that my status never got to my head. Even now I'm sure she'd slap me up side the head if I set one foot in the wrong direction." They both laughed, the sound echoing around the pillars only to be eaten by the sand surround them.

"I like her already," said Maya still laughing at the thought.

"She will like you too," said Nik.

"So even though she's old and frail she's giving you a hard time?"

"Yes. I don't like that she lives alone." Nik paused. "Well to be honest she isn't alone. Father gave her a few servants a long time ago and they are still with her so it's not as if she needs the physical help. I just…"

"You're worried she won't have any loved ones around when her time comes?" Maya asked curling her hand around Nik's arm.

He nodded, "Sometimes I feel like I should just put all my duties on hold and stay with her for a while."

"Maybe you should." When Nik frowned she said, "I've always thought it's a bit of waste of time to pitch up for a funeral when the person is gone. They're not even going to know you're there.

Why not spend some time with her while she is able to enjoy you.?"

Nik wrapped his arms around her and rested his chin on the top of her head. "You have a good point, Maya Rao." Then he sighed. "Maybe once this task is completed I will go to Florida. And spend a few weeks with her. And maybe you can come to meet her. It would probably make her happy to know her son actually does have someone in his life besides demons and gods."

Maya laughed into his shoulder. "How do you think she will feel knowing I'm mortal? It's not as if she's going to be happy knowing her son has a temporary girl?"

Nik stiffened then grabbed Maya's shoulder and held her away, "Is that worrying you?"

Maya tried to shrug although the movement was odd with him still gripping her upper arm. "I guess. I think about it sometimes." She sighed and her shoulders slumped. Her head fell forward and lock of hair came free from her ponytail, fall over her forehead and down her cheek. "Doesn't it bother you?"

Nik lifted the lock of hair from her face and tucked it behind her ear. "It does. I try not to think about it too much. I guess a part of me was hoping you'd have been granted some form of immortality with your powers."

"Have I?" Maya asked, curious. She'd never thought about immortality before. Not until Nik came into her life.

Nik shook his head. "Not that I know of."

Maya shrugged. "It's not important. Why don't we worry about the now and think about the future when we get there."

Nik snickered. "Not sure how that will help."

"I know. But I don't want to think about growing old and dying while you stay as handsome and godly as you are." Maya's eyes grew hot and she was horrified she might cry. She blinked the tears back keeping her face against his chest. She had to admit it had been bothering her for a while but she hadn't accepted how much.

Nik moved back and place a finger beneath her chin. He tilted her head up so she had no choice but to look at him. "I know how you feel. You must know that I have to go through this too. It's not only the people I love that have to suffer." His words were soft and Maya was unable to hold back her tears. Nik bent to place his lips on her forehead, the kiss leaving a mark of heat that Maya prayed would stay forever.

ik cleared his throat. "We should probably get back to work. We only have a few hours before we have to get back."

Maya nodded and took Nik's hand. They disappeared and flickered back to solidity in the valley somewhere in the sand dunes.

"So no more blood smelling?"

"Not exactly," said Nik, slipping his hand into his pocket. He withdrew a long strip of black fabric.

She kept an eye on him as he lifted his hands. "So what exactly arc we doing? We don't really have time to get kinky," she said raising an eyebrow at the fabric."

Nik laughed loudly and Maya grinned, happy to see him experience a little joy. She felt a little stupid considering all her petty and selfish thoughts about where he'd been and what he'd been doing when all this while he was dealing with the imminent death of his mother. Maya resolved to be more understanding and less demanding in the future.

With everyone.

Nik closed in on her, holding both ends of the fabric in his hands. "You're right about one thing. This is a blindfold. But it's purpose is much more serious in this case."

"Okay." Maya laughed, the sound flat and odd as it rose and fell in the sand dune valley.

He picked the sunglasses off her head and pocketed them. "Turn around."

She did as she was told, and waited as he lowered the fabric in front of her eyes. A wave of panic broke over her as the world went dark and the golden shifting sands disappeared behind the black screen. She tried to control the fluttering of her heart, reminding herself that Nik would never do anything to hurt her.

Nik tied a knot at the back of her head. Then placed his hands on her shoulders and turned her around slowly. It was a strange sensation. The utter darkness seemed to swallow her up. It must have something to do with the sand that rose on either side of them. With her sight removed she could almost feel an odd pressure pushing against her from both sides.

"Describe what you feel." Said Nik, sounding as if he stood a few feet in front of her.

"It's dark, I can't see anything."

"I asked what you feel, not what you see," he said dryly.

"Okay, then." Maya said slightly miffed. She inhaled. "I feel like something is beside me, here and here." She waved a hand on either side of her."

"Good, those are the two sand dunes. Anything else?"

"Well, I feel the sun and the heat from the sky. Oh, and also the heat from the sand."

"Okay. Now tell me if you feel this."

A blast of hot air sped by Maya's face, the heat of it more than just a kiss on her cheek. She sniffed and smelled burning hair. "Nik! What the hell are you doing?" Outrage trembled in her voice.

"What do you think that was?" he asked, his voice neutral.

"A bloody ball of fire that's what." Maya shrieked indignantly.

"Good. Now tell me if you sense this." Maya waited but nothing happened. "Anything?" asked Nik.

"No."

"Concentrate. Take a deep breath and calm yourself. Listen and feel," he instructed. "Ready?" Maya nodded.

This time she felt a sense of air moving past her at her left side. "On my left, but it felt a little further away than the first fireball you nearly killed me with." Her response was a little less indignant as before, as she began to understand what Nik was doing.

Nik laughed. "That was nothing. I'm training you for worse. Now one more time." He sent another fireball past Maya and she could tell again which side and how far away it was. Three feet on the left side. "Now, the more you concentrate, the more you train you will learn how to feel the fire the moment it leaves the body of your attacker."

"How will I do that." Nik was silent. "Nik?" Maya called but he didn't answer. Her skin rippled, a thousand desert scorpions scurrying across her skin, pincers tails raised, promising death.

Maya stiffened wondering where the attack would come from. When it did it was the last think she expected. A ball of fire hit her square in the gut. She hadn't even felt it coming.

She sat on the sand in disgust, gritting her jaw and dusting her hands together. "This is a waste of time. I'm no good at it."

"Nobody is good at this when they first start off, now stop feeling sorry for yourself and get your head in the game." Nik said. His tone was firm, brooking no argument. Maya pouted but got back to her feet. Sometime she wondered at how much sense it made for the guy who trained her to be the one she was crazy about, because at that moment all she was crazy about doing was wringing his sorry neck. "Anger and annoyance will only hinder your training. Let go of your frustrations, free you mind. Only then can you call on your ability to see without seeing."

"Okay, Confucius. Let's do this." Maya slapped the sand off her, the rolled back her shoulders.

"I'll stay here," Nik said from a foot in front of her. He grasped her hand then held it close to his. "Feel this." He held her hand close to his, just to the side of his palm. Maya felt an odd pressure appear then flicker with warmth and power.

"I feel that."

"Now you need to learn to detect that power from a little further away. I won't speak this time. I'll just generate the flame and you need to tell me where it is."

Maya nodded and then fell silent. The wind rose around them and she could hear the grains of sand fighting against each other in a wave of solid particles. She listened, opening her mind, waiting. And then she heard it, and felt it.

A rush of air, a slight pressure.

She pointed to her right. "There. But it's faint."

"Good. I'm about five feet away. You need to get better. Not all your attackers will make sure to get up close." Maya nodded. "Again."

She stilled her thoughts and waited, and when she feel the feel of air displacing she pointed to her left behind her. They continued this process for a while. The furthest Nik went was ten feet. Maya was getting the hand of things when Nik blasted her with a stream of fire. She felt the head rush toward her and only managed to raise her palms and call her own fire a breath before his fire hit.

"What the hell?" she shrieked.

"Your attackers will not be nice enough to tell you when and where they will attack."

"Fine," said Maya gritting her teeth. He had a point.

She opened her mind again and waited, and soon Nik began to send barrages of fireballs at her from all directions. She could just imagine what he looked like, appearing, sending a ball of fire before disappearing again. For more than half an hour she worked, paying close attention. She managed to deflect more than half before Nik stopped.

"You're making progress. So far you can sense when someone calls their fire. And now you're able to deflect fire coming at you. Let's step it up."

Maya nodded and waited, then stumbled back as she sensed half a dozen fireballs coming in her direction. Instinctively she threw her arm up intending to send her fire up in an arc to deflect he oncoming balls of fire. Then everything stopped and Nik said, "Wow."

"What?" she asked standing still, afraid to move.

"Take you blindfold off with your left hand and be careful. Move slowly." Maya did as she was told and her jaw dropped when she saw what she'd done.

She'd sent her fire out hoping to defend herself against Nik's flames. Instead she'd created an umbrella with her fire. She stared at the half globe of flame that shimmered before her. The film of fire hung in the air, giving off an intense heat and Maya was in awe. She'd just made herself an umbrella of fire. It had done its job, the balls of fire Nik had sent were nowhere to be seen.

"How did you do that?" asked Nik coming closer to inspect the shape she'd created.

"No idea. I just knew I needed a fire enough to protect me from all the balls coming at me."

"So you could tell how many?"

Maya nodded. "Six. And they were coming in an arc. I didn't think of making an umbrella. It was just instinctive. I called the fire and it did what was needed." She moved her hand and the arc of fire disintegrated into nothing, but the image of it was burned in Maya's mind. "And *Wow* pretty much hits it on the head."

"Yes, that was quite incredible. But we have to get back." He said looking at his watch.

"Oh," said Maya feeling a little deflated. "Just when the going gets good."

"Don't worry we'll practice again, but at least we know that the fire adapts with your needs. You just have to be confident that you will defeat your attacker."

"Easy for you to say." Maya snorted.

Nik laughed. "You possess way more power than you realize Maya." He crooked his elbow. "Now lets get back. We're full of sand so I'll go straight into my bathroom just in case Joss is using yours."

Maya giggled. "Not much chance of walking in on her naked. She's going to be a bawling mess watching that movie."

And true to Maya's assumption, after dusting off and cleaning up in Nik's bathroom, they walked into the girl's room to find a red-eyed Joss sitting on the bed surrounded by a scattering of scrunched up tissues.

CHAPTER 33

"*D*id the invitations arrive?" Nik asked, not wasting a second.

Joss nodded. "The concierge called and said she's holding them." She sounded blocked up from all the tears, making Maya grin.

Nik headed for the door. "I'll go get the tickets. Then we'll know exactly how much time we have."

The final credits rolled on the movie and Maya grinned at Joss. "Good movie?"

Joss laughed. "Stop laughing at me. Man, I never knew these movies were such tear jerker's. I could barely keep up with the subtitles but that didn't stop the tears."

Maya grinned then headed to the closet to scan her wardrobe for something to wear to the party. The skirt and beaded top from the previous night's dinner seemed appropriate. She didn't want to attract any undue attention anyway.

Understated and elegant will have to do.

The phone rang and Joss twisted around to pick up the receiver beside her. She dropped it moments later and turned to

Maya, "Nik says it's at 8pm. So you need to get dressed and be ready by seven."

Maya nodded and was about to head into the shower when she saw the morose look on her friend's face. "Nik's right about you not coming tonight ,you know."

Joss nodded but her expression remained unchanged. "I know. It still sucks."

"You'll get your opportunity to kick some ass soon enough. Don't worry."

"Says you who kicks ass all the time." Joss slid onto her side and propped her head on her hand. "So what did you two get up to?"

Maya quickly described the fire training to her now wide-eyed friend." See?" asked Joss. "I missed all the fun."

"You did get to watch the movie," Maya pointed out.

"Not the same thing and you know it." Joss pouted. "Things better get a little more exciting in the Joss fun department or I'll be wanting to go home."

"Hey. Don't be like that." Maya frowned. "As soon as we know where the bow is we'll be back here and getting ready to go. With you." At Joss's raised eyebrow Maya said, "And if we find we don't need you for anything I'll tell Nik to take you straight home."

"Maya." Joss couldn't hold back her hurt expression and Maya couldn't stop the laughter that bubbled from her lips. She turned and hurried into the bathroom, narrowly avoiding the pillow that Joss sent flying from the bed.

As she showered she thought about Joss. Hopefully, her unfortunate friend will get her chance at the main action.

Joss was dying to proved herself as a Kali Hunter.

AT SEVEN NIK knocked on the door and Maya grabbed her sequined bag and waved at Joss on her way out.

"We'll take a cab. I'd rather we arrive in neutral transport in case things go bad," said Nik as they boarded the elevator.

"Makes sense. A hotel car will bring them right to our door."

Maya found a couch while Nik approached the concierge to order the taxi. Maya watched the girl's expression as Nik spoke. She seemed confused that a guest would request a method of transportation not provided by the hotel but she eventually accepted it, although her lips settled into a tight, disapproving line.

Nik returned and sat beside Maya. "She didn't like it."

"I could tell," Maya laughed. "Did she give you a hard time?"

"Not too much. I had to drop a few hints about you hiding from your tyrannical father. Didn't seem to make a lick of difference to her though." Nik glanced at his watch. "In the end she called. Taxi should be here in ten minutes or so."

They didn't have to wait too long. Less than ten minutes had passed when the bellhop entered the hotel and walked up to them. He smiled and the gleaming white of his teeth made a startling contrast to the night-dark of his skin. His bright red coat did nothing to ease the color disaster.

He beckoned and bowed, and they followed him through the foyer and out into the darkening evening. Night made only a tiny percentage of difference to the thick layer of odor that blanketed the waterfront.

The driver alighted and came around to open the door for them. Maya slid inside, followed closely by Nik. They sat quietly in the back, where every move they made crackled the cheap vinyl of the seats and the windows fogged up so much they couldn't see outside. Maya assumed the view wasn't going to be all that great anyway. A mosquito buzzed in her ear and she smacked at it. Raising her fingers to the weak light for the street lamp she was satisfied to see the little red smudge and the remnants of the dead blood-sucker.

It wasn't long before she had to hold her breath, the reek of the driver wafting into the back seat. Maybe the end of the day wasn't a good time to take a ride in a taxi without air conditioning.

Maya sighed, slapping away at a little party of mosquitoes who'd followed in the tracks of their lone, recently deceased friend. There were a few times in the last few days when she had to remind herself that she was really in India. A place she'd had little interest in visiting until Lord Shiva gave her this task.

The mosquitoes returned with a vengeance and Maya began to shift in her seat, uncomfortable by the barrage of bugs. Ten minutes of suffering later she turned around in her seat to scan the vehicle for the source of the ceaseless supply of blood suckers.

When she gasped Nik turned beside her. "What's wrong."

She stiffened her body, discomfort and bug-dislike petrifying her muscles. "Look at the rear dashboard. There's a frigging colony of mosquitoes living and breeding there." She spoke with her neck stiff and taut, as if the mere movement of her body would bring on the next deadly wave.

Nik looked and grunted, annoyed. "Nothing we can do but keep still and hope we get there fast."

Nik was right and twenty minutes of stiff awareness passed before they arrived and when Maya opened the door she sank into shocked silence. The taxi had driven them inside the gates of a mansion and pulled up beneath the overhanging roof of the entrance to the house. Lights shone from every window and there was no doubt a party was going on.

A liveried guard helped Maya out of the car and waved them up the stairs. As they walked along the red-carpeted steps Maya glanced back to see the taxi driver's very shell-shocked face as he stared up at the house on his way out.

At the top of the stairs another liveried guard gave them a tight smile, unable to disguise his distaste at the taxi driver's presence. "Good evening Sir, Madam. May I see your invitations please?" If the man thought that either Nik or Maya didn't belong, he didn't show it.

Nik handed him a pair of white cards, printed in gold. He quickly ticked off their names from his list and waved them inside. Maya held onto Nik's arm as they walked through a large marbled entrance hall, flanked by brass vases and decanters taller than Nik. At the end of the hall they came to a balcony that overlooked the ballroom one floor down. A gigantic black stone Nataraja statue - Lord Shiva performing the cosmic dance- took pride of place, flanked by two sets of stairs that led down into the ballroom.

"That is one amazing statue," breathed Maya.

"It is. It's hand carved from meteor rock."

"How can you tell?" Maya stared at him, curious.

"Rock that is extraterrestrial gives off a resonance that is immediately recognizable and different from terrestrial formations."

"Woah. ET GPS." Maya was in awe and glanced back at the black statue.

Nik frowned. "ET?"

"Extra-Terrestrial? ET go home?" Maya looked at Nik and shook her head, laughing. "You really need an education in movies. I think I will make it my mission to teach you."

"Sorry Maya, no time to watch movies."

"Of course, you have time. When you visit with your Mom make her hot chocolate or iced tea and put on a DVD of ET and watch it together. She'll remember the movie. And you can both enjoy it together."

"What a lovely idea." Nik nodded, his face serious. "I never would have come up with that myself. We must discuss this in more detail. Although for now I think we need to descend into the morass that is this party."

Maya looked down into the seething mass of people and tried

unsuccessfully to tamp down a shudder. So many people. "I am so going to get hives."

Just before they set foot on the first stair Maya stiffened. Directly across from them a man stood watching their progress intently.

"Don't react, just act normal." Nik seemed super-attuned to her body's reactions.

"What's normal?"

"Just look at me." She looked.

"Who is he?"

"I'm not sure but he is quite likely our host so the best thing is to not react in a negative way."

"What makes you think he's Thakkur?"

"Not sure. Maybe the cigars in his pocket. There is the odd older gentleman walking around with a lit cigar but none have stock in the jacket pockets."

"So he's handing them out. And it would be the host who would do that." Maya nodded. "You're good. Give Bond a run for his money." When she glanced at Nik, he rolled his eyes.

"I know who Bond is. We watched that movie together remember, Golden something?"

Maya giggled. "*Goldeneye*. Fine. You get that one. But it's still not good enough."

She held onto Nik's arm and they descended the staircase. Maya's floor length skirt trailing the steps behind her as she walked. They end up at the left side of the ballroom floor. A waiter glided past, his tray full of bubbling champagne but both Maya and Nik refused. They weren't here to eat or drink.

They mingled, weaving thought the mass of people, pausing every so often to inspect a piece of art set up on dozens of pedestals along the edges of the ballroom. Maya was in awe of some of the pieces, especially if the name-cards claiming their ages were to be believed.

"Nik," she whispered. "Some of these pieces are three thousand years old. Where is he getting them from?"

"Museums. Illegal digs. Black Market. Who knows."

"But if it's illegal won't the government want to reclaim the relics?"

"In some cases perhaps, but Thakkur donates part of his finds to the museums and loans the rest if he is asked. Of course, he gets paid a good sum of money for his efforts."

"So the government is in cahoots with him?"

"Probably. It's not easy to pay your way into the museums. I've read up on him. He was once accused of buying a relic from the Delhi Museum of Ancient art. He'd insisted his piece was a replica and invited his accusers to test the piece."

"And of course when they tested it they found it was really a fake," said Maya. "He got a copy made in time, I take it."

"He is a very clever man. He probably bought the original from the museum and had to cover it up when he was accused. And the copy now sitting in the museum is probably a fake too."

"Must be hard," said Maya studying the people around her as they streamed past, glittering and loud like sedate seagulls.

"What must be hard?"

"Keeping track of it all, getting your head around the whole thing. I can't imagine being able to manage all of that."

They lingered beside a stone carving of an Apsara and when Maya glanced around her again she caught a girl watching her. Dark eyes, jet black hair hanging all the way to her waist, full lips. The girl smiled, friendly and pleasant. Dressed in a black beaded gown with a plunging neckline, the fabric shimmered in the light of the dozens of chandeliers hanging from the two story high ceiling.

The girl weaved in amongst the crowd and disappeared. And Maya turned her attention back to Nik who was inspecting a stone carving of the demon Ravana.

"You think we've mingled enough?" Maya whispered to Nik.

Nik glanced around as if looking for the next artifact to look at, then bent to her ear. "I can't see him anywhere. There's no telling if he has cameras either."

"I can't see any."

"Me either. So I have a plan," he said as he curved his arm around her waist. "We can get a little romantic."

"Ah I see. Using my tricks against me?" Maya grinned and leaned into Nik. The plan was good. A public show of affection before they disappear down a corridor. If caught they would have a good enough excuse.

"Of course. I learn from my experiences," said Nik with a wink. He moved closer, eyes on her lips, and Maya did the same. They were far too close, scandalously close, especially considering the few disapproving glances they were getting already.

Maya stood on tiptoes and whispered into Nik's ear. "Right, we have enough people glaring at our impropriety, so maybe we can get out of here now?" She disliked being a spectacle especially here in India where people were far more staid and strict than they were back home.

Nik tightened his arm around her and drew her close, leading her off the ballroom floor.

CHAPTER 34

$\mathcal{M}$aya leaned into Nik and stared up at him, adoration plastered on her face. "So what does your Heavenly GPS say?"

They moved a short way up a hallway that led off the ballroom. Nik gave her an indulgent smile then used his free hand to trace the line of her cheekbone. "I can feel something. We're moving in the direction of whatever is emitting that pulse." Then he stopped, bent over her and kissed her deeply. Maya froze with shock. When he finally let her go she could almost feel the daggers of the stares in her back. "What the hell was that for? There's got to be at least a dozen old geezers staring at us right now, all a millisecond away of either frying their pacemakers or keeling over of a sudden case of myocardial infarction."

Nik snorted. "That was my intention. They get an eyeful and we have proof of the depth of our passion. Why else would we be running away from a perfectly good party?"

"Very good thinking. I'm beginning to wonder how much you haven't told me about your past escapades." When Nik sent her a curious glance as he led her deeper into the building she said,

"You know, long-lived demigods are notorious for their love 'em and leave 'em ways."

Nik snorted. "Perhaps you are confusing me with actual gods. And beside, my mother would have my head if I behaved disrespectfully to any woman."

"I actually think I like the sound of your mother," said Maya, wondering if she would ever get the chance to meet Nik's mother.

The hallway ended and Nik guided Maya left with a hand at the small of her back. Suddenly she was glad she had fabric covering her body. What would she have done had the garment been backless? "It's getting stronger." He said, walking faster and with more confidence.

"Slow down, dude. You don't want to draw attention to us," she said gripping his arm and trying very hard not to scan the passage walls for cameras.

He slowed to a stroll, "You're right."

Maya glanced around her and was pleasantly surprised. The walls were painted white, the clean lines broken every so often by a a pedestal holding an interesting vase or carving, or by a canvas. "This whole places is a museum."

"And I don't like it one bit."

"What's wrong?"

"My signal is getting interference."

"Are you losing it?"

"No. Not losing it. There seems to be other objects giving off a similar resonance."

"Crap. You mean this guy has other holy objects hidden within this house?"

Nik nodded as he tilted his head as if listening to a far off sound that Maya couldn't hear. Then he nodded in answer. "Yes. There are many more, although its fairly easy to identify Gandiv."

"How?" Maya frowned. "Have you ever been near the bow before?"

"No. It's not that. Gandiv is powerful. It belongs to Lord Shiva so it's resonance is incredibly strong. The other fields of power that I can sense are much smaller. And though there are quite a few of them, they cannot drown Gandiv out."

"That's good," said Maya as they strolled down the passage. They reached an intersection of corridors and Nik bent to Maya, kissing her cheek. "Giggle." He said into her ear.

"Huh?"

"Do what girls do when a guy is kissing their neck."

"Oh," she said then pasted on an adoring smile. She threw back her head and let out a breath, ending it with a soft moan. "Like that?"

Nik cleared his throat. "Like that, yes. But you need to be so convincing. I couldn't tell if that was real or an act."

"That's for me to know and you to find out," Maya winked.

"Not very nice of you, Maya?" he leaned against the wall, his body tense.

"You're supposed to be concentrating on Gandiv." She scolded in his ear, hiding a grin as the warmth of her breath touched his neck.

"How can I with you making these kinds of sounds?"

"I thought that was the job?" she asked innocently.

Nik cleared his throat again then held Maya away. His face was dark and strained as her pushed off the wall and grabbed her hand, pulling her along the hallway, his speed slightly more urgent than before. Maya smiled to herself as she double-stepped to keep up.

They reached a set of double door and Nik made a play of looking up and down in case anyone was coming. Anyone watching the cameras would see a young couple looking for a place to be alone.

Hopefully.

Nik pushed the door open then shut it as soon as Maya walked through it. Then he pushed her gently against the door, his hot breath on her cheek, and said, "I can give as good as I get you know."

"What does that-" asked Maya. When Nik kissed her neck, sending shivers of electricity through every part of her body, all she could do was whisper, "Oh."

For that one moment Maya forgot everything. Nik's lips moved to hers and she kissed him back as deeply as he kissed her. Their breathing turned ragged and desperate very quickly. When Nik pulled away she felt bereft and almost grabbed him to keep him with her when she saw the look in his eyes. He kept his face in front of hers and looked in the direction of another set of double doors to their left.

He was telling her Gandiv was in the next room.

Nik moved his lips to her neck, "We go to the door, open it. If Gandiv is in there, do not react. It's supposed to mean nothing to us, all we are supposed to want is a private place to get to third base. Okay?"

Maya arched her head and sighed, "Yes."

Nik growled, his lips at her ears. "I think you are way too good at this." Then, before she could respond he pushed off the door and pulled her toward the other doorway. He tugged it open and they both looked inside the room. Maya blinked and wanted to fall over. She had to force herself to remain calm, to keep her spine soft, to take her eyes of the most beautiful bow she had ever seen in her life.

Nik pulled her away, then shut the door, as if the bow was insignificant to them. By now they should have been looking for a sofa but this room, that appeared to be a small office, had only single armchairs. The sound of running filtered through to them from the hallway. "Not much time left." He stepped toward Maya and she stepped back slowly until she felt the solidity of the wall behind her. Nik pressed up against her, his chest taking her breath away, the heat of his skin filtering through their clothing until it seared into hers.

Maya's arms moved around Nik's neck pulling him closer. Her heart thudded in time to the sound of footsteps rushing toward them. Nik grunted. "Lift your leg and give me your knee."

"What?" Maya asked as she did as requested. When he scrunch up the length of her skirt and pushed his hand up her leg she squeaked.

"I'm sorry, Maya. We need to be caught in the act and this is as hot as it's going to get to convince them."

"Okay," she answered a little breathless. She lifted her knee and curved her leg around Nik's hip. She knew how it would look when they burst into the room and a part of her was dying with embarrassment. Another part of her didn't care a damn. She wisher the uncaring part would take charge so she wouldn't be so incredible nervous and so strangely ashamed.

When the door slammed open Nik's hand lay midway up Maya's bare thigh, the black chiffon scrunched up on her upper thigh. His lips were press against hers so hard she could barely breath, and her arms were curled around his neck so tight she was sure she would choke him if they didn't get done with this charade soon.

"Don't move." One of the men instructed. Maya shifted her gaze and froze with shock. He was holding a gun on them, as were the three other men who had barged into the room. The look in his eye made Maya's stomach turn to stone and her arms loosened of their on volition, leaving Nik's neck and falling to her sides. She let her foot drop and the expanse of skin she'd just flaunted was now covered by meters of fabric.

The guard was staring at her as if she was a piece of meat.

Maybe they hadn't thought this through well enough. In this guards eyes, Maya was trash. What if he decided he wanted a piece of the action himself? "What are you doing here?" he asked and then he laughed. "Okay, forget I asked. It's pretty obvious what you were doing." He walked closer to Nik and Maya, pressing his gun to the side of Nik's head. "Step away from the girl."

CHAPTER 35

ik gripped Maya's waist. "Leave my wife alone."

"Your wife?" The guard laughed, although there was a nervous hint to it that showed he had not expected a married couple. Nik hadn't removed his hand and the guard didn't press the issue. Instead he stepped away, a look of disgust on his face. "Your invitations, please."

Nik pulled them from his pocket and handed them over. After inspecting them the guard said, "Mr. & Mrs. Malhotra, if you will remain here please, Mr. Thakkur would probably like to meet the couple using his study as a brothel." He turned on his heel, spat out instructions to the guards and left the room. Two guards followed him out, one of them remaining to guard the door, the other hurrying after him.

The third guard glared at them and pointed at the set of armchairs in front of the desk. He turned them around to face the door and placed them side by side. "Sit." He barked the instruction so loud Maya jumped. Nik led her to the chairs and they both sat and waited.

Maya couldn't help wondering why the guards weren't tying them up. Maybe it had something to do with the fact that they were invited guests. She certainly hoped so, but she wasn't looking forward to seeing Thakkur in person. Just looking at him had made her skin crawl.

Minutes past and Maya glanced at Nik, worried. He held out his hand and she gripped it hard. *He could get us out of there,* she thought. *But we can't afford witnesses.* Teleporting out of the room would be their last resort.

After what seemed like hours the sound of heels tapping on the marble tiled floor filtered into the room from the adjoining room containing the bow. Then the door opened to reveal the beautiful young girl who had smiled at Maya from across the ballroom. Maya frowned as she entered but the girl ignored them. Instead she glared at the guard, "Do you have any idea how much trouble you're in?"

"What? Madam. Sorry Madam." He said with a confusing flouring of low bows and side to side head movements. "Adil said to watch them while he fetched Mr. Thakkur."

"I see. Did it ever occur to you dimwits that Mr Thakkur would be extremely upset if his guests were mistreated."

"Sorry, Madam. We haven't done anything to them. They are okay." He held his hands out, placating the fiery woman, his face twisted with shame and fear.

"Okay, yes, but being held gunpoint is not going to make them open their pockets very easily when Mr Thakkur needs their donations." She walked around the guard. "I suppose these things must be explained to imbeciles like you."

"Sorry, Madam." The guard bowed to her, his head poking out a little as if he offered it to her to lop off if she so desired. Maya swallowed a grin at the queer mental picture.

When he hesitated the woman took a step toward him. He shrank back as she spoke, "Leave us." As soon as she spoke he scurried out of the room, shutting the door softly behind him.

"I'm so sorry this happened to you. These men are bumbling

fools. They do everything Thakkur Sahib says." There was a note of distaste in her voice.

"Do you work for him?" Maya asked.

"I suppose you could say that." The girl answered her, then looked directly at Nik. She titled her head, her almond eyes glinting as she stared at him. "I'm going to take a huge risk here. I need help to get away from Thakkur."

"Is he holding you prisoner?" asked Maya, snapping the girl's gaze back to her.

"Yes. In every sense of the word. I am bound to him. Have been for decades."

"Bound? What do mean bound?" Maya asked frowning. She had the strange sense that the girl was going to say something that she should not believe.

"He found me thirty years ago. And he found the spell to bind me to him." She glanced again at Nik, as strange familiarity in her gaze. "My name is Archana. I am an Apsara. My mother was the great Tilotamma."

Nik stiffened.

And so did Maya. The girl hadn't been afraid to reveal her identity to them. To tell a pair of complete strangers that she was a heavenly creature bound as a slave to a millionaire art collector. Nik hesitated then glanced at Maya before saying, "You took a huge chance revealing that to us." He was still hedging.

Archana shook her head, her expression confident and sure. "No, I didn't. You see, I can tell the difference between a human and a half-god. Being from heaven and all." Maya's eyes went wide but she remained silent. This girl can tell a demigod from a human but surely she can't see that Maya has Kali's powers within her. "Anyway, let's get you two out of here. Once you're in the ballroom the guards won't touch you, although I suggest you be prepared for an audience with Mr. Thakkur. He will want to see the lovebirds, face to face."

Maya shuddered at the thought, but thankfully Archana was

looking at Nik. Again. The Apsara held out her hand and on her palm was a folded piece of paper. Nik took it and opened it. Maya leaned forward to see a telephone number. Instinctively she stiffened, narrowing her gaze at the girl. Why was she giving Nik her number?

Then Archana said, "Please keep my number. It's not every day a demigod walks into this house. You have to find a way to get me out of here, out of this binding. " The look on her face, the desperation, suddenly made Maya want to cry. She couldn't even begin to imagine what the Apsara felt, imprisoned and bound to a man for thirty years. "Please. I don't think I could survive another year trapped with him, let alone another thirty years."

Nik glanced over at Maya and she could see he was on the verge of agreeing to help the girl. Maya nodded and said, "We'll try to help you. Give us some time. We'll find a way to get you free."

The Apsara looked over at Maya and for the briefest moment Maya thought she saw a hint of haughtiness in her eyes. And then it was gone. Archana nodded and walked to the door. "Follow me and say nothing until we reach the ballroom."

They obeyed and followed in silence as she led them through a warren of corridors. Maya was thoroughly lost and very glad to have the Apsara leading them. At last the sound of the party began to grow louder and then they were at the edge of the ball-room which still glittered with guest and chandeliers alike.

Nik glanced at Maya and crooked his elbow, "Shall we?"

"Thank you," she said and took his arm.

He led her down into the crush and bent to whisper, "We'll stick around a few minutes then leave through the front door. We can come back later for the bow."

Maya nodded then grabbed a crab roll from the tray of a passing waiter. She popped it into her mouth, nerves getting the better of her. The roll was delicious and went down fast enough.

Only problem she was now left with oily fingertips. "Damn," she said.

"What's wrong?" asked Nik.

"My finger are oily and I don't want to get any of it on my dress." She raised herself on tiptoe in search of a waiter. The last one had had a small pile of mini-serviettes on his tray but Maya hadn't been fast enough to grab one as he rushed by.

"May I be of assistance, my dear," said a voice at her shoulder.

Maya turned slowly and her stomach twisted. Raj Thakkur stood before her, holding out a much needed paper towel.

"Oh, thank you so much," she gushed her thanks, hoping her bright smile convinced him she welcomed his company.

While she wiped her hand he held his out to Nik and said, "Rajiv Thakkur. A pleasure to meet you."

"Nikhil Malhotra," Nik shook his hand, his smile looking so genuine Maya almost believed it.

Almost.

Then Thakkur turned his attention to Maya and said, "And this must be the beautiful Mrs. Maya Malhotra."

Maya wanted to die laughing at the ridiculous monstrosity of a name but instead she gave a husky laugh and said, "Guilty as charged Mr. Thakkur. Although I have to admit I have only had the pleasure of the name for a few days. Nikhil and I are newly-weds." She glanced at her *husband* and sent him a seductive smile.

Nikhil held out his hand and Maya took it, a move Thakkur didn't miss.

"Ah, so that would explain it," Thakkur nodded but when Maya frowned he didn't elaborate. Then he gave them a slight bow, "I do hope you enjoy the rest of your evening, Mr. and Mrs. Malhotra." And with that he turned and disappeared into the undulating shoal.

As he departed Maya let out a pent up breath. She gripped Nik's arm, uncaring that her nails threatened to rip into the tailored suit fabric. "Let's get the eff out of here."

"What's wrong." he asked as they turned to the staircase.

"I think we made a mistake bringing you with us. Joss and I should have come alone and we should have had you outside just in case," Maya said, lifting her skirts as she took the stairs.

"What do mean, Maya?" he stopped her at the top of the stairs but she pulled him along toward the front door.

"He made you. He knows what you are." She ground the words out between clenched teeth.

"How do you know that?"

"You know those bloody vials you made me taste?" When Nik nodded she continued, "Well, he's a demon. A Rakshasa. A very, very, very powerful Rakshasa. And a bloody Rakshasa with freaking powerful glamor." Maya's voice shook as they headed outside into the warm night.

Somehow the odor of the Mumbai night was infinitely more preferable than the air conditioned air inside the Rakshasa mansion.

CHAPTER 36

As soon as they got outside Nik and Maya hurried down the driveway, their shoes crunching on the loose driveway gravel. They ignored the car guy and walked down the road in the dark. The second they rounded the first corner Nik transported them straight into his room.

"Are you okay?" he asked, holding her shoulders gently.

She didn't answer. Instead she said, "He made you. He knows."

Nik shook her by the shoulder. "Don't worry about that right now. We're out and safe. And nothing stops us from trying again." Then he shook her again. "Okay?" he asked.

She just nodded and gave him a weak smile.

They headed for the door and Nik hovered at the shoulder as Maya dug into her bag for the card key. He watched until she shoved the door and entered her room.

As soon as the door shut behind them, Maya heard Ria's voice. She glanced back at Nik who seemed to have heard Ria too. He kissed Maya gently on the cheek, rubbing her chin with his thumb. Then her slipped outside as quietly as he could. Maya held the door open for a moment then let it swing shut on its own, announcing her arrival with a whoosh and a click of the lock.

The voices went silent almost immediately and only when Maya walked into the room did she realize why.

Ria sat on the bed beside Joss who was holding her hand. Both girls had tears in their eyes and Ria had a black eye that made Maya's own face throb with empathy.

Maya breathed slowly as she sat beside Ria, "What happened?" She asked softly but what she really wanted to do was to scream and rant. She knew what had happened. Viren had hurt Ria. But for now she had to force herself to calm down and listen for Ria's sake.

"Somehow he suspected I'd been out of the room. I have no idea how."

"Did he find our room key?" asked Maya keeping her tone soft. She didn't want to upset Ria by sounding accusatory.

Ria shook her head. "No. He didn't touch my personal stuff. He was yelling about how he can never trust me. And said a few disgusting things, like I was a slut and there was only one thing I was good for. And then he started to hit me."

Joss shook her head then stood up and walked to the window. "Show her," she said as she stared out at the water, her voice dead.

Ria looked at Joss and hesitated, then she stood up and reached for the hem of the long overdress of her salwar kameez. Underneath, the drawstring pants was loosely tied and hung sadly on Ria's jutting hipbones.

Maya could see why she hadn't dared to tied the pants tighter. Her abdomen was adorned with blue and purple bruises. "How can you even walk with those injuries?" asked Maya. Ria let go of her clothing and looked up. And Maya saw the fresh bruises on her neck. The marks of fingers that had tried and failed to strangle her friend. "Oh, Ria." Maya's eyes filled with tears but they weren't sad ones. Vile fury filled her and she clenched her fists. She felt the burn in her palms and ignored it.

"Maya." Joss called her, a hint of warning in her voice.

When Maya glanced at her, irritated, she saw that Joss was looking at her hands and realized how close she'd come to showing Ria her true power. She forced herself to calm down, to breath and tamp the fire back down. But she couldn't do anything about her anger. "I want to kill that bastard," she said, her voice vibrating with pure fury.

Ria laughed. "He's gone. No idea where. He left me in the room and grabbed his coat then left. That was just after lunch. I was unconscious for some of the time and when I woke up I figured it would be better to get the hell out of there before he got back. I took the stairs just in case."

"Smart thinking," said Maya, pointing at the bed. "Sit. You don't look strong enough to stand." Ria obeyed and for a moment Maya a felt ashamed. Viren would have ordered Ria around as well and Maya had just done the same thing. "Right so we need to get you out of the hotel without anyone seeing you."

"Easy enough," said Joss. When Maya and Ria looked at her she stalked stiffly to the closet and grabbed one of the Burqas Nik had gotten them. "This should do."

"Brilliant," said Maya, nodding. "You can wear that and leave the hotel. We can't be seen with you so you'll have to leave alone but we can sort that out soon enough. For now I need to make a call."

"Maya, who are you calling?" Ria asked her voice filled with panic and tears.

"Don't worry, it's just my Mom. I'm sure she'll know exactly what to do and where we can take you."

"You can't tell her, Maya."

Maya paused and glanced at her friend. Seeing the fear flickering in Ria's eyes she said, "Please. You have to trust me. If it will make you feel better I won't tell her who you are." Ria nodded and gave Maya a weak smile.

Maya pulling her phone from her pocket and called up her

mom's number. She paced the floor, waiting for her mom to answer, praying they wouldn't already be on their plane.

And sighed with relief when Leela answered on the third ring.

"Maya, honey how are you all doing?" Her moms voice sounded weak and tinny.

"Not time to chat, Mom. Sorry."

"Okay, what do you need?" her mom replied all brisk and businesslike.

"I need a place to send someone. We met a friend here in Mumbai and we need to get her somewhere safe where her husband won't find her."

"Is she being abused?"

"Yes. Badly." Short and to the point.

"You can send her to the mountains, to the compound. They take many women who need safety and hope," said her mom. And for a moment Maya thought she heard a strange hitch in her voice, but she brushed the thought from her mind.

"That will be fine. Text me the address and we'll send here there ASAP."

"Why don't you wait for us, we're catching our flight in two hours. Can she wait for us to take her?"

"I'll make sure she waits. We'll have to figure a way to get her out of here without her being seen with us. We have a Burqa she can wear, but Joss and I can't be seen with her. Or Nik."

"Okay. We'll figure it out when we get there," said her Mom, the calm and comfort in her voice coming through the connection and settling over Maya like a warm blanket. "How is everything going there?"

"We hit a small snag but it's nothing major."

There was slight pause as her mom spoke with someone in the background. "Dad, says hello and be careful."

Maya laughed. "Same to you, Dad."

Her mom rang off and Maya sat next to Ria. "My parents are

coming to Mumbai. They have seats on a flight leaving in a couple of hours. They should be here tomorrow."

"But Maya. They know me." Ria shook her head. "No. No, I don't want them to see me like this."

"Then, that's fine Ria, they won't see you," Maya kept her tone soothing and soft as she held Ria around the shoulders. "Wear the Burqa and just don't remove it while they're here."

Ria looked doubtful, her eyes searching Maya's face for something. Eventually she gave in and nodded. "I'm trusting you. I don't want them to know this happened to me."

"Ria. You do know this is nothing to be ashamed of, don't you? He did this to you. You don't deserve anything he's done to you."

Ria laughed. The sound bitter and harsh. "He didn't just abuse me. He used me too. Now, nobody will want to marry me."

Maya stared at Joss, horrified and unsure of what to say. It made sense though. Ria never mentioned a chaperon and usually an unmarried couple never went anywhere without someone to ensure the girl's honor.

"Oh, don't worry. He made sure it was all legitimate. We were married at the local courthouse as soon as he knew he was coming to Mumbai. My father couldn't have cared less. And my mother, well of course she wouldn't have been allowed to say anything. We were legally married before we left the States so that's all they cared to know."

"And here? Do his parents not care about your well-being?"

Ria shrugged. "His mother is probably in the same position as I am. The most they did was send a doctor to make sure I was one some sort of contraception. Which of course I'd have to stop once the wedding is over. Can't do anything to prevent the babies from coming." Ria laughed again and then she started to cry.

And Maya wanted to cry with her. Instead she swallowed her own tears and just held Ria while she shed hers.

After a few moments, she patted Ria's back. "Wanna have a soak in the tub? Or a hot shower?"

Ria smiled. "A soak sounds good."

"Hungry?" When Ria hesitated Maya said, "We didn't each much so I'm going to order something from room service. Look at the menu and pick something. You need to eat."

"And there is one other thing I think we need to do," said Joss

"What's that?"

"We need photos." Joss looked at Ria, sadness clear in her eyes.

Ria stared at her, all emotion and color draining from her already pale face. "No way. I'm not allowing you to do that."

Maya nodded and turned to her. "I think it's a good idea. Then you have proof of what happened."

"No." Her response was short and sharp, meant to end the conversation but Maya wasn't done. Even when she saw the glint of tears in Ria's eyes.

"Okay, fine. So what happens if they find you here? Kill you and bury you body out in the desert. How does anyone ensure that he gets punished if something were to happen to you or to us?"

"Maya," Joss admonished, shocked at her audacity.

"No, Joss, Maya has a point." Ria sighed as she looked at Maya. "You're right. We need some sort of insurance." She got to her feet and began to undress, pulling the long top of her salwar kameez over her head.

Joss and Maya were much more comfortable taking their clothes off around each other but Ria had always been on the shy side. So, watching their friend disrobe was a strange experience especially when her bare skin revealed the extent of her suffering.

She stood there in her plain white underwear and said, "This is the best you're getting. I am not stripping." She gave them a wry smile, and Maya loved her even more for her strength in the face of dealing with this horror.

Maya stood and said, "I don't think you will need to go as far as that. You ready?" she asked as she got out her phone. Ria nodded although her face remained pale, putting the purple bruises on her cheek and eye into start contrast. "Okay, turn around. Let's start with the back." Maya instructed, thinking it would be better to ease Ria into the pictures.

Ria obeyed and turned away and Maya snapped a few pictures of her bare back and thighs, patterned with bruises and marks. "Okay, turn back when you're ready." When she faced her Maya said, "I'm taking pictures of you which include your face. We need to prove these images are really of you and having your face in the picture is important. Are you ready for this?"

For a moment a stricken look crossed Ria's face and Maya waited, giving her friend as much time as she needed. In the end, it was Ria's decision to make. Ria looked from Maya to Joss and then back again. Then she nodded, although her eyes filled with tears. Joss handed her a tissue and Maya waited while she dried her eyes.

Maya took a few pictures of Ria from head to toe, then snapped a few of the specific bruises on her stomach and her throat. It was over quickly and Maya shut the phone off and tucked it into her pocket. "I'll download that to my PC when I get home and we'll know we have the proof just in case."

Ria nodded and gave both her friends a weak smile then headed into the bathroom. They watched her turn on the taps and then return and curl up on the bed to wait for it to fill. The girls chatted about school and home and nothing until the tub filled and Ria headed into the steam engulfed bathroom.

Maya and Joss headed over to Nik's room to give her some privacy.

CHAPTER 37

*N*ik let them in, and went to his jacket which was folded and thrown over the back of an armchair. He withdrew the notepaper containing Archana's number from one of the pockets and stood still for a moment, staring at the green Post-it.

"You calling her?" asked Maya softly, trying her best to keep the hard edge out of her voice. Just the mere thought of the Apsara sent a million icy prickles racing along her skin. There was just something about the girl that Maya couldn't put her finger on.

Nik nodded and didn't seem to notice Maya's misgivings. "She did ask for our help."

"Yeah, but I wouldn't trust her if I were you," Maya said, folding her arms as she sank into the armchair, preferring not to look at him in that moment.

Nik came around and sat on the foot of the bed, just in front of Maya. "You sound jealous," he said, an amused grin curling at his lip.

"Who's Archana? And who is Maya jealous of?" Joss butted in, frowning as she sat beside Nik.

Maya turned to look out the window, leaving Nik to give Joss the rundown of the evenings events. When he fell into silence, Joss snorted. "I agree with Maya. You need to watch yourself. She's sounds like she does have the hots for you."

Nik shook his head, "I really don't think so. She's just desperate to get out of that demon's control."

"The fact that he's a demon doesn't make me feel in the least bit sorry for her. And as a demigod, you sure are pretty naive," said Maya dryly, her narrow eyed gaze never leaving Nik's face. She wasn't planning on making it easy for him.

Joss cleared her throat. "Who is a demon?" she asked looking from Maya to Nik and back again.

"The rich guy. Thakkur," answered Nik, scrubbing his scalp leaving his hair standing up at a hundred odd angles. Just seeing that gesture calmed Maya down a little. Their relationship was complicated but she was sure they could figure things out eventually. At least that's what she told herself. And yet the hard, tight feeling in the pit of her stomach didn't disappear. She refused to consider what that meant.

"You're kidding." Joss stared at them eyes wide.

"Nope," said Maya. "And he's powerful and knows enough magic to ward himself. But when he got close, I knew. Guess his magic doesn't work on humans with the taste for demon blood."

Joss shudder, "Yuk. Did you have to remind me of your blood-sucking proclivities. That's walking a very thin line, Maya. A very thin line." Joss shook her head, a sad look on her face and Maya just laughed.

Then she turned to Nik. "Maybe you should call her. She might be able to give us information about the bow."

Nik nodded. "But, I do think we need to wait. Let's sneak in and try to get the bow out of the mansion. Once we have it safe we don't have to worry about losing it."

"I agree. Let's go. We'll call her as soon as we get back."

"And I guess I'm staying here?" asked Joss, her cheeks pink.

"You need to stay here for Ria. What if that asshole husband of hers comes looking for her? Go back to our room and don't answer the door for anyone. We'll come directly into the room but we'll stay near the door so we don't scare the hell out of Ria. Keep the chain on the door and keep your Madu's close in case you need to defend her." Joss nodded as Maya spoke, her face serious as she realized, just as Maya did, that Ria's situation is not a small problem. "Look at it this way - you can used you Madus on a real live candidate.

Jess nodded, definitely comforted by the possibility of skinning Viren herself.

Maya hesitated, then looked at Nik. He put a hand on her shoulder, "We won't be long. We know exactly where the bow is."

"Okay, let's go and get this done with." He held out his hand. As Maya took it Joss was already walking out of Nik's room.

THEY DISINTEGRATED and reappeared in the study beside the room holding the bow. What they hadn't expected was for the room to be occupied.

Two men sat in the armchairs in front of the desk. Both turned around as Maya and Nik materialized.

They rose shoving the armchairs out of their way. Maya's nose filled with the odor of the two Rakshasa's as they came at her and Nik. The first demon pounced at Maya, an almost feral look in his eyes. Maya lifted her hand, undulating her palm, the movement pulling the fire from her solar plexus. Then she turned her palm toward the demon and let him have it. A fireball erupted from her hand and went straight for the approaching demon. The white flame hit him in the gut, spurting wider, embedding themselves into his abdomen.

The expression on his face went from feral to confused, a transition that made Maya want to laugh out loud. Instead she pulsed more power into another ball of fire and let it loose. It hit the demon in his chest. The shock of the second impact made him go still, the veins in his neck stiffening as he instinctively resisted the power of the fire. A soft golden shimmer appeared beneath his skin, the fire scorching him from inside. When his eyeballs began to glow Maya let out a sigh of relief.

For this particular demon it was over.

A glance over at Nik's opponent showed he was in a similar boat, about ten seconds away from biting the dust.

There was a faint pop and Maya's demon disappeared in an explosion of glowing embers and slowly disappearing flames. Nik's demon followed suit and then it was just Maya and Nik facing the door into the next room. They moved together and Nik cracked it open. When he stiffened, Maya glanced up at his face, frowning.

"Something is wrong." He spoke softly, so quietly Maya almost didn't hear him. She paused at his elbow and peered into the room. The bow sat on a long table, glittering in the soft yellow light of the three lamps in the room.

"What is is?" whispered Maya.

"It's a bow. It's not the real thing."

"No heavenly GPS?"

"Not a single vibration."

"So we're in trouble?"

"Pretty much."

"Let's get out of here then."

But before Maya could grab Nik's hand the main door to the hallway was flung open and three more demons entered. They ran at Nik and Maya giving them no time to take stock of the situation. Maya sent off two blasts of fire, both connecting to two of the demons. They were flung backwards, but only one landed on his butt, sitting there fire-dazed.

The other stumbled, then regained his footing. He ran to Maya, his eyes glowing red, arms outstretched. His fingernails turned into blades and stretched out in front of him. Maya flashed back to the first time she'd seen similar blades on the Amber-demon's fingertips. That day, Amber had almost killed her.

She ducked just in time as the demon swept over her with his wicked-sharp blades. Low on her knees Maya produced a fiery stream of heat sending it straight into the demon's stomach. He backed off, springing into a backward somersault and landing in a low crouch a few feet away from her. This demon was stronger, smarter than the last two they'd encountered. But Maya was confident her fire won't let her down.

She sent another fireball at him and then had to turn her attention to the second demon who had though it a smart move to creep up on her while her attention was elsewhere. Smart enough, but not so smart as he was dealing with the Hand of Kali.

Nik was busy pummeling the life out of the last demon. Maya glanced at the approaching Rakshasa, whose bladed fingers had fierce looking jagged edges. Maya so did not want those anywhere near her. She spun around, planting a roundhouse kick to the middle of his sternum and watched the look of surprise on his face as he fell on his ass a second time. He wasn't as shocked as Maya though, as she hadn't expected the move to be completed so effortlessly, and with such power.

More confident now, she waited as the first demon came at her again. This time she glanced around for a weapon, her eyes alighting on a ceremonial dagger. Straight and thin, it looked European in origin, maybe French. It lay on a pedestal just a foot to her right. She grabbed it, the rounded, twisting pommel more suited to fencing than dealing with demons but for Maya's purposes it would do.

She called her fire, sending it spiraling into her fingers and surging into the tip of the metal. The dagger glowed with the heat of the flame but neither Maya not the demon paid attention. He simply ran at her, his ego slashed to bits having had to retreat from the fire produced by a girl and a human at that. In his ferocity he was careless, didn't consider a possibly that the dagger would be fatal.

Only when Maya sidestepped as he barreled at her and buried the glowing dagger in his side did he take the time to look at the weapon. For him it was too little too late. The hilt of the dagger remained outside his body, the pulsing fiery blade burned deep inside his flesh. Maya could see the glow through his skin and from the way he stiffened she knew he could see it too.

Pretty.

And deadly.

She looked back at the second demon, leaving the first to die slowly at her feet. She stepped over him but shouldn't have bothered. It took mere seconds before the body disintegrated into nothing, the dagger clattering to the stone floor, free from the constraint of dying demon flesh.

Glaring at him, she saw the moment of hesitation in his eyes as he glanced at the door. Escaping wasn't the plan, though. She squatted and grabbed the dagger from the floor where it lay in a small pile of black embers.

The demon gave the door one last desperate look and launched himself at the exit. Maya caught him in the middle of the back with the glowing dagger. A stream of fire remained attached to the pommel as she continued to send Kali's flame deep into the demon's body.

Seconds later, he exploded into a thousand orange and black flecks. Followed closely by Nik's demon, who stared at the demigod, a strange confused look on his face as the rest of him stood in place, a charred body topped by a conscious and aware head. And then with a puff he disintegrated into dust.

Nik dusted his fingers and Maya stared at the dagger in her hand. "They would have caught that on their cameras. We should get out of here."

"Yeah, nothing to see but a fake."

Maya grabbed Nik's hand as he disappeared. She felt the whoosh, the odd sense of being sucked into a pool of darkness.

AND THEN THEY materialized in the girl's room beside the front door. Maya moved slowly into the room to see Joss on her phone while Ria lay unmoving on the bed, fast asleep.

"She's been out for a while now," Joss whispered.

"Not surprising considering what she'd been through," Maya answered.

"So did you get the bow?"

Nik and Maya both shook their head and Maya flushed with the disappointment of the whole evening. "It wasn't there. They put a fake in its place."

"That was quick," Joss answered, her eyebrow raised.

"Exactly what I was thinking," said Maya. Then she looked at Nik. "Call her. There is still a chance that she could be innocent. We need to know where the real bow is and she's our only lead right now."

Nik nodded and typed the number into the keypad. He waited as the phone rang then made a face and cut the call. "No answer."

Maya wasn't so sure. "Wait. If she really wants to make contact with us she'd be watching her phone. If she couldn't answer she'll make the time to get back to you."

And sure enough, a few minutes late Nik's phone buzzed. "She's sent a text." Maya had to shake her head at the incongruity of a texting Apsara.

Moments slipped away and both Maya and Joss stared at Nik with raised eyebrows. "What does she want?" asked Maya, keeping her voice hushed.

"It's just an address and a time. The Mall down the road."

"What if its a trap?"

"That's why I go alone."

"We can't let you do that," Maya protested, her voice raised a little too loud. She glanced at Ria but the poor girl hadn't stirred.

"Maya, I can leave the mall whenever I want. How can they stop me?"

"Are there any spells that they can use on you? To bind you?"

Nik shook his head. "No, I haven't heard of anything that could bind a god or a demigod for that matter. You can create a ward to keep something in or out. But I didn't see how or why they would ward an entire five floor mall. He can't have that much power."

"Are you sure?" Nik nodded and that left Maya unsure if further protests would be worth the effort. It was true he could just beam out of there if things got dangerous. "Okay, fine. But don't go taking any chances. If it is a setup just get the hell out of there."

"Yes ma'am," he said giving her a small salute.

Maya made a face as he disappeared.

CHAPTER 38

*N*ik reappeared after half an hour.

A half hour that had almost driven Maya insane. Even when she asked herself if she was jealous of Nik being alone with the beautiful Apsara, Maya couldn't answer truthfully.

When he appeared, going from liquid and shimmer to solid, Joss and Maya both stared at him, waiting patiently.

"So?" asked Joss. Maya hadn't trusted her voice to ask the question.

"She confirmed they moved the real one. She gave me the address of its new location."

"But the question is do you trust her?" asked Maya.

"Can we do anything else right now but trust her? If the bow really is where she says it is, then we need to trust her. If only just for the bow."

Maya sighed. "I guess you're right. But let's just be clear on this. I don't think we should trust her so keep a close eye on her. I just think it was way too convenient that she was the one to release us, and that she's asking us to help free her." Maya frowned. "Are we going to help her escape?"

"I think we should. She might be of help."

"And she may just be a mole and be feeding information to her boss all along. He's a very powerful Rakshasa. So powerful I almost threw up when he touched me."

"When did he touch you?" Nik asked, his voice rough.

"When he passed me the serviette. His fingers touched mine. And believe me it's an experience I'd prefer not to relive, thanks." Maya shuddered, hiding a smile at Nik's reaction. She loved when he got all protective and possessive over her.

Within limits, of course.

Before he could say anything, a loud knock sounded on their door. Maya and Joss jumped, Nik whirled around and Ria sat up in the bed, fear marring her features.

"Open up," a voice rang loudly at the door.

Nik stepped forward but Maya held his arm, pointing at his room with her thumb. "Are you sure?" Nik asked, but Maya was willing to risk Ria finding out that Nik had powers. She nodded and walked closer to the door.

"Who is it?"

"It's the concierge Madam. And a Mr. Viren Sen. He believes you are harboring his wife." Maya glanced over her shoulder and watched as Nik held his hand out to Ria. "Go with him," she whispered.

Ria looked at Maya, a worried expression twisting her brow but she took Nik's hand and with a gasp disappeared into thin air.

With Ria safely out of the room, Maya went to the door and opened it. "I'm sorry but we haven't seen Ria since the other night when we saw her at dinner." Maya decided to go with her version of the truth.

Outside, Viren stood with his arms folded, his face red and mottled with anger and no doubt alcohol too. "I don't believe her. I want to see the room."

"I don't think you have any right to come into my room without a warrant."

Viren laughed coldly. "Don't worry. I'll show you a warrant soon enough if you don't let us inside. His eyes flashed, and there was a coldness that Maya saw there that chilled her blood. Now she wished she'd never seen the Viren that Ria saw on a daily basis. This person was capable of far worse than just physical abuse.

The concierge stepped toward the door. "I apologize for the inconvenience Madam, it would make things much easier for all of us if you would allow the gentleman to look for his wife."

Maya looked at the man's face and figured he was afraid too. The way his eyes darted in Viren's direction made Maya worry about what Viren would do if he came inside and found the room empty. "I'm not opening the door until you get the manager here."

"I assure you the manager is on his way Madam."

"Then that's fine. I'm not letting this man into my room without protection. What if he hurts us?" I glanced at Viren, noting the purpling of his skin as his anger was fueled by my delay.

The concierge didn't need to answer. Footsteps from the direction of the elevator made them turn and watch the bulky figure of the hotel night manager as he waddled his way toward us. He had a security guard with him and I wondered who the thin-faced was there to protect. The manager stopped in front of Maya's door and mopped his sweaty brow with his already sodden handkerchief.

"Good evening, Madam." He squinted at Maya as she peered thought he partially open door. "I'm so sorry for the disturbance."

"Miss Rao was waiting for you to arrive before she allowed Mr. Sen to enter the room."

"Ah, you will allow him to check the room?" asked the manager, pippin his head out hopefully.

"Of course. I have nothing to hide. I was concerned for my safety and that of my friend. Mr. Sen looks very angry." And though she didn't say it she could see that both the concierge and the Manager could hear the unsaid words 'and he looks very drunk'.

"Thank you very much for you cooperation, Miss Rao."

Maya merely nodded stiffly and closed the door to removed the chain. The moment she opened the door Viren charged past her, shocking her aside and slamming the door against the wall so hard Maya flinched.

He growled as he entered the room then glanced around into the bathroom. Maya followed and watched and he stalked to the closed toilet door. He flung it open and then whirled around. "Where are you hiding her?" The words were a shriek. He look ready to burst a blood vessel. Then he straightened and smiled, the grin cold and knowing as he nodded at Maya. "I know where they are keeping her."

Neither the concierge nor the manager asked where. They just stared at Viren patiently waiting for his next words. Maya wondered if it was trepidation or were they working for him?

"The boy. The one who is here with them."

"Nik's room is next door, "said Joss from where she stood beside the bed. She was glaring at Viren as if she wanted nothing better than to gouge his eyes out. He gave her a cursory glance and immediately dismissed her.

He turned to the manager. "I want to see that room as well."

"Mr. Sen, I'm not sure what we are doing is withing the regulations of the hotel," the manager stuttered then flinched as Viren stepped in toward his face.

"You will let me into his room." Viren growled the words, making the manager gasp for air.

I cleared my throat. "I'm sure Nik won't mind if it will assure Mr. Sen that we are not harboring his wife in our rooms."

The manager sighed with relief then turned on his heel and maneuvered his bulk out of the room. Viren walked past Maya, giving her a cold glare.

Maya shut the door as they headed to Nik's room. Joss was

already on the phone with Nik. He appeared in seconds with a very pale Ria, then disappeared to answer his door. The knocking was so loud the three girls could hear it in their room. Then there was silence for a long while.

A silence that ended with Viren stamping out of Nik's room yelling about hiding Ria somewhere and that he'd better not find out we were keeping him from her.

Nik appeared soon after that and the four of them stood in a the girl's room in silence.

Ria was the first to speak, "Can someone please tell me what just happened?" she asked, her gaze going from Nik to Maya to Joss, like a fluttering sparrow, unsure where to land.

Maya cleared her throat. "Nik has the power to transport himself from place to place."

"What? Like a teleporting power or something."

"Exactly like that," answered Maya.

"Oh." Ria sank onto the bed as if her legs refused to hold her weight any longer.

"Are you okay?" Maya asked, stepping toward her.

Ria laughed and glanced up at Maya, "A guy just saved my ass from my violent husband and he did it by teleporting me between two rooms. Sure I'm okay. Why wouldn't I be? Happens everyday, right?" She ended on a sharp, high note that made Maya wonder if she was about to freak out. Nik, Joss and Maya remained standing, unsure of what Ria was going to do.

"Don't worry guys. I'm not going to get hysterical."

"You're okay with it?"

"How could I not be? Nik saved me from Viren," she stared at Maya as if Maya were nuts to even ask.

Maya and Joss sighed in relief.

"I think it's time we all got some sleep," said Maya. "Who knows what tomorrow will bring."

"You girls will manage here with just the one bed?"

"Yup, we've had years of training," said Joss

"Training?" asked Nik, confused.

"It's an exclusive thing, invite only. It's called sleepovers." Joss arched and eyebrow.

Maya and Ria cracked up while Joss tried hard to keep a straight face.

"Very funny," said Nik, laughing. "Right. I'm headed to get some sleep. First thing in the morning, we head out."

Maya saluted but Nik had already disappeared.

THE NEXT MORNING the girls rose early, with Maya and Joss dressing in the same clothing from the day before. They handed the Burqa to Ria who made a face. "Not looking forward to being closed up inside of this thing."

"At least you will be safe."

"Point taken," said Ria. Then she studied the two girls. "So where are you two headed? Come to think of it you never said what you were doing here at all. And without your parents."

"We're off to see a temple this morning. And we came early to see the Mumbai sights. My parents are arriving soon."

Ria nodded, evidently satisfied by Maya's explanation.

"Do I come to see the temple or stay and wait for you parents?"

Maya shared a glance with Ria and in that moment made the decision. "You will have to come with us. What if we left you alone and Viren barges inside the room. Without Nik to beam you out Viren will take you with him."

Ria stared as Maya spoke, clearly she hadn't thought of the possibility. Then she cleared her throat. "I'm coming with you." She drew the black garment over the overly long top of her salwar kameez. Soon she was hidden within the safety of black fabric.

"Right, let's get Nik and get out of here." Maya knocked on the wall between the two rooms and Nik appeared beside her.

"Ready to go?"

"Yes. And Ria has to come with us."

Nik gave her a short nod. "I agree. We can't leave her alone. And Joss may not be enough protection even if we left her with Ria."

"I can protect her," Joss insisted, although the flicker of doubt in her eye confirmed she still had a healthy respect for Viren's penchant for violence.

"Not if he comes with his cousins and uncles. Then who knows what will happen to you," said Ria her face serious and worried.

"Right, seems we are all going. And maybe we should split up. Joss and Ria, you take a taxi to the temple, I'll transport Maya there. So all they will see is two women off to see a temple."

Joss stood up and headed to the closet. Maya glanced back at her curious. Joss returned with the second Burqa. She dusted it out and said, "Let's get dressed and get out of here."

They waited only until Joss was dressed. "Right you and Ria leave the room and head to the lobby. Go straight outside and request a public taxi. That way the hotel won't know where you are going. Only tell the driver once you get inside the taxi and close the door. Make sure the hotel staff don't hear you. We will meet you at the hotel."

Joss nodded and took Ria's hand. They left the room and Maya's stomach tightened as she watched them go. What if something happened to them? And now they had Ria involved. Just her knowledge of Nik's powers could be dangerous.

CHAPTER 39

Maya stopped worrying about Joss and Ria long enough for Nik to transport her to the temple.

They stood to one side as a group of people walked thorough the buildings front entrance. The girls were all dressed in matching outfits made of red and gold silk, their faces made up, eyes lined thickly with Kohl. Their hair was bedecked with flowers and jewels. At the head of the procession a man played on the drums, a steady beat that was quite entrancing. The girls passed, the bells on their ankles jingling as they stepped elegantly forward, heel to toe, heel to toe. The troupe disappeared into the darkness and soon the sound of music and bells drifted to them.

The sun beat down on them and Maya felt a drop of perspiration glide down her neck and down her spine. The smell of the street engulfed them, sweat from the crowds, incense and frankincense from the temple and a stench that screamed the lack of adequate toilets. Maya wrinkled her nose and shook her head.

She would never pretend to understand this country.

Nik nudged Maya as a taxi drew up. The black sedan grunted to a stop and Joss and Ria got out, keeping a sedate pace. They were still dressed in their Burqas, their faces hidden from view. A few people threw them some odd looks but the girls pretended not to see.

They stopped in front of Nik and Maya, Joss asking, "Where's the ladies?"

Maya shrugged, "Probably at the back of the temple. Sorry, no idea." She couldn't see any signs announcing the existent of toilets and hoped the girls would be able to find it fast.

Joss shook her head, but Maya couldn't tel if it was annoyance with her or just frustration. Joss held onto Ria and the girls headed for the far end of the temple structure and disappeared into the throng of bodies. Maya paced until they returned five minutes later with flowers in their hair.

Joss grinned and gave the white flowers a little toss. "Aren't they cute?" she asked with a grin.

Maya smiled and shook her head, feeling like a parent watching a child achieve a milestone. "Right, let's get inside. Too many people here right now."

"Too many people can be a good thing," Joss said hurrying behind her.

"Not for what we want to do."

"Right. I hadn't thought of that."

They kept their shoes on as they walked into the temple, intending to remain a good distance from the area relegated to prayer and obeisance. As soon as they entered the building they moved to the right beyond the ropes guiding the worshipers toward the statues seated in various alcoves along the far wall.

Their eyes adjusted too slowly to the darkness. They were jostled by the crowd as they made their way further into the temple, keeping to the right of the crowd who were gathered before the main deities in the large hall. Numerous stone pillars dotted the large space disappearing into the densely dark pyramid type roof.

Maya shuddered as she stared up into the darkness, imaging all the things that could be living in there. Snakes, rats, bats. Bats.

Maya brushed her hair with her hand and pulled it over her shoulder to the side. She cringed at the thought of having a bat struggling within the strands of her hair, caught and unable to fly off. Do bats have claws? She tried to recall the anatomy of the bat, taught by her biology teacher the previous year but nothing came to her mind.

A finger was jabbed into her back and Maya spun around, immediately on the defensive.

"Maya, keep moving. What the heck are you staring at?" Joss hissed the question in her ear.

Maya glared at her and pointed to the dark recesses of the roof. "What do you think is up there?"

"What? You're afraid of whatever could be living up in the temple roof?" Joss laughed so loud she had to immediately cover her mouth with her hand. Then she spoke slowly and calmly. "Maya, whatever lived up in that roof cannot harm you. Unless the bats breathe fire and the rats poop fire pellets and even then you could probably incinerate them all with a flick of a hand."

Maya would have laughed if Ria hadn't spoked. "What do you mean Maya can incinerate them?"

Joss grabbed Ria's arm and pulled her along. "Nothing, just trying to stop Maya from being a scaredy cat. How far will the girl go in life if she imagines bats in every shadow?" Joss snorted then threw Maya a warning glare over Ria's shoulder.

As they reached Nik, Maya stiffened. He'd stopped at the edge of the large hall beside an entrance leading to an unlit passage. He wasn't alone. Joss and Ria slowed down so Maya could catch up. Joss gave Maya a questioning glance. "Archana?" she asked.

Maya nodded. "Yes. I didn't know she was meeting us here." Her voice was tight, and suspicious.

"From Nik's face it seemed he didn't know either," said Joss tilting her head at Nik. Maya had to agree. He didn't look particularly welcoming either but Maya couldn't be sure if he didn't want to be around the Apsara or if he felt uncomfortable with

Maya seeing them together. Whatever the case was Maya didn't like the situation.

"Wait here," she said to Joss and Ria. Then she walked ahead and stopped in front of Nik and Archana. She turned slightly to Archana, who smiled at her, her expression clear and unassuming. Maya returned the smile as pleasantly as possible, her eyes taking in the deep red and gold formfitting churidar. The blouse fitted the shape of the Apsara's body, leaving little to the imagination from shoulders to bust to hips. The top flared out at the hips and filled out into a rich skirt, the hem ending in a gold panel at mid calf. The pants hugged her calves and ankles in the same sexy figure-hugging way.

Maya tried to bury the tendrils of jealousy that rose within her, if only to ensure the Apsara did not see her reaction. "It's lovely to see you, Archana. I didn't know you were joining us."

"I'm sorry. I know I came unannounced, but Mr. Thakkur wanted me to check on the bow so I came. I was hoping I could leave with you."

"I'm not sure. Will it be that easy to get away from him? And what about the spell that binds you? How do we break it?"

Archana's smiled disappeared and Maya almost felt bad for her. "I'm sorry. I didn't think it through very well. All I could think of was a way to leave him." She fell into silence for a moment then brightened. "I could still leave with you and hide out until we find someone to break the spell."

"Where would we hide you that he won't find you? Can't he just summon you and you will have to go to him?"

"I'm an Apsara, not a genie." Arcana smiled condescendingly, and Maya tried not to flush. She'd seen the flicker of cold in the Apsaras eyes and was now more sure than ever that Archana couldn't be trusted. She had to force herself to pay attention to what she was saying. "I am able to go where I please, only the binding spell allows him to find me wherever I am. But, there are places I can hide. One of the heavenly realms should do."

"So you are asking us to take you one of the heavenly realms?" asked Nik. Maya noticed he'd kept his tone even and unaffected but she could tell something was up from the cool detachment in his eyes.

Archana nodded and tilted her head to look up at him, giving him the full effect of her heavily-lashed light brown almond shaped eyes and her full pink lips. No doubt she thought she had him because most men would fall at her feet when faced to such beauty.

But not Nik.

His expression remained unchanged as he looked at the Apsara and Maya was pleased to see the small frown that appeared on Archana's perfect brow. Now she knew she didn't have Nik in the palm of her hands. The girl's jaw tightened and Maya knew they had to keep a close eye on her.

"Let me see what I can do. But remember, I can't promise anything. And you have to be prepared for an answer you may not like." Nik's voice remained even, and emotionless.

Maya frowned, "You mean there is a chance they could refuse to help her?" She was entire without heart, The Apsara may genuinely need help.

Nik nodded. "Unfortunately, yes. The gods don't just allow anyone asylum. There has to be a good reason to give someone a place in the heavenly realms. In the end, it is up to the gods."

"I see," Maya said. She could see Archana watching her, an odd expression on her face. Maya knew that challenging Nik in front of her would make the girl think that Maya was on her side. Exactly what Maya wanted. "I have to say I don't think that's particularly fair."

"I'm not sure what you mean," Nik's brow creased as he played along.

"If they say no, then what do we do? Just desert her when she needs help?"

"I'm not sure. We'll think of something, Maya. Don't worry."

Nik curled his hand around her waist and pulled her to him, his intent to comfort her clear to the the watching Apsara. Her eyes went to Nik's hand at Maya's waist and face whitened, her jaw tightening almost imperceptibly. "Now, let's get moving. We need to get the bow out of here as soon as possible."

Maya nodded, turning to the silent Apsara. "Do you know where they are keeping it?"

Archana tilted her head and smiled but the expression was flat and lifeless, like her eyes. "I'll show you the way. Follow me." She turned on her heel, the soles of her shoes tapping lightly on the stone floor as the darkness swallowed her up.

Maya glanced back at Joss and found she was already hurrying toward them. "Come. We have to follow her."

"What are we doing here?" asked Ria. Her question was soft but Maya knew she wanted an answer. One that Maya didn't want to give.

"We're here to pick up an artifact for a friend of Maya's father," said Joss as they walked deeper into the tunnel. The walls were dark rock, smoothed and well cared for. Here and there, cracks had formed in the neatly planed rock and Maya's gaze drifted to the ceiling. More gigantic rocks. She shuddered as she looked away from the overhanging rocks. How were they staying up there? Surely gravity would pull them down at some point. And knowing her luck now would probably be the time for it to come crashing down.

Ria's voice brought her back to the conversation. "What exactly is it that you are getting for him?"

"It's a bow. Some kind of ancient artifact."

"And he couldn't pick it up himself?"

"Nope. He couldn't get a passport in time." Maya grinned as she stared straight ahead. Joss was good.

But Ria wasn't giving up that easily. "Surely he could have gotten a bunch of adults to come get it for him."

Maya grinned at Ria over her shoulder. "Well, not everyone can boast the fact they have the ability teleport. It's a handy skill."

"I have to agree with that." A shadow passed over her face, he lips forming a tight line. "How can I ever thank him for saving me?"

"I think he already knows how grateful you are," Maya said softly.

They followed the Apsara deeper and deeper into the temple, turning left at varying intervals. Maya tried to recall the shaped and size of the temple and knew that there was something odd about how far they'd walked. She was about to call out to Nik when she noticed they were traveling on a slight downward slope. That made sense. They were going beneath the temple structure and their path kept to the edge of the temples walls.

For the umpteenth time, Maya wondered if they were doing the right thing following the Apsara. But right now it was too late to think about that as they followed Archana into the darkness.

CHAPTER 40

About eight left turns later Maya's ears began to pop and the ground leveled out quite suddenly. The walls and floor remained unchanged, still tons and tons of grey stone bearing down on them. When Archana took the next left, Maya hurried to follow her. The corridor turned out to be a recessed doorway, the door itself was made of solid rock.

They paused in front of it and stared, perplexed.

"How are we supposed to get past this?" Maya asked staring at the door that rose ten feet into the air.

"I'm not sure," Archana responded although she didn't seem in the least disappointed. "The door was open when I was last here. I did saw where the bow was kept, though."

"What exactly is this place?" asked Maya, her voice echoing around her.

"These subterranean rooms were built beneath the temple centuries ago." Although Archana kept her voice low it still echoed around them as well. "They were used to house the priests and of course the valuable contributions of the people. It used to be considered some of the safest places to store gold and other valuables."

Nik bent to look for a lock but there didn't seem to be one.

"Wouldn't people just break in? It seems fairly easy to get inside," asked Joss, glancing up and down the corridors.

"It is easy when there are no gates and no guard dogs. But in ancient times the people feared their gods. And nobody would ever dare to steal from a temple. That would bring down the wrath of all the gods upon the thief. And few people would dare to take such a risk."

Nik straightened abruptly and looked at Maya. "I'll have to go inside and see what we are up against."

Maya nodded and Nik disintegrated. Just when he was gone for what she thought was too long, he slowly materialized in front of them. "Right. I found the bow. I can take Maya inside to fetch it."

"What about us?" Joss asked. Maya could tell she didn't want to be left alone with Archana. Apparently she wasn't the only one who didn't trust the stunning Apsara.

Maya glanced at Nik and saw he'd already made his decision. He held out a hand to Joss and as she took it Maya noticed the hard look on Archana's face. Whatever her goal was she dislike being thwarted. Too bad, thought Maya. Nik blinked back for Ria and then a few seconds later for Maya. As he took her hand he glanced at Archana. "See you on the inside?" The Apsara raised her eyebrows a fraction. She hadn't expected that Nik would know she could teleport too. But even Maya had suspected that as a heavenly creature she would have the ability to teleport.

If Rakshasa's could then so could Apsaras.

She merely nodded and disappeared as Nik and Maya blinked out. They reappeared at the same time on the inside of the room, blinking against the thick, black darkness. Instinctively, Maya brought her fire to her palm, creating a spinning ball of red and orange flames to her hand.

Ria gasped and Maya doused her fire, cursing her stupidity.

How much longer is she going to be able to hide this from her friend? "What was that?"

"A torch. I tried to light it but it went out. Hang on you guys. I'll get it to work." Maya had seen a metal drum containing half a dozen torches at the entrance of the room.

But, before she could move toward the doorway a subtle light caught her eye. It shimmered in the distance, near the far wall, the light almost fluorescent. Maya walked toward it, and felt Nik beside her.

"You can see it?" he whispered.

She didn't reply, just moved until she stood beside a pedestal, large enough to bear the body of a man. It stood between two columns. Torches hung over the pedestal, ready to provide light to view this beautiful object.

But Maya didn't need the light at all.

Gandiv glowed.

The golden bow gave off a bluish fiery light that flickered and undulated across the surface of the weapon.

"Wow," she said softly as she reached out and touched the bow. The metal felt warm to her touch and when she removed her hand she stared at her fingers presuming it would glow too, almost expecting the blue fire to be some kind of strange glowing residue.

But it was all the bow.

"Maya?" Joss's voice filtered toward them, bringing Maya back to reality. She turned and slowly made her way past the group with Nik close behind her.

She felt her way forward using the tiniest bit of light, ensuring it faced away from the Ria. She reached the pot and grabbed two torches, lighting them quickly with fire from her palm.

She returned as the torches sputtered and spat, getting brighter and burning more fiercely as she reached the group. She handed one torch to Joss and the other to Ria, wanting to ensure her both her own hands were free just in case.

Maya glanced at Nik. "The bow?"

He nodded and pointed to the far end of the room for the whole group to see. The entire space seemed to have been created to store or display objects of value. The four walls contained alcoves filled with items that looked, at a glance, to be extremity old. Floor-to-ceiling stone supports beams dotted the floor providing even more space for alcoves and artifacts. At the very end of the hall an are opened up, uninterrupted by columns.

Again, Maya stood before Shiva's bow, this time with the light of the torches to show her the true beauty of the bow.

Joss and Ria gasped while Archana looked on in silence. Clearly Gandiv was wasted on her.

"Right. No point in wasting any more time," said Nik as he reached for the bow. "The sooner we get it and get out, the better for us all."

Maya nodded and waited like the rest of the group as Nik gripped the bow. He strained to move it, the muscles in his neck bulging with the effort.

"It's not moving." He let go of the bow and gasped for breath. He held on to the edge of the table and gathered his strength. His jaw tightened as he looked at the bow and Maya sensed he was frustrated at his failure.

Archana moved closer. "There are only a few people who have the ability to lift the bow. And even then only one person has the power to string and shoot the bow itself."

Maya met her gaze. "You mean an avatar?" At her nod Maya said, "Well that's fine because we don't need to use it as a weapon. We just need to carry it out of here."

"And what if nobody can lift it?" asked the Apsara, an eyebrow raised pointedly.

Maya was stumped. She glanced at Nik. "Can't you just transport it out of here?"

He shook his head. "Not unless I can carry it. Myself."

"Right, I guess we all need to try our hands at lifting it," she said.

"Me first," said Joss nudging Maya out of the way.

Maya stood beside Ria, watching Joss put her hands beneath each limb of the bow. She flexed her fingers, opening them wide, then closing them over the rounded limb. She rocked slowly from one foot to the next then pulled with all her strength. As with Nik, Maya could see the amount of strength Joss put behind her attempt. Her spine was stiff, the muscles in her neck dangerously tight.

But she also failed to lift the bow even one hairs-breadth off the stone table.

Joss sighed, her shoulders slumping. She stepped back disappointed. At that moment Maya glanced up, straight at Archana and she didn't miss the look of triumph on the girl's face. What was the Apsara up to and where did her loyalties truly lie?

Joss's spoke softly beside her. "Sorry, Maya. No can do." Joss folded her arms, her face still red from her effort, red too from her failure.

Maya patted her shoulder and stepped toward the table. And stared at the bow. This was it. She was their last option. She glanced up at Nik who had moved to the opposite side of the table to watch her. He gave her an encouraging nod.

Maya took a deep breath and moved to rest her hips against the stone table. Her heart knocked against her ribs, an ominous thudding stirring dread in veins. What if she couldn't lift it? If she failed they were pretty much doomed. But she had to try because there was always a chance that she would be able to lift it. Shiva wouldn't have asked her to come if she couldn't even move the bow.

Her hands shook as she placed them beneath each of the bow's limbs, the way Joss had done. She gripped the bow tightly and lifted, putting all her strength behind it. The bow moved and

Maya stumbled back a foot, straight into Joss and Ria. If it hadn't been for them she would have landed flat on her ass.

She froze when she looked down at the bow in her hands. Even though she hadn't expected to move the huge bow of Rama herself, she'd managed to carry it so easily, as if it didn't weight more than her handbag.

The room remained silent as they all stared at Maya and the golden bow she now held in her shaking hands.

"How did you do that?" asked Archana. Her voice held a sharp, almost accusatory, note to it that made all eyes snap to her face.

"What do you mean, Archana?"

The Apsara didn't get the chance to answer. The ground shuddered and began to move, tilting precariously. Maya bent at the knees, trying to maintain her balance while holding tightly onto the bow. Despite her efforts she began to slide along the steep incline.

The entire floor beneath the long table that had so recently held the bow, had shifted. And now, one end of it opened like a ramp sending all five intruders tumbling into the dense blackness below.

CHAPTER 41

They tumbled over each other and landed in a confused heap.

Maya pushed to her feet, careful of Ria and Joss who sat stunned on the cold stone. "You guys hurt?" she asked as she glanced up at the booby trapped floor. Her heart sank as it began to slowly lift, shutting them inside the trap.

"We're fine," said Joss standing and dusting herself off.

Archana got to her feet too, and stared with frustration at the slowly closing trapdoor. She sighed, annoyed as she glanced around, as darkness engulfed her.

"Look at what you did," Archana whined from somewhere in the dark. Maya could no longer see her face to judge what the girl was thinking. All Maya knew was they now had a viper in their midst and they had to be careful. She distrusted the Apsara now more than ever.

And Maya's patience had also worn thin. "How was I supposed to know the floor was rigged? That's something you should have told us." Maya flung the accusation at the Apsara knowing she had a valid point.

"I didn't know anything about the trap," Archana answered defensively but something in the girl's voice made Maya wonder if she really didn't know. Had she been aware she certainly would have kept far enough away from the trick floor so as not to get caught when it slid open. That would make sense as to why she was so pissed off.

A movement beside her alerted her to Nik's presence. "We need light," he whispered in her ear.

Maya nodded, reaching out to create a ball of fire but Nik beat her to it. Half a breath later a ball of white fire floated two inches above his outstretched palm.

Maya glared at him until Ria spoke. "What the hell is that?" asked Ria, staring at Nik open palm. She frowned as her eyes followed the floating ball.

Nik cleared his throat. "Sorry I didn't want to spook you earlier so I let Maya find the torches instead."

Ria's eyebrows shot into her hairline. "You can make fire too?"

"Just a little. I know a few people who are much more powerful than I am," Nik said, a smile curving his lips as he glanced at Maya.

"So what now?" Ria asked. She seemed to accept his powers with such ease that Maya began to wonder if she'd soon get hysterical from the overload. "Can't you just teleport us out of here?"

Nik nodded. "I could take you and Joss out but I won't be able to move Maya while she has the bow. I can only transport what I am able to carry myself."

Maya stared at him, realizing slowly what that meant. If they wanted the bow they needed to find another way for her to get out of there with the bow in her possession.

Easier said than done.

Her concern was interrupted but the beeping of her phone. She tugged it out of her pocket and nodded to herself. "Mom and

Dad have arrived. They're about ten minutes away from the hotel."

"Good," said Nik. "Then I can take Ria straight to the hotel room. I'll take Joss first though. We can't chance leaving Ria alone at any point." Joss looked about to protest but then she closed her mouth. With the Apsara watching Maya couldn't talk to either one of her friends.

Nik held out his hand and waited until Joss grabbed hold. Then he tensed, ready to teleport out of the trap with Joss and return moments later for Ria.

Nothing happened.

Maya waited longer for Nik to disappear and for his light to go out, but still nothing happened. Nik frowned, his confusing only enhanced by the strange bobbing light of his fire.

"What's wrong?" Maya asked, stepping closer to him.

"I can't seem to move out of here," he said frowning and staring at his body as if the explanation lay somewhere in his flesh.

Maya glanced at Archana. "Can't you get out of here too?"

"I can but I won't leave you here alone. Who knows what could happen to you or to the bow."

"Why do you care what happens to the bow. Thakkur won't be in control of you much longer."

"I want to make sure that the bow is returned to its owner."

"That's what I am doing," said Maya. She stiffened wondering what it was that the Apsara was trying to do. "And of course you will get credit for helping us return it if that's what's worrying you."

"I'm not worried about that," she said then turned to examine the cell.

"Then at least try to get out of here. We need to know if there is a reason Nik can't teleport out." Maya's tone made it clear that it wasn't a request but her words seemed to have the required effect on the Apsara. Archana nodded giving Maya a cool glare before she lowered her eyelids, ready to transport herself out of the cell.

Nothing happened.

Archana opened her eyes shaking her head. "It didn't work," she said in disbelief. She stared at her hands in much the same way as Nik had done, then stiffened her muscles as if trying to make another jump. Again she relaxed, frustrated. "It's not working. I'm stuck here too." She growled her anger and glared at the trapdoor above. "This is not supposed to happen."

Nik frowned at Archana's outburst then drew closer to Maya. "We need to get out of here," he said, keeping an eye on Joss and Ria. He walked with Maya the few feet toward the stone wall.

"But how?" Maya asked. "These walls are solid rock." She placed a palm on the stone and felt the age-old solidity of it against her skin.

"You can get through it. Think about your fire," Nik urged softly.

"You mean blast a hole through the wall?" she whispered watching Ria and the Apsara over Nik's shoulder. "But that would reveal what I am to Ria. And to Archana." The latter of the options was the most distasteful.

"We have to take that chance, Maya. It's not as if Archana can leave, even if we asked her to."

"Yeah. She seems to have some kind of agenda that she's not sharing. And I don't trust her at all," she sighed and glanced up at Nik. "Keep your enemies close and all that?"

"I agree." He peered over his shoulder and they both saw that Archana was watching them, a bold challenge in her eyes. He turned back to Maya. "And Ria? Well, someday Ria will have to find a way to deal with the truth about you. And you don't have any choice if someday happens to be today."

Maya considered Nik's words. Ria had already seen Nik teleport, and seen him produce fire from his palms. Despite the tightness in Maya's stomach, she knew she had little choice but to do whatever she could to save them. She would have to deal with the consequences later. "Fine. No time like the present." She glanced at the bow. "I'd love to let you carry the bow but you'll understand if I don't."

"Very funny, Maya." Then he faced the wall. "Let's do it together. I can give you some fire power, But the full power will come from you."

Maya nodded and hefted the bow over her shoulder. The string sang as she moved it against the fabric of her clothing. With Gandiv secure she held her hands out, palms facing the wall. Nik's ball of fire puffed out plunging the room into darkness for a moment. Together, both Nik and Maya sent out individual blasts of fire, focusing the two streams on one point. Heat rushed into the rock and soon the stone wall began to shimmer.

Maya heard the Ria's gasp of shock behind her, and like a coward hoped that Joss would give her a quick explanation before she had to face the music. Especially, since she needed to focus her attention on the wall. She was beginning to tire. Beads of perspiration dripped down her back and her arms began to shiver with the effort.

The glow from the dual fires lit up Nik's profile and she saw he was tiring too, and not for the first time she realized how much more powerful she was then her demigod boyfriend. She'd always assumed he had more power than she did but looking at him now she accepted how wrong she'd been. Just a short time of concentrated power seemed to have stripped Nik of all his energy. He looked about ready to fall flat on his face and that made Maya worry. What was this going to do to him?

Her concern for Nik's wellbeing strengthened Maya's resolve and she focused her attention back on the stone wall. Cracks had begun to appear, slowly widening and filling with glowing molten rock.

The concentrated heat had melted the rock into lava.

Maya didn't expect it when the wall finally flew apart, the

explosion sending her flying three feet back and pelting them with rocks of every size. Maya had landed on her butt, fire still spurting from her palms, lighting the room. A rock flew past Maya's face and her eyes widened to see that it was bigger than her head. Just one inch to the left and it would have done major damage to her face.

As the last bits of rock and dust fell, Nik touched Maya's arm and her fire sputtered out. With a sofa sigh she regenerated a small ball of flame and pushed it away, allowing it to hover in front of her.

"Are you alright?" Nik asked, his forehead scrunched with lines of concern. When she nodded he put his arm around, helping her to her feet. "We should go. Who knows if Thakkur's men heard the explosion. We need to get out of here fast."

Maya got to her feet, scanning the room for Archana and her friends. The Apsara rose from the dust untouched by the explosion, except for a patch of soot on her cheek which made her look mysterious and a little dangerous. Maya snorted silently. She knew exactly what she herself looked like. A mess. She had a hope in hell of pulling off any kind of disaster and emerge from it looking anything like a goddess.

A few feet from Archana, Joss stood with an arm around Ria who looked a little shell-shocked, what seemed to be her most recent look of choice. Maya beckoned the girls who hurried to her immediately. Now steady on her feet, Maya followed Nik out of the cell with her friends and the Apsara following close behind her. Lit by Maya's hovering flame-ball, the corridor outside appeared no different to the one that led to the room full of arte-fact's and Maya was uncertain of which way to go.

"Just pick one and move," Nik urged and Maya was off and running to her left. The bow sang at her shoulder but she didn't miss a breath. Neither did she miss a heartbeat.

Adrenalin pulsed through her body and she sped down the tunnel, listening to the sound of her friends following her, trusting her choice. She paused only when they came to an inter-section of tunnels. Here the walls had a film of moisture and seemed darker towards the bottom. The stone floor also seemed more moist than the rest of the tunnels they had already come through.

Still unsure of which route to take Maya followed her instinct.

CHAPTER 42

They jogged along the tunnels, deeper and deeper into the bowels beneath the ancient temple. The further they went, the more water surround them and soon the walls began to weep. Dull green moss clung to the corners of slick stones and the temperature began to drop so low that Maya shivered.

She needed warmth.

Her skin was moist and clothing damp. Her hair clung to her face in wet tendrils. She glanced at Nik but he seemed focused and unaffected by the cold. Archana hurried up behind them and made the journey looking like she was ready to walk down the runway. Only Joss and Ria looked like how Maya felt.

Cold and miserable.

Maya clenched her jaw to prevent it from chattering. How useless was she. She'd blasted her way through a wall of solid stone but she was about to freeze to death before she returned the bow to Lord Shiva.

Then she wanted to laugh.

Fire.

Maya shook her head and forgot to shiver. She called her fire from her solar plexus and sent streams of it to her fingers and toes, allowing the heat to simmer at the surface of her skin.

And just like that she was warm.

Now that she was comfortable Maya could focus a little better. She turned and waved Joss and Ria forward. "Hold my hand," she said opening both her palms and waiting for them to take a hold of them. Joss took a hand without hesitation but Ria frowned, then met Maya's gaze. "It's okay Ria. I'm going to try to get you warm. I'll send my fire into you, just enough to take the cold away so you can keep moving."

She watched her friend's skeptical expression, worried that she would refuse her help but despite the ripple of fear in her eyes Ria took Maya's other hand and held on tight. Maya sighed softly. She knew she had some explaining to do but for now it was okay. For now Ria was okay.

Maya breathed deeply then called her fire gain, channeling it to her fingers and her skin exactly the way she had before. Only this time she allowed the heat to seep through the pores in her skin, to connect with each hand that she held. Their hands felt heavy in hers, their skin clammy and icy cold, but as her fire penetrated their skin she could sense the change in temperature, the growing warmth in their hands and the change in the expressions on their faces.

Ria gasped. "I'm warm," she said in amazement, staring at her hand in Maya's, and then at her own body, her abdomen. "How did you do that?" she asked softly but it didn't seem she really wanted an answer as she was too busy grinning at Joss and enjoying the welcoming feeling of warmth.

"Right, now that you're warm again we can keep moving." The girls nodded as Maya moved to the front where Nik waited. Filled with new energy she was able to move fast enough to keep up with Nik's long strides.

She'd gotten a steady pace when she was suddenly ankle deep in icy water.

Maya gasped and so did the girls behind her, including Archana. *So the heavenly creature wasn't immune either,* Maya thought.

"Where is all this water coming from?" asked Maya no-one in particular. She was not expecting an answer.

"Probably an underground lake? Or from the water table," said Nik as he moved forward peering into the dark tunnel. His feet sloshed in the deep water but he didn't seem in any way disturbed that a third of his body was immersed in pitch black liquid. They couldn't even tell if anything dangerous lurked in the murky depths. Maya shuddered and tried to keep those thoughts out of her head.

Maya moved deeper into the water, her ball of fire floating just above the water's gleaming surface. "Guess we have no choice but to keep going. This water must come out somewhere."

Behind her Archana grabbed her arm. "I don't think this is such a good idea. What if there isn't a way out?"

"Then we turn around and come right back," said Maya, tugging her arm out of Archana's grip. "We have to keep going. You feel free to turn back if you want to. We aren't stopping you." It was a challenge and the Apsara knew it. She gave her a vicious glare but said nothing.

They kept moving, and the level of the water kept getting deeper and deeper. Soon the darkness was broken only by the shimmer of the ball of fire on the ever-rising surface of the water. Gandiv glowed behind Maya and she felt somewhat comforted by the light. For the first time in a long time she prayed she would be able to get the bow back to Lord Shiva, prayed that she would not fail him.

When the water reached her neck and she doubted where her feet would fall next Maya instinctively kicked off and treaded water to stay afloat. "This is not good." She turned slowly in the water to check on Ria and Joss. Both were treading water and subdued.

Nik coughed as a wavelet of water entered his mouth. "Wait here. I'll go further into the tunnel to see if gets worse or better."

"No, Nik. You could drown," said Maya. Archana snorted behind her and though Maya wanted to turn around and slap the girl she managed to restrain herself. From the expression on Joss's face it was probably a good thing she was too far away from the Apsara, because Joss looked like she wanted to slap her too.

Maya hid a grin and turned to Nik. His face told her he was confident he would be fine. She gave him a small nod and he sank into the water in one smooth move. She watched him generate a ball of fire below the surface of the water, watched the white light swirl about and then move down the tunnel lighting the hollows of his face as he moved further and further away. Soon the glow below them faded and they were left in semi-darkness, treading dark water and thinking dark, dark thoughts.

He was gone too long.

Maya sucked in a breath as panic took over. But the bow vibrated on her shoulder, short steady pulses almost like a soft heartbeat, sending her comfort and confidence. She choked back a sob and breathed deeper and the panic fled.

Suddenly, the water in front of her shuddered violently, dozens of little waves broke the surface and Nik popped out of the darkness, taking a deep breath. "The tunnel goes for about fifty yards more before the water fills it to the roof. Then it's underwater for twenty yards and then out the other end. There's some broken walls and what looks like it used to be a temple or something. We can make it there easily. Girls, you can swim so it should be a piece of cake." His ball of white light remained submerged, dancing eerily within the inky water.

Maya nodded along with the others. She felt confident that they could make the distance. "I'm ready. Let's go."

Nik looked past Maya at the Apsara. "Can you handle it?"

"Of course, I can." Her voice held a sharp defensive note and Maya grew concerned. Was Archana being overly confident?

Maya looked over her shoulder and hoped the girl wasn't going to do anything stupid. Not that Maya cared should she overextend herself and drown her vain ass in the process.

"Right, let's go," said Nik. He treaded water and moved forward slowly. His submerged fireball following like a loyal pet. Very soon, the distance between the tops of their heads and the roof of the tunnel went from two feet to an inch, snuffing out Maya's flame and plunging the tunnel above the water into shadowed darkness.

Lit from the white fireball below, their faces were strange and ghostly. And the tunnels had the smooth, slick look of a whales belly. They were barely able to keep their mouths out of the water. And they had no choice but to submerge.

A nod from Nik, and Maya took a deep breath and sank into the water. She went below the surface comforted by Nik's floating ball of fire. Maya didn't bother to light another one. Nik's underwater torch provided sufficient light to allow then to move through the tunnel well enough. Maya swam through the dark water, putting all her strength behind each thrust of her legs. She moved fast through the water despite the bow on her shoulder and when she popped through the choppy surface she was half surprised it had ended so quickly.

She blinked against the sudden intrusion of light against her eyes. She'd been so used to moving around in darkness that the light hurt and she wanted to shy away from it. Thankfully the transition took only a few moments and she was soon comfortably treading water beside Nik, studying the shambles of this part of the warren of tunnels.

Water stirred behind them and Joss, Ria and Archana surfaced, gasping for air. They remained silent as they followed in Maya's waker and swam to the edge of the water. They dragged themselves onto a shelf of stone, exhausted.

Maya lay on the floor, one hand holding onto the bow, breathing deeply and enjoying the feel of solid ground beneath her. Nik was propped up beside Maya, staring at her with a strange look in his eyes. She flushed when she registered the state of her sodden clothing, the material clinging to her body in all the right curves and hollows. She got to her feet, unsettled, nervous and blushing while Nik rose beside her grinning at her discomfort.

Maya glared at him, then turned her back on him to study the large cave like opening. It looked like someone had built an open auditorium that had slowly filled with water. The group stood at the top where the steps ended And behind them lay the remains of a temple. Statues that had once adorned the carved pyramid roof of the temple had fallen on every available surface.

Maya stepped closer to the ruined building then stopped in her tracks.

"What is it?" Nik asked.

Maya frowned as she stared at the closely packer mounds of brown soil inside the remains of the temple. It rose in a almost a bee-hive shape, with a round opening at the top. A few dozen other smaller opening dotted its surface. "It looks like a snake burrow."

"A temple to Nagini? But that doesn't explain what happened to it. Why would the temple have been destroyed?"

Maya barely heard Nik's words. "Something terrible happened here," she whispered. "I can almost feel it."

"What do you sense, Maya?" asked Nik softly, as Ria and Joss drew closer, their faces filled with worry and concern.

"I feel grief and tears, and then fury. Lots of suffering and pain." Maya's eyes filled with tears as she stared around the cavern wondering what horrible event had taken place here to leave such a powerful imprint of emotion on the place that even she could feel.

A slithering sound drifted to Maya's ears.

Slow and scaly and sort of familiar. Maya stiffened and beside her she saw Nik stop moving as well. She hoped Archana had the sense to be careful too as she had a pretty good feeling what was behind her.

When she turned she took in a breath. Not one of surprise, but more of recognition and appreciation. A gigantic snake slithered toward them curving one the ground moving in the sensuous s-shape of all the snakes in the world.

CHAPTER 43

The cobra stopped in front of Maya and raised itself up, its head held over Maya like a giant umbrella. The serpent's head expanded outward like any cobra about to strike and Maya winced, waiting for the impact, knowing she would not be able to dodge the bite when it came.

She heard Ria's gasp and Joss calling out for her to run, but the strike didn't come. Instead, Maya felt the cool touch of scales around her legs. She let the bow drop slowly to the ground fearing it would be crushed against her body if the snake decided she needed crushing. She remained still, barely taking a breath, reluctant to anger the animal in any way.

The cobra continued to wind itself around and around Maya until she stood covered from feet to neck in a tight spiral of a serpent's body. Only when the cobra tightened its grip did Maya begin to worry. What was its intention? So far it hadn't seemed to want to harm her, but the tightness around her body worried her. Soon she had to hold her breath and then she was more than cocerned as the snake squeezed again.

Maya sent a questioning glance at Nik who gave her a slight

nod. She took it as tacit agreement that she needed to take measures that were a little more than drastic.

As the gigantic snake went in for the third constriction Maya pulled her fire from her core and expelled it to the surface of her skin, slowly building the heat more and more until she could almost hear the sizzle of it searing into the snakes scales.

In one sinuous undulation of its body, the snake hissed, rearing its head, its coils falling hard and fast, thudding to the ground at Maya's feet. Maya, short of breath, bent over to inhale deeply.

"Are you hurt?" Nik called from beyond the pile of the snake's injured body.

"I'm fine. Just stay where you are. I don't think it wanted to harm me."

"Are you kidding? It was squeezing you to death, Maya," said Joss, her protest ending in a high-pitched squeak.

"Your friend is right, little girl. I had no intention at all of hurting her." Maya looked beyond Nik and her jaw dropped open.

The snake was gone and its place stood a beautiful woman. Her complexion dark, her cheekbones high, her eyes the deepest black. Her black hair hung at her back parted in the center and pulled away from her face. Her beauty was simple but stunning. But what shocked Maya were her injuries. The dusky skin on her face, neck and arms were burned so badly that the skin pucked and the white flesh beneath was clearly visible.

Maya knew instinctively she'd cause the burns. Without thinking she ran to the woman. "I'm so sorry. I had no idea." She stood in front of the snake-woman and stared at her injuries, horrified that she'd caused someone such harm.

"Do not worry, my child. I will heal. And I can see your heart. It is pure and true. And now I know why my sister chose you to bear her gift." The woman smiled and as she did she seemed to glow.

Maya gasped as she watched the woman's burns heal right in front of her eyes, the white flesh disappeared and the skin smoothe and within seconds not a sign of her injured remained.

Maya was still staring dumbfounded when the woman spoke again. "I am Nagini, ruler of the serpent realm."

"My name is Maya Rao," Maya said, feeling a little ridiculous introducing herself to a goddess.

"Hand of Kali, it is my pleasure to meet you," Nagini tilted her head at Maya then glanced over at Nik. "Hello, Nikhil. It has been a long time since we last met." When he frowned she laughed. "You won't remember me, child. You were a little baby when I last saw you. That should explain why you didn't sense who I was."

Nik look relieved and Maya understood his confusion. He should have sensed who they were dealing with immediately.

"These are you're friends, I presume?" the goddess asked as she glided closer to Ria and Joss. To their credit they neither flinched nor stepped back as Nagini stopped inches from them.

"Ria and Joss. Yes. They are my friends." Maya was sure to make the point clear. Archana was not a friend.

"Good. It is a blessing in itself to sacrifice ones own freedom for a worthy cause. Even when that cause is not ones own. Be brave, girls. You will need it if you wish to support the Hand of Kali."

The goddess moved away without another word and when she frowned Maya's stomach clenched. When Nagini hissed and spun to face Archana, Maya flinched both at the sudden action and the fury in the goddesses eyes. She glowed from within and the faint images of her four other hands could be seen shimmering at her back.

"Archana, daughter of Tilotamma. What are you doing in my realm?" Nagini voice was gravelly and it echoed around the stone cavern.

"I didn't meant to come." The Apsara stiffened beneath the

scrutiny of the goddess but found a moment to shoot Maya a dark glare.

"You know Archana?" asked Maya wondering if the goddess would help them free the girl from her binding spell.

"Yesss," Nagini spoke the word, her s's sibilant and musical yet filled with anger. She hovered close to the girl, her hands held forward as if she were about to pounce on her. "I know this Apsara very well. In fact, I have been waiting patiently for the day that she and I will cross paths. I believe I owe you my thanks, Maya Rao."

"What did she do?" Maya asked softly, wondering if she should even be talking to the goddess who now vibrated with fury and who was hovering three feet off the ground right in front of the shaking Apsara.

"She took my child from me. And I will make her pay for it." Nagini reached out and grabbed Archana's throat, her fingers closing tightly around the girl's pale neck. Archana grabbed at the goddess fingers wide eyed and struggling as Nagini lifted her off her feet.

"What happened to Nagini's daughter?" Maya shouted at the Apsara. Archana's gaze darted at Maya and for an instant it seemed she would refuse to talk.

But Nagini shook her, and like a rag doll her arms and hands trembled in midair. "Talk or you die a horrible death."

"Okay. It wasn't my fault. He made me do it." Archana stammered the words out, fear twisting her features into something almost unrecognizable. Gone was the stunning beauty. What remained was just a terrified husk of an arrogant and self-centered girl.

"Who made you? What did you do?" Nagini asked, her enraged voice echoing around the cavernous space.

"Ravana." The named fell on Maya's ears like a blow, stunning her for an instant, and she stepped back. The Lord of the Rakshasa's, Ravana, the evil king who stole Sita from her husband. Archana's voice broke through Maya's shock. "He owns me. He made me betray her to bring her to Lanka."

Nagini screamed, the grief in her voice almost palpable as she brought Archana's face close to hers. "Where is Malini." She asked the question so softly that Maya had to lean forward to catch her words.

"She's still in Lanka, as far as I know." Archana grabbed at the goddesses fingers, panic filling her eyes and her movements. She kicked desperately as if she knew that her end was close and her usefulness no longer existed. "Help me," she pleaded with Maya, eyes bulging as she sucked in every bit of air that she could.

Maya stepped toward the goddess but Nik held her arm. "Don't get between a mother and her vengeance."

"The little god is right, young Maya. This creature has caused me centuries of pain, endless days and hours and minutes of agony and fear and grief. Of not knowing where my child was or even if she were alive or dead. This creature has no loyalty. She had the blood of Tilotamma in her veins and yet she has nothing of her mother in her heart."

And than the goddess Nagini broke Archana's neck with one twist of her hand.

Maya swallowed a gasp as the lifeless body of the the Apsara dropped to the ground in an inelegant heap. Behind her, Ria let out a strangled shriek and Joss gasped, neither expecting the girl to be killed so efficiently. Or so quickly.

Maya stared at the body, unsure of the goddess now that she had just seen her kill so ruthlessly.

Nagini turned to Maya and lowered herself slowly to the ground. "I pray you will never know a mother's grief Maya Rao. Now, I owe you a great deal for bringing my daughter's betrayer to me. I finally know where Malini is. Is there some way I can help you?"

Maya nodded. "I need to get the bow to Lord Shiva."

CHAPTER 44

"That is easy enough to do, my child." Nagini disappeared, slowly fading into nothing.

It seemed she'd been gone for far too long and Maya began to worry that the goddess won't be returning. And then she reappeared in a shimmering haze. "The lord of lords will be here soon." Nagini smiled and Maya bent to lift the bow and hang it over her shoulder. For some reason she wanted to keep it close until Lord Shiva had it in his possession.

When she lifted her head she caught a strange look on the goddesses face. Almost one of apology, but Maya thought she must be mistaken and ignored it.

It didn't take long for the air to shimmer again. Even the surface of the water rippled with the impending arrival of the god of gods. Shiva materialized in front of them, a serene expression on his face. Today he wore a red and gold coat the reached to his knees.

He bent his head in a small greeting, "Hello Maya. I believe you have succeeded in your mission?"

Maya placed her hands together and bowed before the god. "Yes, my Lord. I have Gandiv."

"Then come with me, Maya Rao." He held out his hand and Maya glanced at Nik. Nik who was frowning as he stared at Lord Shiva, the strangest look on his face. His eyes widened and at the same time Maya caught a whiff of dead meat and spices. The smell of the Rakshasa. Something was terribly wrong.

When she looked at Nagini she knew. The apology was clear in her face and Maya moved to step backward, aways from the god in front of her.

And then Lord Shiva transformed into Raj Thakkur, the demon art collector.

But it was too late. He grabbed Maya's hand, and transported her right out of Nagini's lair.

THEY ARRIVED ON SOLID GROUND, the room almost a duplicate to Lord Shiva's hall in Mt Kailas. A glance at the god confirmed what she'd thought she'd just imagined. The man who stood before her and the demon Ravana were one and the same. Mr. Thakkur, venerated scholar, esteemed collector of ancient Indian artefact's was none other than the earthly persona of the hated and fear King of all Rakshasa, Lord Ravana.

Maya took a step back, instinctively wanting to turn and run, but Ravana held out his forefinger and shook it at her. "Uh unh. Don't be foolish and make a run for it. This is Lanka. You have nowhere to go."

Maya glared at him and tried to swallow the lump of fear in her throat.

She had no friends, not backup. All she had was Gandiv and the bow was little protection against the demon standing before her.

"Hand the bow over." Ravana opened his palm and beckoned her with two fingers.

"And what if I don't?" she asked, playing for time even though she wasn't sure she should even bother.

"Then all that will happen is you will get very hurt. Or maybe I will hurt someone else. Like little Malini, for instance."

"No," yelled Maya. She glared at the demon. "You can't hurt her. Nagini made a deal with you didn't she? Gandiv in exchange for her daughter?"

"You are most astute, my dear. Yes, we made a deal but the goddess of serpents never clarified that her daughter be returned to her alive. You see, my child, it's all in the fine print." He said, laughing maniacally. His laughter echoed around the room so loudly that Maya almost didn't hear the two demon guards come in, dragging a girl between them.

"Maya, meet Malini, daughter of the goddess Nagini."

The girl raised her head. She seemed weak yet unhurt but she stared at Maya sullenly, as if she didn't even consider the possibility of being saved.

"Why did you take her? Or do you just have a habit of abducting innocent women?"

He sneered. "She had something I wanted. And, no. You can stop thinking dirty thoughts, not that they have never occurred to me." He walked over to the the defeated girl.

They had dressed her in a pale blue short sleeved beaded blouse and floor length skirt, demure and simple, but still beautiful. He ran a finger down the bare skin of her arm and she shuddered, drawing away in fear. "You see, the daughter of the queen of serpents has an interesting power. She produces a venom like nothing ever created on earth. In its various potencies it can be used as a painkiller, a hallucinogen, a sleeping drug and a deathly poison. And the beauty of it is it's truly undetectable. Even those forensic doctors won't be able to find a trace of it in a victim's blood. So yes, this young one has been very useful."

"So you won't give her back?" Maya stomach clenched at the

thought of Nagini's wrath and her grief if she didn't get her daughter back after such a huge betrayal.

"Oh, I have no further need of her. You see, humans have their uses too. Especially the ones who can replicate the venom. But it's up to you whether she returns home alive or dead."

The girl stared wide-eyed at Maya, having finally realized what was going on around her. "What are you doing?" she glared at Ravana, anger stronger in her gaze than fear and Maya knew this girl was stronger than she looked.

"Just giving the girl a choice. It's always interesting what people do when faced with choices they dislike."

Malini shook her head, pulling away from the guards. "Don't. Don't let him win. Whatever he wants it's not worth what he's asking for."

Maya snorted. "It's your life in exchange for a bow. I'm sure Shiva will understand."

Malini gasped, shock making her face grow so pale Maya could almost see the outline of scales beneath her skin. "Shiva's bow? That's Gandiv you have there?" When Maya nodded, Malini shook her head so hard the strands of her hair flew in her face. "Don't give it to him."

"Oh, how heroic of you, little serpent. I didn't think you had it in you." Ravana moved closer. He ran a finger along the girls cheek moving it slowly to her chin. Then he slipped it under her chin and lifted her face until she had no choice but to look him in the eye. "Don't worry. She will give me the bow. You see, she is human. And she knows how important life is."

"He's right," said Maya bringing the bow round and slipping it off her shoulder. She held it out to Ravana and he smiled, teeth gleaming in the wide, satisfied grin he gave her. "He can have the bow. But only when he lets you go." Maya stared Ravana down stiffening her spine. "Call her mother. When Nagini takes her away then you can have the bow."

"Very well. You drive a hard bargain but I am willing to keep my end." He snapped his fingers and a moment later Nagini appeared, her expression slightly confused. "My lady, you may have your daughter. Please take her and leave."

Malini ran to her mother and melted into her arms. The serpent goddess rubbed her daughter's back but the expression on her face was hard and angry. Maya suspected she wasn't done with the demon lord but she had to get the goddess out of there now. "Take her somewhere safe. I'm fine."

Nagini hesitated her gaze flicking from Maya to the bow. "But Gandiv. Are you going to give it to him?"

"I don't have a choice, really. What's done is done. At least Gandiv is one step closer to its master."

Maya gave Nagini a smile and it seemed the goddess understood because she took one last furious look at Ravana and said, "Someday I will make you pay for what you did to me and my family." Then she disappeared with her daughter held close to her bosom.

"Don't they always say the nicest things?" Ravana asked, smiling. He behaved as if he hadn't stolen her daughter from her, hadn't drained the girl for a deadly poison, hadn't kept a family apart and caused endless grief for hundreds of years. He was a psychopath. Now, he turned that charming smile on Maya and said, "Ttime to hand it over my dear. Or are you going to break your promise."

She shook her head. "Of course not. Take it," she said holding it out.

Ravana laughed, taking a step further down the hall. "You know, it's quite amazing that you are able to carry a bow that few men on earth have ever been able to hold. A long time ago, another women stood here in this very hall. She was also able to carry Gandiv."

Maya frowned. "You're talking about Sita?"

"Ah, she knows her history," Ravana laughed and clapped his hands together.

"She was another woman you stole away from her family. You seem to have a certain pattern, don't you?" asked Maya, the look she gave him full of distaste. She was so tempted to look at her watch. *How much longer will they be,* she wondered.

"Very well, let us not waste any more time. Bring the bow and place it here. It's a special place that's been waiting for so long for Gandiv." Ravana waved a hand at a pedestal a few feet further into the hall.

Maya walked to it and placed the bow on the stone table. As soon as she set it down and took a step back the guards descended on her. Maya drew her fire sending two blasts are each of the demons, fire so powerful that it incinerated each Rakshasa on contact.

"Oh, my. You are much more talented than I ever expected. I do think you will come in handy."

Before he could say another word, an enormous ball of light appeared beside the bow. The light lengthened and grew slowly into the shape of Lord Shiva. Within the protective force of the swirling white light, Shiva reached out and grabbed hold of the bow. He turned to Maya and gave her a small smile. Then with a tiny nod he disappeared. When the white ball spun around and around and eventually fell in on itself, Maya felt as if all her hopes had just left with the God of Gods.

He'd come for the bow but he hadn't saved Maya.

Ravana growled, shrieking so loudly that the entire room vibrated, carvings and painting fell to the floor around them. "Now, what did he go and do that for?" the demon lord asked as if he had no idea why Shiva would want his own bow back.

"Maybe because it belongs to him?" Maya offered. The words flowed so easily past a throat filled with tears of abandonment.

He smiled as he clicked his fingers and time seemed to slow

down. The iciness of his eyes seemed to go on forever although his toothy smile soon disappeared to be replaced with a thin unfeeling line as he stared at her. Maya felt her stomach twist, her breath whoosh from her lungs. She felt her body disintegrate, watched the richly decorated hall disappear.

CHAPTER 45

*W*ithin the same breath, she reappeared. Somewhere pitch dark, somewhere not a flicker of light penetrated.

Beneath her she felt stone and as she moved metal jangled beside her and behind her.

She clicked her tongue, fed up with the lack of light, called her fire into a ball of light, then flicked it off to hover in front of her.

The light brought her situation to her shocked gaze. She sat in a darkened stone cell, her hands shackled, the rusty chain attached to a wall behind her. She sank slowly to the floor, her heart heavy in her chest, thoughts of abandonment overcrowding her spinning mind.

She let out a soft sob as she scanned the cell desperate to see a face or hear a voice, to know she wasn't alone here in this barely lit dingy cell.

"Well, you're certainly the last person I would have expected to see here," said a voice from the shadowed corner at her right.

Maya's head jerked up hard and she frowned, studying the shape of a man she could see shackled to the far wall, forcing him to remain standing for his entire incarceration. Her heart clenched. She knew that voice. "Kas?" she asked the shadows, suddenly wanting to laugh at the absurdity of it all.

"Maya?" he mimicked her, although not unkindly. "Yes, it's me." He sighed.

She shifted on the floor and something metal hit the stone beneath her. Chayya's brass container.

Maya's way out of this hell hole.

She'd have to use it before they decide to search her, though.

Kas's voice broke through her rush of excitement. "What the hell are you doing here?" she asked as her eyes adjusted to the dull light and she could at last see the face of her once-enemy, the demon Narakasura.

"Probably the same thing you're doing here," Kas suggested with a superior tilt of the head.

"Chained to a wall and still arrogant," Maya mumbled to herself. She watched him, her gaze narrowing. "Ravana threw me in here after I gave him Gandiv. Not that it mattered, because Lord Shiva arrived and took the bow away anyway. What are you here for?"

"Ah, I knew it wouldn't be long before he lost the bow. He'll be pretty pissed," said Kas, his shadowed gaze focused on Maya's face. Maya moved her hand and her ball of light floated closer to him. His jaw clenched as he filched from the brightness; a jaw encased in a heavy rough of a tangle beard. "And I'm here because I failed to fulfill the master's command to cut off your pretty little head. So you see, you are to blame."

Maya snorted. "I love it. Won't take the blame for anything will you?"

"I tell it like it is, Maya Rao. You thwarted my plan but I failed to kill you. Those were his instructions. Make sure the Hand of Kali is dead. And I failed. Hence my current address." His teeth shone in the darkness and Maya detected a movement of his shoulder that could have been a shrug. She almost felt sorry for him. Almost.

"Have you been here ever since then?" she asked, thinking about their last encounter a few weeks ago.

"Came straight here. And haven't left," Kas said softly.

Maya's eyes had adjusted well enough by now to see he still wore the blue handwoven overcoat she'd seen him in when they'd last fought, when he'd stabbed her in the back. The sleeve of his left hand was cut open, old brown blood darkened its edges. His bare bicep revealed a thin line, the memory of her poison-tipped dagger scarring his skin.

Buttons were missing in his overcoat and it hung open, revealing the left leg of his trousers, ripped and bloody where she'd struck him in the thigh.

"So, this is what you got for failing to kill me?" He nodded. "Guess loyalty works only one way with him doesn't it?"

"So it seems," Kas said sagging his head sadly, although Maya knew him well enough to see through his feigned despair.

"Now what?" she asked glaring around the cell.

"Now, nothing. They bring food, release us to use the toilet. And we're back here, day after day."

"You haven't tried to escape?"

Kas laughed, the sound jetting around the room, bounding flatly off the stone walls. "There is no escape."

"You mean you haven't tried," said Maya firmly scanning the room again for the slightest show of weakness in the walls, in the metal bars of the cell door.

Metal. That was it. She could melt the metal with her fire and free herself. But she needed a plan.

Footsteps sounded from the passage outside and with a flick of her hand Maya doused her fireball. The footsteps stopped in front of their cell, a shape held a torch while another fiddled at the lock. Two Rakshasas stopped in front of their cell, their faces oddly lit by the lone torch. One held a tray piled with plates and sealed silver containers, along with a jug of water and two silver cups. The first demon opened the door and allowed the tray-bearer to move inside and set his burden down in the middle of the cell.

Without thinking, Maya summoned her power and sent two fireballs at the pair in quick succession. The first hit the demon at the door full in the face. She'd been careful to imbue as much power as she could into the fire and it achieved the result she'd wanted. The fire slammed into the demon, sank deep into his bones and flesh and burned him up from the inside.

All while the second demon looked on in horror.

He was so transfixed by the death of his partner that he didn't see his very own fireball hit him square in the ribs. Within seconds he too evaporated in a flurry of orange embers and flakes of black dust.

"That sorts them out," she said dusting her hands together. Then she drew her fire and threw out a fireball to light the room again.

"There's more where they came from," said Kas dryly although he didn't fail to look impressed. The metal door hung open and Maya frowned. "We should get that door closed before someone comes by."

"I'm thinking." she snapped. It took only a moment for her to make the decision. She concentrated her fire in the palm of her right hand, sending it into the metal shackles. The iron began to glow and then she stopped. "No. I can't do this. If it melts off one of the demons will see it and just lop a different shackle on." She spoke almost to herself. Kas had nothing to contribute.

Staring at the cell door she had the tendrils of an idea.

She called her fire again, aiming her palm at the bottom of the iron cell door. She sent a stream of the flame into a thin line, focusing the energy of the fire at the bottom corner. With a powerful thrust she pushed the door shut. It clicked as it hit the lock but without the key it didn't shut completely. Maya made a face at the bottom corner of the door.

"Don't worry. They won't notice." His attempt at comforting her failed miserably.

She snorted. "They can't be that dumb. Eventually someone will see that."

"Let's hope by the time they see it they will be too late," said Kas with a smile that Maya considered a little too friendly for her liking. She shot him a narrow glare then focused on the food. Her stomach turned at the thought of eating anything that Ravana provided.

"How long before someone comes for the tray?"

"A couple of hours. We don't rank highly on the service list."

"I'm sure we don't," said Maya. She shifted again and reached a hand into her pants pocket for Chayya's brass container. She supposed she should be grateful they hadn't shackled her to the wall the way they did Kas.

She glanced at him frowning. "They left food. How are you supposed to eat?"

"Well, if you hadn't made them go poof they would have exchanged my shackles for ones like yours. And don't worry. It won't take too long before they put you in shackles like mine. It usually happens after the first meal."

"Then I supposed I have no time to waste," she said firmly as she unscrewed the lid of the container and watched in awe as a thread of black shadow swirled up into the air. It seemed to grow larger and larger until Maya blinked at the sight.

A Shadow Girl stood in front of her, everything from her face and hair to her clothing and skin were a shad of grey, from gunmetal to slate to dull smoke. She shifted as she floated, waiting for Maya's command.

"Please tell the Goddess Chayya I need her help. I'm in a jail cell in Lanka. And there is also one other person with me who needs to be freed."

The Shadow girl bowed and broke apart into a million tiny

little flecks of darkness. The scraps of shadow danced this way and that and then simply blinked out of sight.

"Pretty. But how helpful a Shadow will be I really can't say," Kas said not in the least hiding the sarcasm in his voice.

"You just be quite and wait," Maya snapped and pulled her knees up. She rested her chin on them and waited, listening hard for the sound of footsteps that would end this escape attempt.

It seemed like forever had passed when the air shimmered and shadows, both dark and light, coalesced, coming together to take the form of the goddess Chayya.

"I apologize for taking so long," said Chayya her face serene and seemingly unaffected by the delay. "I had hoped the cell would not be warded, but unfortunately that would have proved too easy."

"Then how did you break through?" asked Maya coming to her knees.

Chayya sighed, "I had to speak to the god of gods but when he knew it was to save *you* he was most happy to break the ward," she said as she glanced around the cell. Her eyebrows rose as her gaze settled on Kas. "I am assuming he is the other person who needs saving?"

Maya nodded. "Don't ask if he deserves to be saved," she said with a wry smile. "Can we get going? Before the guards return?"

Chayya nodded and leaned forward to help Maya to her feet. With a nod Chayya began to disintegrate into grey and black shadow. Maya watched as her own body took the form of satiny rips of darkness and then fell away into nothing.

SHE BLINKED and then she was standing in her room at the Oberoi. Ria and Joss sat at the foot of the bed while Maya's parents were in the middle of a meal. They both looked tired, jet-lagged from the journey but as soon as Maya solidified into herself they came straight to her.

"Maya," said her mom as both her parents jumped to their feet and hurried to her. "Are you alright?"

She nodded, "I'm fine. Nothing damaged, not even a drop of blood taken."

Joss snorted. "This time," she said giving Maya a stiff glare.

But, before Maya tackled the wrath of her family and friends she turned to Chayya. "Kas?"

The goddess nodded. "I will return for him."

"Where will you take him?"

"To Patala. Yama has a few things to discuss with the boy."

"Boy? Isn't he older than Nik?"

"Only a little. And in demigod years that doesn't mean much." Chayya smiled and placed a hand on Maya shoulder. "Don't worry about him. He will receive due punishment for his actions but I have no doubt that he will be fine."

Maya shrugged. "I don't really care either way."

"Yeah, why should you care. The guy stabbed you in the back," snapped Joss. Maya's mother turned to hide her smile while Dev wiped his mouth in an effort to hide his own amusement.

"What are they talking about?" asked Ria. To Maya's relief she looked curious and not confused. Then Maya blinked at her Friend, suddenly aware that Ria was uncovered, her identity plain for her parents to see. She made a mental not to check what happened to change her mind about keeping her secret from Maya's parents.

"Long story," Joss patted her shoulder. "Don't worry. You'll know every detail soon enough."

"I had best be going. He must be growing frantic," said Chayya.

Maya laughed then dipped her hand into her pocket for the little brass container. When she handed it to Chayya, the Goddess shook her head as she took it. She held her right hand over it for a moment then returned the vessel to Maya. "Please hold onto it in case you need me."

Maya nodded, smiling. "Shadow messaging."

Chayya nodded then disappeared in a flurry off black and grey silken shadows.

Maya sighed and glanced over at Ria who was still staring at the spot that Chayya had just occupied. "Why does that no longer surprise me?"

Joss nudged her. "Don't worry it gets worse. Trust me."

"And better," said Maya as she forced herself a space between her two friends. She held them both by the shoulders and squeezed.

"You alright?" asked Joss.

"Never better."

CHAPTER 46

*M*aya's mom and dad rose from the small table by the window. "Right, we have to make plans for our trip to the refuge tomorrow," said Dev.

"Where exactly is this refuge, Dad?" asked Maya, as curious as she was tired. All her life she'd heard of the refuge but she'd never once thought of finding out exactly where on the map it was. Funny how things which often seem insignificant can someday be of great importance.

"It's near a place called Varandha Pass. It's in the Western Ghat or mountain range, about four hours south of Mumbai."

"Oh, good. Not a long drive."

"Sort of." Her dad smiled and when she frowned he gave in. "The car will take us to the foothills of the mountain but we will have to walk the rest of the way. It's about a two hour trek to the temple itself."

There was a chorus of weak groans from all three girls and Dev laughed. "Get a good night's sleep ladies. Boot camp starts at four in the morning."

"That early?" Maya complained.

"Come on, Maya. You battle demons on a regular basis and yet an early start defeats you?" Her mom raised an eyebrow.

"Kali gave me her fire power not an Early Bird alarm clock," Maya said with a pout.

Everyone laughed at that and her parents left soon after.

Maya immediately rounded on Ria and Joss, both her own eyebrow raised questioningly at the two girls.

"What?" they both asked in unison.

Maya looked at Ria. "What happened to keeping things from my parents?"

Right sighed. "You know how amazing you parents are. And Joss thought it would be a good idea if they knew who they were saving, if only for my own safety." She shrugged.

Maya was satisfied with Ria's answer so she turned to Joss. "Kali's fire power? Demons?"

Joss raised both her hands in defense. "Hey, we were alone. And it seemed a good a time as any to tell her. Sorry."

"Good," said Maya, happier than she'd been in a while. "One more person I no longer have to tiptoe around." She smiled at Joss who seemed strangely shy all of sudden. Then Maya sighed and said, "Shower."

"Go. When was the last time you bathed," asked Joss.

"The black streams of the serpent plane, remember?"

Maya headed into the shower and turned the taps as hot as she could manage. It still felt as thought the cold water from the tunnels had gotten deep into the marrow of her bones. The scalding shower revived her somewhat while she dealt with the odd emotions fighting for space in her mind.

She'd been confused and deflated when Lord Shiva had arrived to take the bow away. And left without her. She hadn't had time to think about it while she'd been making plans to escape from Lanka, but now that she thought about it she wasn't sure she liked it too much.

It made her feel used and dispensable.

Had the God of Gods even cared if she had a means of escape from Lanka. Would he have put an escape plan in place had she not had her emergency call to Chayya? Maya wasn't entirely sure. Lord Shiva had been helpful with the wards but would he have done anything if Maya had been stuck in Lanka without a way out?

Maya sighed as she dried off. Should she even try to figure out the god's motives or was that a pointless exercise. Yes, she had been given a task. And yes, she had fulfilled it. She really needed to leave it at that.

But one niggling thought remained.

The thought that she wasn't as appreciated as she expected to be. Maya shook her head. But wasn't that arrogant of her? Who was she in the greater scheme of things. Her real duty was to fulfill Kali's expectations of her. None of the other gods owed her anything.

Dressed, much more relaxed, and waiting for her room service order, Maya was just sitting down to talk to the girls when her parents returned. Nik appeared in the girl's room minutes later. Ria let out a soft shriek when she noticed him standing beside her.

With a hand on her chest she said, "I will get used to that. I promise."

They all laughed at that and Maya brought them up to speed on everything from Nagini's betrayal to Kas as a prisoner in Ravana's jail.

"So you don't seem surprised that Nagini betrayed me?" Maya asked after they asked all their questions of her.

Nik shook his head. "As soon as you disappeared with Shiva-turned-Thakkur, Nagini apologized and explained what she'd done. She'd felt she had no choice and that was the only way to get her daughter back. What she didn't realize was that was probably the best way she could have done it. Getting Ravana to take you to Lanka it meant the bow was in the heavenly plane."

"Making it easy for Lord Shiva to simply walk in and take it back," Maya nodded. "Which he did do in the end."

"And once he had the bow he told Yama about your situation and set things in motion for a rescue. My father contacted me immediately because, of course, he thought I was with you."

"So how did you all get out of Nagini's lair?"

"The magical ward that Thakkur, or rather Ravana, had set didn't work so far away from the trap below the artifact room. I was able to bring the girls back almost immediately and then go home to see what plans were being made to get you out of Lanka. When I got there it seemed a rescue plan was premature as you were already saved by then."

"I was lucky that Chayya had given me a way to contact her. Had it not been for her I would still be in Lanka waiting for you to save my butt."

"And it appears you managed to capture Narakasura as well." Nik nodded proudly.

"Ha. I had nothing to do with it. He was simply imprisoned with me. Or me with him, rather. Right time and place, nothing more."

"So he's been in Lanka all this while?" asked Joss.

Maya nodded. "In that very cell from the looks of it. He was still wearing the same clothes."

"Er, Maya. You were pretty observant to recall what he'd been wearing weeks ago," asked Joss raising a doubtful eyebrow.

"Yeah, you tend to recall these things when you slice the guys arm and leg open. Ripped and bloodied clothing are memorable things."

"Oh," said Joss and Ria together.

Dev got up and bent his back. Maya rolled her eyes at the sounds of cracking bones that came from her father's body. "Dad, you're falling apart."

"Parenthood will do that to a man," he said as he walked toward the door. "Get some rest kids, wakeup call is at three."

Maya's mom gave her a tight hug and followed Dev out the door.

Before long Nik had disappeared and the girls were wriggling in the bed trying to get comfortable. Maya didn't have to worry about how long it would take her to fall asleep.

The moment her head hit the pillow, she closed her eyes and fell into a deep exhausted sleep.

CHAPTER 47

The next morning their sleep shattered at three and they dragged themselves out of bed, packed and headed to the lobby. Nik met the girls at their door and walked them to the elevator. Even at that hour, with Ria covered from head to toe in the Burqa, all four of them were on the lookout for Viren.

Thankfully they didn't run into him. Maya had to admit to herself that she wasn't entirely sure she'd be capable of holding back if he tried to take Ria from them. She could picture it all ending with a very crispy Viren Sen.

Minutes later they were all in the hired four-wheel-drive, heading out into the Mumbai darkness. At first, silence reigned as they all slowly went from groggy to fully awake. Nik sat up in front with Dev while Leela had chosen to sit in the back with the girls.

She turned in her seat so she could Ria and Maya in the back. "Before we get to the refuge, there is something you need to know. But first, Maya I have to say I'm really sorry I didn't tell you this before but since you've been exposed to Ria's experience I thought I could finally talk about it to you."

"Okay, Mom. You're getting me worried here." Maya inched forward on her seat and held on to the back of her mom's seat.

Leela patted Maya's hand. "It happened a long time ago Maya but it's time you knew." She took a deep breath and looked at each of the girls in turn. Then she settled on Ria. "When I was seventeen my father arranged a marriage for me. He was handsome and from a wealthy family, and as innocent as I was, I thought that my life would be perfect. I was eager to make my parents happy. They had always been loving and supportive and I still believe my father honestly thought he was doing what was best for his daughter. Securing her a good future both socially and financially.

"What he didn't know was they underneath the handsome face, my future husband had a sadistic streak. I was blind to it too. The wedding arrangements, the engagement, even the wedding passed in a blur of happiness because, even though I had always been against arranged marriages, I truly believed everything was going to work out fine." Leela stopped and took a shuddering breath and Maya's fingers clenched. Her gut was telling her what her mother was going to say next.

"My wedding night shattered all my dreams, all my hopes." Leela's voice fell to almost a whisper and she looked out of the window. "He force himself on me. He wasn't kind or patient at all, and when I resisted he became enraged. I couldn't go out of the house for two weeks after that night. That was how long the bruises took to heal. He gave me a black eye, a bust lip, two broken ribs and a fractured finger.

"His mother was horrified and so was his father but this was the heir to their estate, to everything they had ever worked for throughout their lives. How could they admit that he abused his wife?"

"So they covered it up for him?" Maya asked, her throat so tight she could barely breath. Maya's glance at Ria confirmed the tears falling slowly down her cheeks. She knew how Leela felt. And Maya's heart swelled with pride for her mother's strength.

Leela nodded "Only until his mother couldn't handle it anymore. It took almost a year. And it took the loss of my first pregnancy." If she heard the trio of soft gasps from her audience she didn't react. "My mother-in-law became ill, refused to eat or drink. And my father-in-law knew he would lose both his wife and new daughter if he didn't do something. So he sent me to the Kali refuge."

"*He* sent you there?" Maya asked, shocked. "Why would he do that?"

"Because he could see what it was doing to his wife. He had seen the loss of his first grandchild. His son was spoiled and entitled and quite vicious when it came to women. Not his mother though. I don't believe he'd ever abused his mother. Just me, because I was his wife, his possession.

"And his father knew that sooner or later I would pay for his decisions with my life. So he did what he had to do, arranged transport, gave me old clothing to disguise myself and sent me on my way. All the way to the train station I looked over my shoulder constantly afraid he would have found out, that I'd see him running after me waving his fist at me.

"In the end I boarded the train and made my way to the refuge. Inside the bag they'd packed was a small case filled with money. Ten lakhs. I was in shock. I knew they were a wealthy family but that was more than twenty thousand dollars at the time. I knew then that they blamed themselves for what I'd been through. I was never more grateful to anyone than to them. What they did for me was incredible and I can never thank them enough. I often wonder what would have happened to me if they had been a different sort of people.

"Although I tried to give the money to the temple, the Mother insisted on keeping it for me. She was certain that someday I would need the money for my own life. And true to her word, a time came when I had a new husband and a new life. A time when that money helped us to move to the States and begin a new life."

"Haven't you ever worried that he would find you? That his parents would one day tell him the truth?" Maya asked.

Leela shook her head. "I knew I could trust them not to say a word. Because they knew my life hung in the balance. If he ever found me I would be dead."

After a long moment of silence, and as the first light of the dawn pierced the night sky, Ria took a shuddering breath. "Thank you for telling me that. It's so easy to feel like you're alone in the horror of it all. So easy to forget there are other women out there going through the same thing."

Leela nodded. "The refuge will be good for you. You can train, become stronger, learn self-defense. And you can change you identity too. When you return to the States you will be someone else and your family and Viren will never find you. But remember Ria, that is a huge step to take. It would mean you can never, ever see your mom and brothers again."

"That explains why we've never met your parents, right?" asked Maya. She immediately regretted the question when she saw the shadow of sadness blot her mom's face.

Leela nodded. "I could never contact them. It would have been too dangerous, for them and for me and my own little family. I still have no idea what my father-in-law told my husband, or my parents. Whether he faked my death or said I ran away? I'll probably never know."

Ria smiled and looked up ahead at Maya's dad talking to Nik and driving along happily. "And you have happiness now."

"Yes, Ria. You can find happiness too. Be a different person but still be yourself. But only if you want to."

Ria nodded and Maya leaned forward, putting her arms

around the seat and around her mom. She squeezed tight and said, "You totally rock, Mom.You're a real inspiration to me, Mom. "

"Me too," said Joss.

"Me three," Ria piped up trying to hide a sniffle.

Leela patted Maya's hand. "And honey, are you okay with me telling the girls this at the same time as you?"

Maya frowned and shook her head. "Why wouldn't I be? You had you reasons for not telling me and you would have told me eventually. Now was just the right time because Ria needed to hear that from you. Beside, these girls are my sisters."

Leela laughed. "Maya, you're pretty amazing yourself."

Everyone laughed at that and Nik turned around, "What's so funny?"

"Girl's stuff," said Maya. "Don't worry about it."

He made a face and turned back to his conversation with her dad. And Maya smiled.

The rest of the trip went by fast enough, interrupted only by a short stop for breakfast at a roadside shop that looked ready to fall down on itself. Maya worried about the hygiene of the drinks and fried food. But she enjoyed the sweetness of the strong tea anyway.

When they reached the end of the trip they stopped at what looked like a simple lookout area. They got out and stretched and then stood staring around at the green hills and valleys. In the distance, Maya pointed out the white slash of a waterfall as it fell into the valley below.

"It's beautiful," she said, shading her eyes against the morning sun.

"Let's get going," Dev said. "We leave the car here and walk the rest of the way."

"We leave it here? Out where someone can just come by and steal it?" asked Maya, slightly worried about their ride back.

But her dad shook his head. "Just get unpacked and I will show you," he said being mysterious.

After they were all ready for the walk, bags on their shoulders, sunglasses and hats on, Dev got back into the car, calling Nik to join him.

When Nik got in, he started the engine and turned the car a little to the left. Then he inched forward slowly to the edge of the cliff. Leela walked beside the car and lifted the long overhanging fronds of a giant banana tree.

Dev guided the vehicle through the opening and down the incline and then the car disappeared. When Maya's mom dropped the leaves it looked like nobody had driven that way at all.

"There's a shallow cave down the incline. We always use it to hide the cars." She winked as Nik and Dev scrambled up the slope and through the banana fronds.

Dev dusted himself off and said, "Right. Off we go."

Maya rolled her eyes, not sharing her father enthusiasm about the climb but she refused to whine and complain about it. One foot in front to the other and they would get there soon enough.

It took them just on two hours to get to the clearing as the edge of the refuge. They were all exhausted but when they stepped through the screen of trees into the clearing they were all incredible relieved.

Up ahead of them the roof of the temple poked out of the forest in the distance and suddenly Maya felt lightheaded.

It was the oddest feeling and the last thing she expected to experience.

She stared at the refuge, with its temple and houses scattered around it, all half swallowed up by the evergreen forest, and felt the strangest emotion. Something that she knew to be true, deep, deep down in her soul.

She had finally come home.

~ TO BE CONTINUED ~

Thank you for reading. The Hand of Kali Series continues with Time & Fate.

ACKNOWLEDGMENTS

To my favorite girls the Inklings- thank you for your constant support and inspiration.

Thank you to my editor Cassie Kelley McCowan and my proofreader Karen Mead- for all your hard work in polishing Blood & Gold for publication.

To Sel & the girls- nothing ever gets done in my book world without your support.

To Sandra Valente who won the Fashion Designer name giveaway. Thank you for contributing to Maya's fashion sense.

And to my readers. Don't stop reading…

FREE STARTER LIBRARY - JOIN MY NEWSLETTER

Get the following titles FREE when you subscribe to my newsletter.

Tee's Newsletter

http://smarturl.it/TeesMailingList

ABOUT THE AUTHOR

I have been a writer from the time I was old enough to recognize that reading was a doorway into my imagination. Poetry was my first foray into the art of the written word. Books were my best friends, my escape, my haven. I am essentially a recluse but this part of my personality is impossible to practice given I have two teenage daughters, who are actually my friends, my tea-makers, my confidantes… I am blessed with a husband who has left me for golf. It's a fair trade as I have left him for writing. We are both passionate supporters of each other's loves – it works wonderfully…

My heart is currently broken in two. One half resides in South Africa where my old roots still remain, and my heart still longs for the endless beaches and the smell of moist soil after a summer downpour. My love for Ma Afrika will never fade. The other half of me has been transplanted to the Land of the Long White Cloud. The land of the Taniwha, beautiful Maraes, and volcanoes. The land of green, pure beauty that truly inspires. And because I am so torn between these two lands – I shall forever remain cross-eyed.

Stalk Tee here:
www.tgayer.com
tee@tgayer.com

facebook.com/TGAyerAuthor

twitter.com/TGAyerAuthor

bookbub.com/profile/t-g-ayer

9 780099 511268 1